FAMILY MEETING

For Lucy + Kip
A bit of Southern warmth
for a decidedly Northern
Family!

Chile LaDeMott

205/2500

FAMILY MEETING

MILES DEMOTT

FAMILY MEETING

Miles DeMott

Word Truck Books

Post Office Box 11031

Montgomery, Alabama 36111

www.wordtruck.com

This book is a work of fiction. Any references to historical events, real people, or real locations are made in the spirit of fictional creation. All other names, characters, places, and incidents are the sole fabrication of the author's imagination, and any resemblance to real or actual people or places or events is coincidental.

ISBN 978-0-9829358-0-4 (hardcover)

For my bride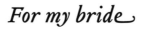

CHAPTER ONE

Tony Gordon tugged at his emerging beard and squinted discerningly, studying the man at the next table who seemed to be engaged in genuine discourse with a cheeseburger. For Tony, fresh out of grad school, this was an opportunity. The ink on Tony's Ph.D. wasn't even dry yet, but his mission was clear and his call to counsel the psychologically impaired was reinforced here before him at the Wendy's at Hartsfield International Airport, Atlanta's Gateway to the World. So much to learn. So many questions to ask. An academic trained in the mechanisms of intellectual and psychological inquiry, Tony chomped at the bit to get inside this man's head. Instead, though, he observed from a safe distance, attempting to retain empirical objectivity, and watched as his neighbor progressed through what appeared to be a heated conversation with his lunch. It began with nodding agreement joined with inaudible mumblings, and Tony recorded that the man and his cheeseburger seemed to be in agreement. All at once, though, the man's nods would shift from vertical to horizontal, he would look at his cheeseburger with great contempt, and the mumblings would become entirely audible as most of the travelers in the main terminal would hear him shout, "I did not say that, and I have no idea where that is coming from."

Tony found two aspects of this conversation especially disconcerting. The first of these, of course, would be that a man would engage a cheeseburger in conversation in the first place. On this point, though, there seemed to be clarity forthcoming, if only because the man seemed increasingly to be including the entire happy meal in the conversation. The second and most disconcerting element would be that the man seemed no more conscious of his surroundings than he seemed aware of the edible nature of his verbal opponent. In these days of heightened security in airport terminals, it seemed unlikely that Tony would have time to finish his extra-large fries. Still, he watched with an intense academic interest, noting that few if any of the passersby even took notice of the interesting repartee. Instead, the people shuffled rapidly through the terminal, pulling their lives and carry-on luggage through the cattle gates that led to security checkpoints and longer, more confusing lines beyond them where shoes and belts, watches and pens would all be removed for intense inspection. Meanwhile Homer, which was probably not his name, continued to wax poetic in a manner fit for a straitjacket, turning his attention to eternal salvation in an effervescent sort of way.

"The Bible is very clear on these points," he said to his cheeseburger. "Jesus is the one way, the whole way, and nothing but the way. Those who don't understand this will surely burn in hell. That was the whole point of Him coming down here, to tell us that God loves us, that He holds a place for us, and that He sent His only son to die for our sins. What part of that doesn't make sense?"

"Amen, brother," replied an elderly woman seated at the table beyond him, waiting patiently for her next flight, or maybe not. She struck Tony as the type who might simply go to the airport to be close to people with whom she would never be very close. The type who would strike up a conversation, follow it to its natural end, and then artfully strike up another conversation with the next participant in pinball fashion. After all, she seemed to have no luggage, held her purse tightly in her lap, and had hardly made a dent in the iced tea on the table in front of her. Tony was settling in to watch this next game of pinball when, through the noise of the crowd, a pleasing computer-generated female voice announced the pending departure of his connecting flight, "Ladies and gentlemen, Delta Airlines Flight 1024, non-stop service to Charleston, South Carolina, is now boarding at Gate C-23."

Without disturbing his neighbor, Tony rose from his seat and made his way to the gate. The planes were usually loaded from the rear, and Tony checked his ticket to confirm his memory that he was seated near the rear of the airplane. Indeed, his boarding pass confirmed that seat 39D awaited. All the way back and by the window, he assumed, and the smell of the lavatories leapt immediately to mind. As he entered the first wave of security and prepared his boarding pass and photo identification for the surly, middle-aged woman in uniform waiting at the other opening of the cattle gate, Tony recounted the events of the last couple of weeks, trying not to make eye contact with the other cattle. He regretted waiting to make the arrangements, but this had, after all, been a last minute gig.

Two weeks before, Tony had walked in the front door of Pacific Mergers, Inc., a venture capital firm with a unique niche in the mergers and acquisitions trade. They were in the family-business-issue-resolution business. Prior to taking an equity stake in the companies they considered, especially those with strong family ties to the company founder, Pacific Mergers would underwrite the controlling family as well as the business. The philosophy behind this approach suggested that business dysfunction was systemic and not merely fiscal. In other words, they argued that the relationships within controlling families were, more often than not, reflective of core management decisions and organizational culture, past and present. From an investment perspective, the process of overcoming the organizational dysfunction might be more complex than simply changing out management. To accomplish this, Pacific Mergers would contract with psychologists trained in the recognition and resolution of family issues to conduct a series of family meetings. Tony's doctoral research on the emotional connections between families and the businesses they controlled seemed a perfect fit, and the fact that he had conducted this research at UCLA, almost around the corner from Pacific Mergers, emerged as an incredible, if not completely accidental, stroke of luck. Remarkably, Tony Gordon had been surprised by their call.

"Dr. Gordon, my name is Michael Kelley, and I've got a proposition for you if you have just a minute," the voice on phone seemed to say. Tony had been trying to finish the last paragraph of his most recent dissertation spin-off article when the phone derailed his train of thought. His mind had not completely let go of the article when the voice drew his attention into the receiver.

"I'm sorry. Who did you say you were?"

"Michael Kelly, Dr. Gordon. I'm a principal with Pacific Mergers, a venture capital firm based here in L.A."

Tony's brow furrowed further as he tried to assimilate this information.

"Okay. Are you calling to get me to invest in something, because you should probably know right up front that I'm not one of those doctors, the ones that make all the money and actually have capital to venture." The voice on the phone broke into a laugh and Tony looked around the room as if he might be able to make others in the room laugh a little. There was no one else in the room. In Tony's world, there rarely was.

"No, Dr. Gordon. I'm well aware of your credentials and I'm not calling with an investment proposition."

"Okay. Glad we got that straight. What can I do for you?" As Tony asked this question he began to run his eyes back over the words on the laptop screen in front of him, trying to get back into the groove of the closing paragraph, committed to passive listening to what he assumed was a cold call. He had tried to be a stock broker himself many years before, right out of college, and his pain through that experience had evoked in him a misplaced sympathy for telemarketers, though he found political pollsters insufferable. He paused to consider, again, the distinction between the two when a turn of phrase reached through the receiver to grab his attention.

" . . . opportunities with us here at Pacific Mergers, if you'd be interested in talking with us at some point. I realize that your interests may be more academic, but a part of what we do . . ."

"Back up a minute," Tony said, stopping the voice short of completed thought. "This call, the proposition you mentioned, concerns a job offer?" Now he really was confused, and he scratched the back of his head and moved his eyes from the laptop screen to the large bookshelf across the small room, letting his back settle into the rumpled sofa that served as office chair on this day.

"Why, yes, Dr. Gordon. May I call you Tony?"

"Please. You've piqued my curiosity. Tell me who you're with again?"

"Pacific Mergers. We are a venture capital firm based here in L.A., though our asset base extends pretty much across the country at this point. Are you familiar with our firm?

"No," replied Tony, "Can't say that I am. But I am familiar with the concept of venture capital, so you can skip that part. Jump ahead to the part that involves me."

"Okay, Tony. I'll do this in phases. You tell me when you're no longer listening. We take equity positions in businesses that, for whatever reason, are poised precariously between generations of family control. We have begun an innovative program of conducting due diligence on the controlling families of potential acquisitions, but our staff is ill-equipped for this specialized type of inquiry. I ran across your work in this area in one of those dry, academic journals you're required to publish in and thought the two of us should share some time and thoughts. Still interested?"

"Do you have your boarding pass and photo ID?" Tony's eyes quickly focused on the stern face of the woman in front of him, dragging his consciousness kicking and screaming back into the present, back to the airport and the front of the cattle gates where he was apparently holding up the line trying to recount the previous two weeks in his mind. He reached into his jacket pocket and retrieved the required items, showed them to the transportation authority, and the woman extended her left hand toward the lines forming at the metal detectors. Tony paused, only briefly, to take in the large, claw-like fingernails on the extended hand. Each of the nails appeared to be painted in a different but collectively bright fashion. When he didn't move quickly enough, the woman intoned loudly, "Next in line, please."

Tony Gordon was a true Californian. Born and raised in and around Los Angeles, Tony had been educated at Berkeley and UCLA, and his professional experience was limited to west coast endeavors. Up until two weeks ago, he hadn't given much thought to working anywhere but California. He wasn't opposed to it, but it had never really crossed his mind. He was happy, accustomed to his lifestyle, and comfortable in his achievements. His bicoastal travels had been limited to professional conferences in Boston, New York, and Indianapolis. He had never been to the South, and Tony didn't feel the lesser for it. Perhaps, he reasoned, he was adventurous in other ways, though the evidence to the contrary was mounting.

Tony lived alone in his late 30s, surrounded by relics and furnishings from his college days. His most recent relationship with a woman, the third in a series of disastrous relationships, had been punctuated with a restraining order. The fact that it was against her offered little consolation. Neither were the corduroy blazers that lined his closet or the Honda hatchback that had several times over the last decade transported his entire existence from rental to rental. The apartments had evolved through the years to include more amenities and higher rent, but Tony really only needed the parking lot and the mailbox. His only trip to the pool at his current residence had yielded, in the end, the restraining order. So much for that.

After passing through the metal detectors, turning on his laptop, retying his shoes, and claiming his wallet, watch, and keys, Tony made his way to the gate and boarded the plane to Charleston. As he ensured that his window seat was fully forward, that his briefcase was stowed correctly beneath the seat in front of him, and that his tray table was in the upright and locked position, Tony made every effort to eradicate the lavatory smell from his consciousness and doze off. His seat could not have been any farther back without a sink and flush mechanism. Just as he suspected.

"Good afternoon, my good woman." A familiar voice from a conversation taking place several rows in front of Tony tugged him back from the restful, though its distance made it almost dreamlike. "May I disturb you long enough to occupy my assigned seat there by your side? I won't bite unless you ask me twice."

"Certainly," replied a voice hushed with formality and consternation. Tony moved his head to the left to look between the seats in front of him, and he was not alone in wanting to connect the voice with a face. The viewpoint between the five rows of seats in front of him were filled with inquiring minds, and he only got a glimpse of the back of a head before the voice occupied the seat, a window seat, six rows up. The back of the head was enough, though, for Tony to connect the voice with the cheeseburger at Wendy's just a few moments back. And the sheer volume of the voice seemed to make it likely that Tony might have to continue his analysis of this character in flight, perhaps even discover what a cheeseburger might know or need to know about salvation and deliverance, Tony thought with a chuckle. Hopefully, though, the old guy would fall asleep on the short flight and allow Tony to get some last-minute rest. Why did he feel compelled to analyze everything and everybody? Damn. Tony shut his eyes against the question and listened passively to the flight attendant's explication of the seat-pocket guide to in-flight safety.

Walker Middleton settled into his seat near the back of the plane and pulled his New Testament from the vest pocket of his blue blazer. It was not the words of the Lord that beckoned him at this moment, as a very attractive flight attendant was pulling the oxygen mask down to simulate an emergency. Rather, it was his own agenda, his schedule and list of primary contact information that was printed on a folded piece of paper inside the small text. As he fished the papers out of his pocket, he watched the flight attendant, his eyes squinting over the top of his reading glasses to get a closer look. A more efficient man would have welcomed the rapid advances in technology to collect and display the important information surrounding his daily endeavors, but Walker liked to think of himself as old fashioned. This masquerade helped him to forget that he had dropped two different PDAs into the locker room toilet at the country club, choosing both times to leave the fishing to the maintenance staff. The loss of the second wonder-gadget ignited his newfound desire to be considered old fashioned, and Walker reverted to the relatively primitive combination of ink and paper, always keeping a stash of index cards, new and used, in his shirt pocket for recording pithy comments and creative ideas. He considered himself a veritable wellspring for both. He had also, at least until recently, made good use of those comments and ideas in his weekly sermons.

As the flight attendant completed explaining the safety features of the DC-9 and stretched to return the sample seatbelt and oxygen mask to the forward overhead luggage compartment, Walker pulled his New Testament and folded agenda from his vest pocket. In the process, though, he leaned a little too far toward the aisle seat next to him to get a better look at the stretched form of the young flight attendant. This became apparent as he settled back into his seat and caught the raised-eyebrow look of the "good woman" to his left who had followed his line of sight and now offered silent but critical commentary, shifting her eyes between Walker's eyes and the small Bible recently fished from his coat pocket.

"Just admiring one of God's great works of art," he said, grinning self-assuredly, like a young Italian man rebuked by a passing female American tourist. This seemed to do little to assuage the look of condemnation, and Walker let the moment pass without further comment, settling back into his seat and shifting his weight toward the window. He pulled the folded agenda from the small Bible and opened it. Even at the last minute, Walker's secretary, Darlene, had taken the time to prepare a detailed agenda. Darlene took such good care of him, thought Walker. The last item on the agenda revealed that his plane was scheduled to land in Charleston at 5:45, bringing to a close a day that had proven to be extraordinary in Walker's 62 years. He made every effort to retrace the steps in his mind as his eyes scrolled down the printed agenda of the day's meetings and the plane shuddered down the runway, lifted off, and tucked its landing gear.

The day's journey, though, had begun almost a month earlier when a letter had arrived at the church office on a glorious fall morning. It had been a Tuesday. There was typically a lot of mail on Tuesdays, as the church office was usually closed on Mondays. Darlene, who had served as the church secretary for almost a dozen years, was initially surprised because the return address on the overnight envelope was the Southern Baptist Association, the governing and accrediting body for Baptist churches, headquartered in Atlanta. Walker's own church, Trinity Baptist in Charleston, had been a charter member of the association in 1827, and Walker had been affiliated with the SBA throughout his 35-year career as a Baptist minister. An overnight package was rare, and the presumed importance of the correspondence certainly evoked a sense of urgency in Darlene's Tuesday morning routine. Walker was taking his time at the barber shop that morning. He usually began his work week with a trip to the barber shop. Personal grooming was important, certainly, but the barber shop also represented an opportunity to take in the local criticism on the previous Sunday's sermon and also to listen to the local gossip that usually offered great fodder for the next Sunday's sermon. Walker's research on that Tuesday, though, was taking longer than usual, and the anxious weight of the overnight package threatened to reduce the corner of Darlene's desk to splinters. She was nervously peeling mailing labels and sticking them on the nursing home newsletters when he walked in.

"What a great morning, Darlene," Walker said as he walked through the outer office on his way to the lead pastor's office. "The birds are singing, the leaves on the trees are showing great color, and all is right with the world!"

"Yes, sir," replied an anxious Darlene. "You're right about that." She paused from her mailing labels as Walker reached for the inbox at the corner of her desk. "Hope it stays that way," she said in a lower tone as she turned and resumed her labeling while Walker shuffled through his mail without comment and walked the remaining seven steps to his own office. He customarily worked with his door open, unless a member of his flock required some private time, and today was no exception. Darlene listened as the familiar squeaks and sounds of heels hitting wood suggested that Walker had assumed the mail reading position, reclined in his chair with his heels up, reading glasses down, and mail in his lap, envelopes arranged by size, smallest to largest. He opened each letter with a Boy Scout knife given to him by Troop 103 for his many years of sponsorship. Today had been a relatively light mail day, and Darlene had taken care to eliminate as much of the junk mail as possible, but the overnight envelope was the largest and would likely be the last one he opened. She was almost startled by Walker's question from the next room.

"Darlene, do we think this is the final invoice from Dixie Painting and Decorating?"

"I'll call Dewayne and check to be sure, but I think it is," Darlene replied. As she began to look the number up in her card files, she remembered a conversation with Dewayne at the end of the previous week, and she continued, "That is the final invoice. We talked about it last week, and Dewayne said that he would send the final bill."

"All right," Walker mumbled as he shuffled some folders on his desk to find the appropriate place to file the invoice. Darlene returned to her labeling. After three more newsletters were ready to mail, Darlene heard the muffled zipping sound of the overnight envelope being opened. The silence of the next several minutes was broken only by Walker's turning of the multiple pages found in the envelope. Darlene found herself strangely comforted by Walker's lack of response, and she took a deep breath as she heard the collection of papers hit the desk alongside the other daily business. Maybe the mistake in the title had been simply that, a mistake. She resumed her labeling with a renewed spirit, the burden of ambiguity lifted, and the day was set to regain its momentum when the squeaky chair prefaced the phrase she knew, in the pit of her stomach, was coming. Walker walked through the door and handed her a file.

"Have Betty review these invoices and send a check to Dixie," Walker said, though his bright, sunny demeanor appeared to have taken a turn. "And find Margaret for me, please," he added as he walked back through to his office, closing the door on what had been, to that point, a wonderful Tuesday.

"Would you care for anything from our beverage cart, sir?" The sultry voice drew Walker's eyes from the clouds over Upstate South Carolina to the eyes of the young flight attendant, though he paused indelicately over the portion of her uniform that should have included a name tag. This, too, did not go unnoticed by Gladys Kravitz, or whatever the woman's name was that was seated between him and the aisle. She rolled her eyes and mumbled something under her breath.

"Why, yes, I most certainly would," he said, dropping his tray table in front of him and placing the small Bible there, in clear view of the flight attendant and the Kravitz woman. Walker relished his perceived role as an agitant, and he loved to shake things up. He often thought he should have been a Roman Catholic or an Episcopal priest, just so he could leverage the collar that his Protestant denomination denied him. "I'll have a gin and tonic, please, Marcie," Walker said, finally catching sight of the nametag.

"That figures," said the Kravitz woman.

"Okay. That will be five dollars, and exact change would be great if you have it. Anything for you, madam?" the flight attendant asked, as she leaned over toward Walker to put a napkin on both tray tables.

"I'll have a Diet Coke," she replied, and Walker would have sworn her eyes glanced toward the small Bible as she made the request. As Marcie smilingly put the drinks on the tray tables and the Kravitz woman sneered self-righteously at the bubbly tonic and miniature gin bottle, Walker was reminded of the double-edged sword of womanhood, especially the woman he'd been married to for the last 40 years or so.

"Darlene said on the phone that you really needed to see me," Margaret Middleton said with bright eyes as she walked into Walker's office, leaving the door open as if to say she didn't plan on taking her coat off to stay a while. The gap in time between Walker's request and Margaret's arrival had been only about 20 minutes, but it had seemed both longer and shorter to Walker. "What do you need, Sweetheart? I'm on the way to the Service Guild coffee." She smiled, but Walker, especially Walker, could feel the sting of the razor-sharp implement that Margaret used to divide her time between various civic and social interests. Walker had long given up on slowing down the whirling dervish in red lipstick and St. Johns business casual. He began to wonder why he'd even asked Darlene to call her, but he got up, walked around the desk and his wife, and closed the door.

"I thought we might take a minute to talk through some things, if you have a minute," Walker said as he pointed to the chairs by the window at the far end of his office, the chairs he used when helping members of his flock through tough times.

"Of course I have a minute, sweetheart," Margaret replied, looking at her watch as she walked over and took a seat by the window. If gloves had still been fashionable among Southern women, one could imagine this to be the point at which she would remove her gloves one finger at a time and place them in her pocketbook. Walker followed her to the window and took the seat across from her. He looked out the window, hoping the spirit would move the right words. She looked past him to the small clock on the bookshelf behind him.

"I'm thinking it might be time to make some changes," he said, though those had not been the words he was hoping for.

"Okay," she replied, hoping and pressing for a little specificity, and bracing herself for another of Walker's philosophical tangents. "What did you have in mind?"

"Retirement, for one thing," he said with a shrug, never making eye contact. This was a subject that they both knew was coming, and they had been through the machinations too many times before. He knew she would be impatient at the thought of discussing this one more time.

"Sounds like a good idea, but do we have to discuss this right now?"

"Well, some things have come to my attention that weigh heavily on this decision," he replied. He toyed with the idea of showing her the letter, but decided against it. "Things that could possibly make this a good time to give it serious consideration." He wanted to say "run like hell," but thought "serious consideration" was strong enough for now. He was, after all, practiced in the art of judging a word's impact.

"Are these things," replied Margaret, "what we need to talk about? Or did you just want to get my opinion on retirement?"

"Really just the retirement issue, I guess," Walker said, feeling himself sliding back from the confrontation that he had known was coming, especially with the Service Guild waiting in the wings. Conversations with his wife had, for as long as he could remember, required a calculated effort to balance the risk/reward equation. His determination to get it all out had chilled considerably during the 20-minute gap between the request for and arrival of his wife. "Are you sure it's something you'd be comfortable with?" He was searching now for a safe place to land.

"Yes. Sure, I'm comfortable with that, if it's the decision you make," replied Margaret, her brows drawn together with a combination of confusion and empathy, both sincere. "You give it some more thought," she continued now, adding a hint of compassion that might have been patronizing, "and let's talk more about this tonight. What do you think?" She, too, had sensed a profitable pause in the conversation and was looking to exploit it for the good of the Service Guild.

"That sounds good."

"Okay. Wonderful." This is the part where, in an earlier period, Margaret would have begun the process of putting her gloves back on, punctuating a really confusing conversation with the propriety it deserved. In the absence of gloves, she looked at Walker with eyes wide and brows raised, put her hands on the arms of the chair, and stood. "I don't know what the urgency was, but I hope it helped to talk this through again. I stand behind you, whatever you decide, but it is your decision. Talk more tonight?"

"Sure. That sounds good," Walker repeated, rising from his chair, glad the moment had come and gone.

"Great," Margaret said, taking a step toward him and rubbing the outside of his left arm. As if on cue Walker stepped forward to kiss her on the right cheek. As they parted, Margaret smiled reassuringly, turned, and walked toward the door. As she turned the knob, a final thought made her pause and turn.

"Don't forget that tonight we have the cancer benefit and a late supper with the Thompsons," she said as she opened the door. "We'll catch up after that."

"What time does the benefit start?"

"5:30 at the country club. Coat and tie. Your hair looks nice. Did Coach have any good gossip for you?"

"No," Walker replied with a half smile. "Just a haircut and a shave."

"Well, it looks good. See you this evening." Margaret walked through the outer office, and Walker listened as she exchanged pleasantries with Darlene.

Walker turned to look out the window, scratching the stubble on the back of his neck and looking down the street toward the barber shop. Coach Ferguson had turned to barbering after he retired from the public schools. Proprietor of one of the rare remaining barber shops in Charleston, Coach's second career had been an interesting choice. The locals liked to recall that Coach had been completely bald by his early thirties. This assertion was usually accompanied by an accounting of his coaching record, a less-than-stellar career that led many to assume that he had actually pulled his hair out one loss at a time. Despite the losses, Coach had been a favorite of generations of students and parents. Walker had been a friend and fan of Coach Ferguson through both careers, and he realized early on that if anybody had his finger on the pulse of Old Charleston, it was Coach. Approaching 75 and his second retirement, Coach knew everybody's business, mostly because he knew what parts to share and what parts to lock away forever. He gave the Catholic priests in town a run for the confessional money.

Coach had probably seen the letter coming, Walker thought to himself as he turned back toward the desk to resume his day. On a Tuesday morning back in the spring, Walker had witnessed the depth of Coach's omniscience up close and personal. In for his weekly haircut and shave, Walker was unprepared for the question that filtered into his ears through the steamy hot towel Coach was pulling from around his face.

"Everything okay at the house, Preacher?"

"Far as I know, Coach," Walker replied as lightly as he thought Coach had inquired. After a pause, he pressed a little harder, and Walker began to think that Coach wasn't just making conversation.

"You and the Mrs. getting along?" Walker looked around to see if any of the other Tuesday morning regulars had arrived and caught Coach's eyes in the mirror as he was stropping the straight razor.

"You know something I don't, Coach, I'd be obliged if you'd just come on out with it," Walker said with a half smile, not knowing what Coach did or didn't know.

"Ain't none of my business, but . . . ."

This was a standard Coach preface, but Walker was wholly unprepared for the words that followed. He shook his head now as he thought back to that spring morning and pulled the letter from the envelope to read it one more time.

Mr. Middleton:

It has come to the attention of this organization that relationships may exist between you and others that might be considered inappropriate and, in some cases, illegal. The information that forms the basis of these allegations is confidential, and we are not at this time in a position to pursue judgment on the legality of these alleged relationships. The possible presence of such relationships invokes Article XVII, Section 4 of our Articles of Incorporation, and requires that a full investigation of these matters be conducted and concluded within 90 days of the initial allegations.

As a part of this investigation, you are asked to appear before the Pastoral Ethics Commission at our offices in Atlanta, Georgia on Thursday, September 28 at 10:00 a.m. Your cooperation is appreciated.

Sincerely,

Mortimer Hamby, Ph.D.

Executive Director

Southern Baptist Association

Margaret Camber Middleton woke early, as was her practice, and immediately leapt into action. There was much to be done on this September morning, and she approached the beginning of the day with her usual fervent sense of purpose. Customarily, she was the first to rise, leaving Walker to sleep for at least another hour. It was during this time that Margaret cut fresh flowers from the garden, recorded her thoughts and scraps of dreams in her diary, or simply read from her collection of daily devotional books. Today was different, though, as Walker had risen very early to catch a flight to Atlanta, saying something about a meeting with Dr. Hamby when they had discussed the matter the night before as they ate their dessert. Margaret had been angry with Walker for scheduling a meeting in Atlanta on a day when they had so much going on.

"Why couldn't you have scheduled it at a time when we both could have gone, made a weekend of it, even," Margaret had argued. "Instead, you've chosen to leave town on the very day that the kids are coming home."

"I'll be home before dinner," he had replied, "and I typically do little in the way of preparing for the family weekends. You always make that point very clearly. I don't see the problem."

"You never do, Walker," she had said. "You never do."

"Well, throw a dog a bone," he continued, "and tell me what the problem is. I step in it either way I turn. I told you three weeks ago when you were scheduling this weekend that I had a meeting in Atlanta, and that I would be making a day trip. You didn't seem to think that was going to be a problem three weeks ago. Why is it a problem today?"

"It is not a problem," she said. "There is just so much that remains to be done, and I had hoped you might help out a little. You've said you were going to let Buddy assume more of your responsibilities at the church, and I thought that meant you'd have more time to look after some things around here. I guess I was wrong."

"No, you were right about that last part," Walker said. "I have given Buddy more responsibility over the last couple of weeks." Walker didn't want to go into the details surrounding his decision to assign most of his duties to his associate pastor, most importantly that it had been strongly suggested, if only as a temporary move, by Hamby in a call following the original letter. Walker let all that slip by the wayside, choosing instead to fork a solid piece of red velvet cake and await his wife's next rhetorical advance. After 40 years of marriage, Walker had learned that, when talking with Margaret Camber Middleton, the less he said the better. His inability to communicate with his own wife during the most recent years of their marriage had proven to be one of the most frustrating parts of Walker's daily life. It had not always been that way, but Walker had to work hard to remember the happier times.

This particular morning held everything but anger for Margaret, though. The previous evening's conversation was hardly a memory, and she approached her morning rituals with renewed fervor, driven mainly by the pending arrival of her children that afternoon. She had an agenda, a list, and a set of goals for the early portion of her day, leaving the mid and late afternoon free for giving the appearance that the day's production had required little to no work at all. She was a driven woman.

Margaret Camber was the only surviving child of Augustus Camber, IV, but the burden of that lineage had only recently become an issue with those who knew her. The death of her father, at 91, had thrust Margaret into positions for which she had been, arguably, ill prepared. From the outside, it looked as if Augustus, intolerant of the less formal "Gus" used by his father and grandfather, had been grooming his only child all along. The real story, though, was to be told following his death.

The Guses had been lawyers and planters through the years that straddled the 19th and 20th centuries. Their relative success had led to moderate wealth, held primarily in the form of real estate in and around Charleston. After the dust had settled on the market collapse in 1929, the

Cambers formed Plantation Trust, a banking company designed to leverage their holdings against the inevitable economic recovery of Charleston. The war years and the prominence of the Naval Base combined to facilitate steady growth in the Charleston economy, and the small bank flourished. Augustus Camber assumed control of the bank and related holdings in the late 1940s and was carried out of his office in a box, as was his wish and intent, leaving his only heir, Margaret Camber Middleton, to serve as chairman.

Born in 1940 to a life of conservative affluence, Margaret Camber grew up in the sunshine of her father's restrained adoration but in the shadow of her older brother, Augustus V, whose accidental death preceded and probably necessitated the effort for additional children that brought Margaret into the world and demanded her mother's remaining years as payment. The compounding trail of mortality in pursuit of heirs thrust an already reclusive Augustus Camber deep into his own thoughts and world, leaving the early raising of young Margaret largely to the small staff of the Camber's pleasantly appointed Charleston home. Her formal education followed the prescribed course for young ladies of Margaret's position. Private school in Charleston, finishing school at The University of Virginia, trips abroad to explore the art and architecture of the cultural centers of Western Europe, and presentation, at the age of 21, to polite Charleston society. While her debut fortified her social connection to an established tradition in Charleston, she found the prospects there to be limiting. Margaret found that she lived in a Charleston of about 250 people, and she saw the same people over and over again; they seemed only to change clothes. She longed to explore the larger world that her education and travels had introduced her to, though she was unsure of how her father would receive an idea that she couldn't yet articulate with the clarity he expected.

"Daddy," Margaret began one evening after dinner, "I feel like I need to do something that takes me beyond Charleston for a while."

"What did you have in mind, love?" Augustus replied over the top of the evening paper and his reading glasses as the staff cleared the dessert plates and closed the swinging kitchen door behind them.

"I'm not sure, exactly," she continued, "and I know that frustrates you. I've been trying to put together a plan that might meet with your approval, but I'm not at a point where I could claim a plan defensible."

Augustus folded the paper neatly into his lap and continued to eye his daughter over his reading glasses, brows raised and mouth curled into a contemplative but supportive tightness. Obsessed with the daily operation of a growing enterprise and not entirely sure what to do with a grown daughter whose endeavors and supervision could no longer be outsourced, Augustus had anticipated a conversation of this nature following Margaret's recent graduation from college.

"Have you surveyed your strengths and interests," he asked. "Given thought to both a short-term plan and longer-term goals that might be met?"

Had the staff been listening, which they might have been doing from the other side of the kitchen door, they would have shaken their heads with wonder at how a father could talk to his child with a tone and words they recognized from the many business dinners they had served at the same table. Recognizing a similar tone, though hesitant to mention it, Margaret was accustomed to formal, almost forced conversations with her father.

"If you mean 'Have I thought about what I might want to do next,' the answer would be 'yes,'" she replied.

If he sensed a sarcastic twist to his daughter's reply, Augustus's facial expression did not betray it. His gaze continued steadily from across the table, awaiting the substantive reply he thought to be forthcoming.

"I've been thinking it might be good experience to live and work in New York for a while," continued Margaret, "though I don't have any specific job prospects at present." Hearing herself say "at present," Margaret caught herself trying to imitate her father's tone. "It doesn't seem possible, though, to get a job in New York without leaving Charleston in search of one."

"That's not entirely true, but I see where your line of argument is going," he replied. "How and when do you plan to leave Charleston in search of opportunities in New York?"

"Alice Greevy, my roommate from junior year . . . ," Margaret began, waiting for her father to recognize the name of her former roommate who had actually been to Charleston to witness Margaret's debut. He didn't seem to remember, so she continued, "Anyway, Alice lives in Manhattan and has offered her extra bedroom. Her roommate just married and left the City for Connecticut. Alice seems to think she'll be able to help me find a job at one of the publishing houses doing editorial work."

Margaret allowed a silence to fill the backspace behind the spoken plan so far, and Augustus appeared to be mulling it over. He removed his reading glasses and his consideration of the issues was manifest in his thoughtful manipulation of the frame temples—open and close and open— for nearly a minute as his eyes watched the small chrome hinges on either side of the frame.

"We have friends," he said at last, still looking at the glasses, "in the banking industry in New York who would be willing if not eager to entertain your arrival and introduce you to key people in the City. I'm not certain, though, what opportunities might be open to you without more specific training. And I should also be clear that I'm not imposing this scenario on your plan as a condition of my consent."

"I know you're not, Daddy," Margaret was quick to reply, "and I appreciate that. I also appreciate your willingness to call upon your friends in New York."

"They're your friends, too," he replied, now looking her in the eye. "They've known you since you came into this world, and they knew and loved your mother. But that doesn't make it the right path for you. I bring it to your attention merely to illuminate an option."

"That option would make more sense if the long-term goal included my involvement at the bank," Margaret said cautiously, "but I can't say with conviction that my long-term goals include any role in the family business. And I know that probably meets with your disapproval."

"You needn't worry about either, the bank or my approval," Augustus replied, his face softening briefly in recognition of the implicit pressure felt by his only child to eventually shoulder the family business. "While it has been my hope that you would one day take an interest in our affairs, I have things well in hand at present, and the business will be there should you ever be inclined to examine it more closely. And family businesses can always be sold. In the near term, my hope is that you remain safe, healthy, and happily in pursuit of your own passions. Evidence to the contrary would be an intolerable burden. You have your mother's spirit, and I long to see it flourish."

Margaret had not chosen to examine the family business in any detail until her father's death and her appointment as chairman. Luckily, Augustus had stacked the board of directors and senior management of Plantation Trust with loyal men whose grasp on the operations and opportunities provided Margaret a soft place to land. The Augustan prophecy that a family business could always be sold proved to be incredibly true. At the time of his death, and perhaps awaiting his death, Augustus entertained several corporate suitors who had recognized the undervalued potential of Plantation Trust. His final wish and directive to the board was that, following his death, Margaret would be entrusted with the leadership of the bank as the board negotiated the sale to the highest bidder. This wish and directive was revealed to Margaret at her first board meeting, one week following her father's burial in the churchyard of St. Philip's Episcopal Church, spiritual home to the Camber Family for more than six generations.

Tony Gordon was unable to sleep on his relatively short flight to Charleston, partly because the man five rows in front of him kept the conversation going as if surrounded by heretic cheeseburgers and partly because he felt the need to review the file he had been provided on Plantation Trust and the Augustus Camber Family. What a name, he had thought on his initial review of the file, seated on the small couch in the small living area of his small California apartment. Augustus Sterling Camber, IV, last man standing in the long line of Carolina Cambers. The name carried a breadth and girth that reminded Tony of early 19th-century American history, a notion reinforced when Tony had shared the generalities of his pending mission with a former colleague over a Tex-Mex lunch close to the UCLA campus.

"What was the name again?" the bewildered colleague had asked.

"Augustus Sterling Camber the Fourth," Tony had replied with a grin, reaching for a couple of tortilla chips and washing them down with a pull on a sweaty Corona.

"And this man is the patriarch of the whole clan?" he continued, "a term I choose intentionally."

"Was," Tony replied, noting the innuendo with a raise of the eyebrows. "He died earlier this year."

"Is there a Fifth?"

"Not that I'm aware of," Tony replied. "His daughter has been installed at the head of the board, but the sense is that the old man ruled with an iron fist to the very end."

"And the suits want you to fly to South Carolina and crawl inside the heads of these people, examine the various dysfunctions, and report back on the potential threat of the family dynamic to their investment in the family's bank?"

"For which they seem prepared to pay me handsomely."

"That's great," the colleague replied, "but if I remember correctly, they're not terribly fond of foreigners in that part of the world. And you are a foreigner, you understand." He waited for confirmation as if he thought it necessary to stamp Tony's passport. When he sensed that Tony might have thought the remark condescending, he offered a lightening bit of levity, "Do the slaves wear shoes in South Carolina?"

Now, as the plane began to descend toward the opposite end of the New World, Tony began to wonder by what mechanism he could engage what he perceived to be Southern aristocracy in thoughtful dialogue. His review of Murray Bowen's Family Systems Theory over the previous week had reminded Tony of key concepts and paradigms, but it had not armed him to reconcile psychological theory with people named Augustus Sterling Camber, IV who operated a bank called Plantation Trust. Somehow the shoe comment carried more weight than his colleague had intended.

Tony thumbed through the file looking for the family members that were to be included over the course of the long weekend's meetings. Rather than the narrative that he would have preferred, the listing of interested parties read more like a prospectus or annual report. The death of Augustus Camber, he read, left his daughter and only heir as the controlling shareholder. Margaret Camber Middleton owned 51% of Plantation Trust stock outright and controlled an additional 20% held in trust for her benefit and that of her descendants. An additional 20% was controlled collectively by each of her two children, Augusta Middleton Thomason and Benjamin Walker Middleton, Jr. The remaining 9% was held by directors, present and past, who apparently enjoyed no connection to the family. Noted in the margin was a comment from Michael Kelly with Pacific Mergers, written in the reader's questioning scrawl: "Family ≠ Board?" Had Tony noticed the comment prior to leaving Los Angeles, he would probably have asked Michael about it. He could only assume that Michael questioned whether any family members served on the board. Seemed a logical question since they controlled a large majority of the shares. But Tony, admittedly, wasn't terribly familiar with the world of investments and stocks and boards and such. As far as he knew, Tony had never owned a share of stock in any company. The opportunity hadn't seemed plausible until he was through with school, and Pacific Mergers didn't include a retirement package among their benefits until the end of the first year of employment. At that point, according to the human resources director that had processed Tony's employment paperwork, the retirement and profit sharing programs were quite lucrative. Remembering the raised eyebrows and cheerful facial expression—though not the name—of that person, Tony began to feel the pull that the private sector had over academe, a pull that he had never thought he would experience. The pull became an outright yank when he read at the bottom of the page that the bank managed more than $500 million in assets and that the total market value of the bank stock held by the listed stockholders was over $150 million. Raising his head to completely digest those figures, Tony caught sight of the ground rising through the window as the Delta Airlines flight began its final approach into Charleston. He thumbed back through the beginning of the file to the cover letter that included the agenda and accommodations, noting the hotel and the indication that the immediate family would meet him for dinner at the hotel that evening. The immediate family, according to the cover letter, included Margaret Middleton and her husband Walker, their daughter—the oldest child—Augusta Thomason and her husband Ellis, and their son Ben Middleton and his wife Twinkle. Twinkle, thought Tony, as the landing gear made smooth contact with the runway. Where the hell do these people come up with these names?

After pulling up to the gate, Tony waited patiently as everybody, absolutely everybody, removed their personal items from the overhead bins carefully, as the contents might have shifted during flight, and began the polite ritual of deplaning. As he waited among the lavatory fumes at the very rear of the cabin, the salvation machine cranked up ahead of him, though this time it appeared to be aimed at a human rather than a cheeseburger. Tony listened passively but made no effort to connect faces with voices, preferring to stretch his legs and keep his eyes and facial expressions uncommitted, fearing that a Twinkle, a Bubba, a Roscoe, or a Sue Ellen was surely among the other cattle that waited with heads at odd angles beneath the overhead bins waiting to begin their plodding along ahead of him toward the exit of the chute.

Baggage Claim and baggage claimed, Tony hailed a cab and set out for the Planter's Inn, a conspicuously pleasant hotel, according to the partners of Pacific Mergers, that would provide more than adequate lodging and meeting facilities for the extended weekend. Tony found his room—a Governor's Suite, whatever that meant—was not only much nicer but also quite a bit larger than his California apartment, and he initially thought he should feel awkward carrying his own single bag. He didn't feel awkward. He just wondered if he should feel awkward, as if he should have arrived with a steamer trunk or two full of white linen suits and tales to tell. Part of that whole Southern thing, he realized, but he caught himself playing into the myth.

Tony's room looked out over the central market area in the heart of Old Charleston, which appeared to be a thriving commercial district with great old buildings, open markets, and the smoke stacks of docked cruise ships creating a diverse view from the windowsill to the horizon. In between those buildings and markets that had attracted and defined the experiences of tourists throughout the years, Charleston's charm and history oozed from the sidewalk cafés, old homes, and small shops that had fed, housed, and employed the locals for centuries. Where once the slave trade had thrived, the merry wives of Windsor (Connecticut) could now grab a bagel and a latte and enjoy the crisp fall breezes coming off of the Atlantic Ocean and bouncing over the Battery and splashing against the colorful houses that frame it. They might even stand along the Battery and look out toward Fort Sumter where, not so long ago, shots had been fired that cast the boys in blue against the boys in gray and, in the process, redefined their nation. Some of this Tony thought about as he looked out the window. Some of it he remembered reading in the travel book on Charleston he'd bought and read over the last couple of weeks.

Turning from the window, Tony's eyes caught the small basket on the antique coffee table dividing the soft-looking chairs from the even softer-looking sofa. Appearance became a comfortable reality when he sat on the sofa to investigate the basket and its contents. In a small hotel envelope was a card signed by Margaret Middleton welcoming Tony to Charleston and reminding him of their agreement to meet for cocktails and dinner at 7:00 that evening, downstairs in one of the private dining rooms of the Peninsula Grill, an adjoining restaurant and another favorite of the partners of Pacific Mergers. In the basket were an assortment of crackers and nuts—mostly pecans—and something labeled cheese straws that proved to be quite tasty. Also in the basket were some of the marketing fare—pen, paper, insulated drink holder, and key chain—from Plantation Trust. Nice touch, Tony thought, reaching for another cheese straw. Quite tasty.

Showered and dressed, Tony took the elevator from the third floor to the lobby and front desk, admiring the oil paintings of what he assumed to be previous governors of South Carolina that lined his walk. A lot of thirds and fourths, he noted, and some of the portraits also featured well-mannered dogs and firearms. Reaching the front desk, Tony met the eyes of a very pleasant young lady.

"Good evening, Dr. Gordon," she said with a slight hint of the drawl Tony was told to expect, though the fact that she knew his name took him completely by surprise. He didn't remember meeting her when he came in. "How may I help you?"

"Hello. What a wonderful hotel you have here, Ellen," Tony replied, looking down at the name tag at the last minute and stabbing the words toward a face he was trying to connect with the tag.

"Thank you, sir. Can I point you toward the Peninsula Grill? I believe your party is waiting for you there."

"That would be great, but could you also point out the meeting rooms we'll be using over the weekend?"

"Certainly," Ellen replied. "Or Eueland could show you the room if you like. It's on the second floor," she replied, gesturing toward a tall, thin black man in attendance at the edge of the desk.

Tony followed the gesture and caught the eyes of Eueland orbiting above a broad and friendly smile. Almost without thinking, Tony glanced down to the bottoms of Eueland's legs looking for footwear. When his glance quickly and guiltily returned to Eueland's face, the smile was still present and unassuming.

"No thanks, Eueland. I'll stop by there on the way back to the room after dinner," Tony replied, and Eueland nodded and returned to his lobby vigil.

"Very well, then," Ellen continued with a smile. "The Peninsula Grill is through those doors to the left, and I hope you have a great evening. Let us know if there is anything we can do."

Tony paused to see if Ellen's smile or enthusiasm would fade, but she held his gaze until he turned and walked toward the door to the restaurant. After a series of steps, he turned to look back at the desk, and Ellen had a phone to one ear and had launched her smiling eagerness on an older couple. He shook his head and walked through the doors to The Peninsula Grill. He walked through a dimly-lit entry hall with more oil paintings of famous dead people and was met once more by a smiling face, this time a sharply dressed hostess working a small podium with an even smaller light casting a glow over a thick reservation calendar. She was just ending a phone conversation, replacing the receiver on the phone hidden somewhere in the podium, and greeting him again by name.

"Good Evening, Dr. Gordon," she said, before Tony could get a chance to read her name tag. "The Middletons have already been seated. Please follow me."

Tony hadn't even spoken to the hostess, but he followed her into what appeared to be a very nice restaurant. More oil paintings of hunting scenes, horses, dogs, and presumably long-dead white guys. The lights were dim, but as he wound his way through the rooms in the wake of the snappy hostess he could make out clearly the fresh-faced, smiling groups of affluent diners he would expect in a place like this, with pastel-colored dresses and jackets, cocktails in one hand, fingers extended from the other out over the table stressing a point or a punch line. And yet there was quiet, a cacophony of many conversations revealing the details of none. The hostess turned to face him as they approached a large corner table situated beneath a large oil painting of a hunt scene and what appeared to be an oriental tapestry. As the hostess gestured to the table, an attractive older woman who had been facing in the direction of the door rose from her seat and extended her hand.

"Dr. Gordon, I presume," Margaret Middleton announced, tongue-in-cheek, casting literary pearls before swine. The reference was lost on Tony, still trying to take in the room, the people, and the fact that everybody seemed to recognize him.

"Tony, please," he replied. "Call me Tony." There was for him, then, an awkward moment when the hostess remained and the introductions to the larger table had not begun.

"Okay, Tony," Margaret continued. "I'm Margaret Middleton. Welcome to Charleston. We're glad you're here. Would you care for something from the bar?" The hostess didn't seem bothered by the breach in protocol. She seemed to have been standing there waiting to ask the same question herself.

"A glass of wine would be great," he said, looking at both women, not sure who to pass that request on to, Margaret or the hostess.

"Certainly," said the hostess, excusing herself now to the task at hand.

"Thank you Shannon," Margaret said as the hostess slid behind Tony in business-like fashion. As she slid behind him, Tony moved forward and put his hands on the back of the chair immediately in front of him, leaving an empty chair to his left between himself and Margaret, noting that a neatly folded napkin rested on the back of that chair. At the same time, Tony's eyes began to make contact with the other members of the family now rising from their chairs and posturing for the introductions. Margaret extended her left hand toward the four other, much younger people at the table. Just when she was about to proceed with the introductions, her eyes left Tony's and moved across his left shoulder to a spot behind him. Before he could turn, a voice from the recent past made the small hair on the back of his already tense neck stand up.

"This must be the infamous Tony Gordon," came the voice of Walker Middleton, husband of Margaret and pastor to airport cheeseburgers. Tony turned to greet Walker's extended hand and shook it with some trepidation.

CHAPTER TWO

"Well that was a glorified load of bullshit, if you ask me," Walker said, opening the conversation as he and Margaret drove away from the valet stand in front of the Peninsula Grill, "though I recognize that you didn't ask me." Margaret eyed the shop windows as they passed the Charleston Place Shopping Mall and worked their way through the historic buildings. The streets were wet and the people were few. Dinner had taken a long time, she thought, but she couldn't quite figure out why. The conversation had been pleasant enough, the pace kept constant by Walker's characteristic—and largely self-absorbed—stories and Augusta's tales of private school parents and the effects of affluenza. After giving Walker's opening comment time to register fully, she was prepared to offer her thoughts, just as their pickup truck rolled past the old churchyard at St. Phillip's Church.

"It's what Daddy would have wanted," she said, less a rebuttal than an affirmation, looking across the cab of the truck, past or through Walker, toward the family plot where Augustus, she thought, rested peacefully. The moment wasn't lost on Walker. He chose to drop that line of discourse, and he chose wisely. Instead, he maneuvered the truck through the tight streets toward their "house in town."

"Getting harder to drive this through the streets at night," he said, shifting the focus back to his own idiosyncrasies. Walker had always driven a truck, from the earliest days of their marriage to the present, though their life together had never really afforded him a proper use or need for a truck. He held firm that it provided a connection to his rural background, though his childhood days in South Georgia had been anything but rural. Walker's grandfather had been a farmer, but not in the usual sense. It would be more accurate to say that he owned farms. He never actually tried to plow the fields from the front seat of the Lincoln. Walker's father had been the first in his family to go to college, an accomplishment never fully understood by Walker's grandfather and complicated further by his decision to use all that education to become a preacher. Walker's grandfather had little use for formal education or preachers, so the confluence of these ills in his own son left the two estranged from one another for most of their adult lives. Walker's connection, then, to a rural background was more a nod to what might have been, a fiction perpetrated by a man caught between the sensibility of a practical grandfather and the call of an educated father. We all have crosses to bear and plantations to inherit. Walker's was a pickup truck. Luckily, Margaret had managed a comfort with that oddity that had eluded her father, and she smiled as the old truck passed the churchyard and she imagined the discomfort of the dead. Some days you're the dog, some days the hydrant, but Augustus Camber was rarely the hydrant.

"What exactly were you expecting?" Margaret asked finally. "He seems like a nice enough fellow. New at this kind of work and not very comfortable around people, but he seems to know what he's talking about. All that family systems stuff."

"I agree," Walker replied, walking the edge once again. "I think Augusta had a good question, though. What's in it for us? He didn't really have a good answer for that one. I see the purpose for the California people, and Dr. Tony gets some lab rats to work his family systems voodoo on, but at the end of the weekend, what's the take-away for our family?"

"Augusta's in the school business, Walker. This is about the bank and the folks that want to buy it. It's not important that we understand all the moving parts. They want to understand the history and the family history, the connection of all that to the bank. That's obviously the focus of the weekend, and I need you to hold off on your analytical, close-minded judgment until the weekend is over."

"But," Walker began and was immediately cut off.

"No buts, Walker," Margaret insisted. "I don't want to talk about this right now. You've had enough Scotch to argue with God about creation, so let's drop it. If nothing else, the weekend will give us an opportunity to be with the kids and figure out some way to be more involved in their lives."

Walker drove on in silence, reaching the townhouse and navigating the truck into the side yard reserved for its berth. As they walked through the side yard toward the back door, Margaret resumed the conversation without the slightest recognition of the ball-peen hammer she'd swung against Walker's psyche only moments before.

"How did your meeting go in Atlanta? What was it about, anyway?"

"It went as well as could be expected, I suppose. But let's talk about that next week, after Dr. Granola has finished dissecting our motives and management styles. One thing at a time."

Augusta Thomason sipped from one of the many bottled waters she always carried in her suitcase and stared out the third-floor window of the Planter's Inn at the silent, dark marketplace below. In only a half dozen hours or so, the locals would fill the open-air bays with wares of all description, and the tourists would shuffle through, wallets in hand, searching for the perfect piece of Charleston to carry back to the cruise ship and to the nieces and nephews waiting back home. For now, though, the transactions were an unknown, a mystery. As she finished the water, she turned and walked from the living area of the suite to the bedroom where Ellis had just completed his bedtime ritual and was climbing into the large four-poster bed.

"Snazzy place," Ellis said as he fluffed up his pillows and reached for the remote. "Nice of those folks in California to spring for the rooms. Otherwise, I don't think we would ever have stayed here."

"Probably not," she replied, though Augusta's mind was immediately connected to the thought she had searched for out the window and over the dark streets. She had stayed here before, here in the Planter's Inn, though probably not in this room. She couldn't remember. It had been her junior year at U.Va.

"Have you ever stayed here?" Ellis asked.

"Only once. My debut year. We got some rooms for out-of-town guests and some of my college friends." In the silent pause, she realized she was staring at the empty water bottle and made her way to the bathroom. She heard the television click on in the bedroom behind her. More and more of her conversations with Ellis seemed to be ending that way.

It had been her debut year, and she had shared her room with her college sweetheart, the boy she was supposed to marry, the one who looked great on paper and who had won the unspoken approval of her father. Of course that was before he knocked on her hotel room door after the queen's breakfast. Augusta smiled to herself as she thought of how the Reverend Walker Middleton might have reacted to that. She looked up at the bathroom mirror and caught her smile, remembering the old adage that preachers' daughters were always the easiest. But that had been the only transgression, and her sins had been washed away with graduation.

He had been a senior and the siren song of Yale Law had thrown a whole lot of real estate between them. Almost seventeen years had passed, dotted by marriage, two children, and a career in education, but Augusta could still remember his smile and his dapper look in heavily starched khakis and button downs. She always wanted to pop his pocket, the starched pocket of his shirt. In the end, she thought, he popped hers as well.

Ellis mumbled something from the bedroom and Augusta squeezed toothpaste from the bottom of the tube as her toothbrush led her back to her husband.

"I only heard part of that," she said to Ellis.

"What was the name of that little inn just outside of Charlottesville? We had dinner there with your folks the night before graduation."

"I can't remember. Why?"

"This place reminds me of it. At least an urban version of the Georgian Manor. The detailing and millwork is spectacular. The only place they seem to have scrimped would be the bathroom."

Augusta brushed her way back into the bathroom to spit. She looked around critically while scrubbing her bottom teeth, but she thought the bathroom met the standard set by the rest of the room. She hadn't really given it much thought until now. She rationalized that architects just had an eye for that kind of stuff.

"What do you make of Tony?" Ellis mumbled from the bedroom. Augusta was formulating a response when her husband filled the silence. "Tough to really make sense of his mission, but he seems like a nice enough guy."

"You can tell he's an academic," she interjected at what appeared to be a pause. "Seems out of place here, both in terms of setting and purpose."

"And Old Gus knew all this was coming, all these meetings and consultants? Makes me wonder if he didn't die just to avoid all this."

"Mom and I never really talked about the process and where it began," she replied, noticing that she had begun to choose her words carefully when talking about family business with Ellis. "My hunch is he knew something would happen, but I doubt he expected a Tony Gordon to show up and try to make sense of this family."

"I think I can hear him laughing from the churchyard."

"I doubt it. He wasn't really the laughing type."

Augusta finished up her bedtime ritual in the apparently underwhelming bathroom and turned out the lights as she made her way to her side of the bed, closest to the bathroom. Ellis had turned off the television and was making an attempt to set the hotel alarm clock on his nightstand.

"I stopped on the way up and scheduled a wake-up call," she finally said, tired of him trying to find the right buttons on the clock radio.

"Oh, right. That was a good call."

As they lay there in the dark, the sounds of Charleston emerged as a sharp contrast from their suburban Greenville neighborhood. Muffled voices, bus engines, squeaky brakes, and the faint sound of footsteps from the room above. The sounds were lulling Augusta to sleep almost immediately when Ellis, wide awake, broke the silence.

"When we break out for individual interviews, what are we supposed to say?"

"What do you mean?" Augusta didn't open her eyes. She knew what he meant but wanted to avoid confirming that fact through eye contact.

"Well, there always seems to be some line I'm supposed to toe, but I'm always the last to know. Rather than sticking the whole foot in my mouth, I'd love to know what I'm supposed to say."

"Let's just play it by ear."

"Easy for you to say. You're not the son-in-law."

"What'll it be, folks?" the bartender asked, placing napkins on the bar in front of the young couple.

The young man helped the woman to her seat aloft on the barstool, climbed onto his own, and responded with a practiced tone, "Jack and water," Both men looked at the young woman who patiently replied, "I'll have a glass of red wine," without taking notice of either man. Her eyes had been drawn to the oil painting over the bar, a landscape with a really tall horse, set on a horizontal canvas that made the animal seem larger than life. The bartender set about his business and the young man followed his companion's eyes to the strange painting.

"I'd love to have some of what that artist was on," he said, mostly to himself. She offered no response. They continued to examine the art in silence until the bartender returned to break the gaze.

"Ben Middleton, right?" said the bartender as he placed the drinks on the napkins.

Ben met his gaze and searched for a point of connection. None was forthcoming.

"Yeah, that's right," he replied. "Fill in the blanks for me though." It was only with his response that the woman seated to his left stepped from the painting to the present.

"Jim Taylor, or Jimmy. We made a couple of mission trips together back in the day."

Ben's face lit up like a switch had been flipped to make the connection. "Jimmy, right. Man you look different without the hair," he replied, prompting an awkward recognition of Jimmy the bartender's receding hairline. Jimmy, or Jim, caught himself looking up past his own forehead and smiling it off. To break the awkwardness, or so he thought, Ben introduced the woman next to him.

"Twinkle, meet Jim Taylor, one of the few who knew me when and lived to tell about it."

Twinkle had apparently heard that line before and revealed no change of facial expression as she made eye contact with the bartender.

"Nice to meet you. Glad you lived through the experience of knowing my husband in the early years," she replied with a blank facial expression. "If you'll excuse me, though, I think I'll skip what is shaping up to be the second reunion of the evening and head on up to bed." Again, without a change of expression, Twinkle Middleton picked up her glass of red wine and the napkin underneath, descended from her barstool, and made her way through the small bar into the lobby of The Planter's Inn and, presumably, to her room above.

Ben and Jim watched her leave the room and then turned back to each other as the confusion was lessened by the unspoken recognition that women sometimes do really strange things. Ben took a long pull on the Jack Daniels while Jim moved down the bar checking the status of the few other patrons. He returned with a fresh drink for Ben.

"So where have you been since we saved all those souls and made things right with the Lord?" Jim asked. "You got a hot wife and you're staying in this place, so you must be doing something right."

"Don't let it fool you," Ben replied. "I spend more time than not with my balls in a vise working for the man."

"Yeah. I guess it makes life on this side of the bar look pretty good, huh?"

"I wouldn't go that far," Ben quickly replied, "but you seem to be doing alright for yourself."

"Been at it a long time. Just now starting to see daylight. I figure a big tip from you tonight might just put me over the top."

"Here's your tip, then. Don't marry a woman you don't love. Sounds simple, but with women it's never simple." He punctuated his philosophical tip with the last of his initial drink, moving on to the second glass with hopeful eyes.

"Ouch," Jim shot back softly. "Guess that explains part of what you've been up to." And he walked down the bar to fill a drink order for a waitress waiting patiently between the two chrome rails that marked the waitstaff's domain at the bar.

"You don't know the half of it," Ben replied under his breath as the swizzle stick turned the water into wine right before his eyes. When the glass glowed a consistent shade of golden brown, Ben pulled the swizzle stick out and planted it firmly in the ice of the empty glass on the bar in front of him. Naturally he thought of his wife.

"So where and when did you hook up with Twinkle," Jim asked, returning to Ben's end of the bar, "because I'd probably have remembered that name if you had mentioned it in the jungle."

"Somewhere between the Scylla and Charybdis," he laughed, taking a long drink to revel in his own cleverness. "Twinkle was a teacher at my sister's school up in Greenville. My sister put us together, thought we made a cute couple. Simple math, really. Teacher plus banker equals Volvo wagon and house in the suburbs."

"A banker, huh. I thought your old man was a preacher."

"He is. Or was. I'm not really sure anymore. He may have retired recently. Tough to say for sure, at least without asking him directly." Ben shook his head and stared into his glass as the pause dissipated.

"You never felt the same tug of the cloth, the need to carry on the family business?"

"Nope. Not that family business anyway."

"Too bad, I guess. I always thought your old man was a real kick in the ass, though I only knew him for those couple of summers. Maybe it was the work or the play down in the jungle that makes that section of tape memorable."

"I don't remember much about the work, but I can damn sure vouch for the play. Left a lot of my tape blank, as far as I know."

"Damn straight," Jim replied, hiking a leg up on the footrest of the stool behind the bar. "I rode that wave a long time. Tried all kinds of shit through college. Talk about blank tape." Jim looked out over the bar, across the top of Ben's head, and out toward the dining room where dessert was guiding the final courses of the evening. He appeared to be remembering the old days but also to be formulating a transition. A patient bartender, though, always lets the other side of the bar lead. After a long pause, Ben picked up the cue.

"Twinkle and I rode that wave for a while, too. I always thought it ironic that a prim schoolteacher—especially one that worked for my

sister—could walk both sides of that line successfully. We never hit the really hard stuff together, but she was a wild one on blow. We were tight."

"Pardon the observation," Jim interjected into the pause, "but there
seems to be some space creeping between you now. What's up with that, if
you don't mind me asking—at the risk of losing my big tip!"

Ben chuckled and raised his eyebrows at the punctuating levity, while
he turned the near empty glass in his hands and tried to distill a response.

"It started to get chilly after the equation added up to the Volvo in the
suburbs and wouldn't go any further. She got high on the Lord and blamed
me for not filling the wagon with our own little private-schoolers. I think
she bought into my old man's line of shit as well as his selective forgiveness.
Been a slow train wreck ever since."

Jim the barkeep let all this sink in, made his way down the bar, and
returned with a fresh drink for Ben.

"On the house," he said, putting the drink down and removing the
empties.

"You are a sucker for dysfunctional bullshit," Ben said without looking up.

"Occupational hazard."

Ben worked the swizzle stick magic again and raised the finished
product in a toast.

"To old friends and old habits, both of which die hard." With that, Ben
took a long pull that almost drained the glass. When Jim didn't respond,
Ben looked up out of the corner of his eyes.

"You still in the business?" Ben asked in the tone of a practiced consumer and potential customer.

"Got out years ago, finally," Jim replied with patient eye contact. "I
don't even drink anymore," he said with a laugh.

"Holy shit," Ben said, almost under his breath. "Strange career path
you've chosen."

"Been a series of strange choices, some good some bad. Like I said, just now seeing daylight. It was a good wave for a while, though, til I lost sight of who was riding who."

"Whom. Who was riding whom," Ben replied, missing the forest for the trees.

"Right. I thought you said your wife was the teacher." Jim turned to answer the phone that was beeping in a muted fashion behind him. "This is Jim. May I help you? Good Evening, Mrs. Middleton. Yes, he's right here. Would you like to speak with him? Certainly, Mrs. Middleton. Right away." He had been looking at Ben through the short conversation but turned now to hang the phone up.

Ben, who had watched this little tableau play out, looked curiously at Jim as he turned back to the bar. "Speaking of my wife, the teacher," he said.

"Made it to the room before she remembered that you had the only key. Said you should come let her in the room."

"But how . . . "

"Called from the hall phone."

"Well, there you go," Ben said as he began lifting himself off the barstool and finishing the last of his drink.

"Should I have a fresh one for your return?"

"No, I'm done. But it's only Friday. The weekend's young yet, and this one promises to be a real cluster fuck," Ben replied. He pulled a $100 bill from his wallet and tossed it on the bar. "Hope this takes you over the top."

"Every little bit helps," Jim replied with a smile. "See you tomorrow."

From his third floor window, Tony Gordon scanned the Charleston skyline, replayed the dinner in his mind, and waited for his voicemail to connect. Three messages. A lot for Tony, even on a Friday. The first was from his landlord, though the call had nothing to do with late rent, as most of his previous calls had. The message acknowledged the landlord's receipt of Tony's 30-day notice, and Tony caught himself smiling at the reminder that his new job afforded him the opportunity to leave academic housing for nicer quarters a little higher up the food chain. The effect was so exhilarating that Tony saved the message so he could listen to it a couple more times over the course of the weekend.

Next came a message from his immediate past love interest, Suzanne, a busty blond grad student with a gift for statistics and an abundance of emotional baggage. As she stammered on through the awkward "How've you been?" portion of the message, Tony considered how his previous several romances involved women who seemed to have swapped sex for therapy before leaving him to pursue apparently functional relationships elsewhere. This spoke, he thought, to either his vocational prowess or his inability to sustain personal relationships free of dysfunction. He was hoping for the former when the message from Suzanne seemed to hit pay dirt. "Anyway," the message continued, "I was wondering . . . ." Suzanne was calling to invite Tony to a wine tasting and fundraiser for some organization that he didn't recognize, homebuilders for cancerous hearts or some such outfit. Tony had never been involved with non-profits and had long considered organized gatherings of the well-intentioned to be distant and dangerous propositions. Plus, he had never really had any money to give them. Rather than entertain the possibility that Suzanne simply wanted to see him, Tony concluded that an ulterior motive was in play. When Suzanne had reached the end of her message, Tony deleted her in strikingly cathartic fashion. On to message three.

As Michael Kelley's voice, the voice of Pacific Mergers, emerged from the phone, an ambulance made its way under Tony's window and down through the streets of the open market toward the cruise ships. Having lost the first part of the message, Tony replayed the message from the beginning.

"Tony, Michael here. Hope you found Charleston. I'm looking at the itinerary and see that you're having dinner at the Peninsula Grill. I recommend the fish. I'll be checking email late this evening if you get a chance to send some initial thoughts after dinner. Time change works in our favor for once. Remember to focus through the weekend on any involvement the family might have had, professionally or socially, with senior management at the bank and in the community. Let me know how it went. And when you get to the restaurant, take a look at the big painting on the back wall of the dining room. Ask the waiter to tell you about the donkey in the picture. There's some funny story about that. I heard it last year but can't remember the details. E-mail. Thanks, Tony."

As Tony leaned down to delete the message and hang the phone up, he caught sight of blue flashing lights on the wet pavement. A police cruiser following the tracks of the ambulance without the wailing sirens, down through the market toward the river beyond. He watched the lights and tried to remember seeing the painting of a donkey anywhere in the restaurant. Nope. No memory of a donkey on the wall, Tony thought, but the strange preacher had come close to making an ass of himself through most of the evening. That was a detail he'd probably need to leave out of his e-mail to Michael Kelly, his boss of less than a month. Tony turned away from the window and fished his new laptop out of its new leather briefcase. He set the laptop on the antique desk in front of the window, opened and started it, and while he waited for it to start up he turned toward the closet to lose the new blue suit and tie, the new dress shoes, and the new dress shirt removed from the box for the flight today. He was thankful he'd told the Middletons to dress casually for the Saturday and Sunday sessions. He had another suit, a new olive green with shirt and tie to match, but he didn't want to put it on unless he had to. Reduced to boxers and t-shirt and with his evening hygiene ritual complete, Tony sat down in front of his laptop and hammered out a summary e-mail that he hoped would capture the spirit of the evening.

From: Tony Gordon [t.gordon@pacmerg.com]
Sent: Friday, October 6, 2006 6:43 PM
To: Michael Kelly [m.kelly@pacmerg.com]
Subject: Middleton Dinner

I had the fish, and I appreciate the recommendation. I did not, however, see a painting with a donkey or hear a story about such a painting. I think we're scheduled to eat there again at some point this weekend, so I'll keep an eye out.

Dinner was very pleasant and everyone seems at least interested in the process. Margaret, as you described, seems to be an active matriarch for the family, and she made every effort to guide the conversation through the inevitable lulls. Her husband, Walker Sr., was actually on my flight from Atlanta to Charleston. Apparently he was returning from a meeting with the Southern Baptist Association. Both of the children were present with their spouses. Augusta, the oldest, is the director of a private school in Greenville, about four hours from here. She seems to have a good grip on the business side of all of this. Much more so than her parents. She asked a lot of good questions. Her husband, an architect, didn't say much. In fact, neither of the children's spouses said much. Twinkle Middleton responded to direct questions but didn't participate in any other way. Her body language suggested that there may be tension between her and Ben, or with everybody at the table, for that matter. Ben talked a little about his banking experience, but none of it related to Plantation Trust.

For my part, I opened with the explanations as we rehearsed them last week. I told them that our meetings this weekend would serve two purposes. The first and less significant of these was prompted by an agreement that had been reached with the Board of Plantation Trust for Pacific Mergers to acquire the bank. I was the first wave of due diligence, though the remaining waves would likely not engage the family directly. My purpose in this role was to meet with controlling shareholders—the family—to uncover any specific issues that might need to be addressed prior to closing. In that role, I was simply a representative of the company, and I was all ears. The second purpose, as I explained to them, stemmed from the fact that Pacific Mergers had worked successfully within the family business arena for a number of years and that an interesting by-product of the underwriting and due diligence process was working with the families to help them transition through the sale of their family asset. I was uniquely trained, I suggested to them, to help with that process, and I went through my background and some of the research I had done in family systems theory. My job, as I explained it, was to focus their attention on their family history and attachment to the bank, separate from the financial asset it represented on their personal balance sheets, and to help them talk about how it may or may not define them as individuals or as a family. The Reverend Middleton seemed immediately skeptical, but Margaret seemed taken by the opportunity to share the family history. She traced the origins of the bank to her great-grandfather, but didn't share much beyond what we already know, and I'm not sure she's as excited about sharing family history as she is about having the opportunity to share family history. As you anticipated, she'll be the toughest nut to crack. The others just don't seem to know much. At least that's the feeling I got over dinner.

I closed with a brief explanation of the agenda, explaining that we would begin with opening questions in the morning, some rotating break-out sessions in the afternoon, and some individual interviews Sunday morning. Our wrap-up session is scheduled to follow lunch on Sunday.

I'll e-mail updates as time permits, and I hope to have a summary memo to you by Wednesday. Let me know if there are specific questions you'd like to add to the mix.

Tony read the e-mail once through and sent it on its way. The clock on his computer said 7:04, but the clock radio on the table beside his bed read 11:06. Michael Kelly was right. The time change worked in somebody's favor, certainly, but it wasn't Tony's. He was tired but not sleepy, his body still working on California time. He closed the laptop and moved from the desk to the bed, setting the alarm clock and grabbing the remote before putting his head down on the pillow. He surfed through the channels once and found nothing worth watching. He was tempted to reach for his briefcase and the book he'd brought along. He decided against it and nodded off to sleep within a couple of minutes. So much for not being sleepy.

CHAPTER THREE

"Rhapsody in Blue," thought Tony, as the elevator slow-danced toward the lobby and Gershwin's trademark cadence and mournful clarinet tried to take his mind off of the fact that he was in a controlled fall. Tony had never been very good with heights or small, confined places, so elevators always proved to be a particular challenge, especially the elevators at the Planter's Inn. With barely enough room for a couple of adults and minimal luggage, the size of the elevator cars, for Tony, wasn't even their most disconcerting feature, the full litany of which he found himself reviewing in time to the Gershwin. It was, rather, the uncanny ability of the elevator car to present to the passenger even the smallest bump in the shaft and grain in the cable, framing these small flaws in life-threatening terms and proceeding up and down the shaft with all deliberate speed, the same pace exercised by the racist southern school boards in desegregating their schools. Tony remembered that turn of phrase from a recent article celebrating the 50th anniversary of Brown v. Board. That's a lot of shit to be thinking about, Tony thought to himself as he tried to collect his thoughts and snapped his fingers to the Gershwin. He detected a small bead of sweat emerging from his brow. It wasn't as much the height—he always chose a window seat on airplanes and often enjoyed the bird's-eye view from buildings of reasonable height—as it was the height experienced in a small space of uncertainty, where the distance between him and sudden death wasn't readily discernible. Luckily for him, no other guests occupied his small cell and he wasn't forced to attempt the inevitably futile polite conversation, which would have been quite a feat considering he found himself holding his breath for the full descent, exhaling only when the elevators opened on the lobby level, revealing Eueland's smiling deference. Damn, thought Tony. This man always catches me at my weakest. He nevertheless caught himself looking down again to check Eueland's feet for shoes and quickly brought his own smiling eyes back up to meet Eueland's.

"Morning, Dr. Gordon," Eueland said through his bright smile. "Find everything to your liking in your room?"

"Yes, Eueland. The room seems perfectly appointed. Thank you for your concern."

"Just doing my job, Dr. Gordon. You let me know if you need anything."

"I will. Thank you, Eueland.

"My pleasure, sir."

Tony had stepped out of the elevator by this point, swapping places with Eueland, who was now holding the elevator door open and watching Tony look left and right across the small lobby.

"Breakfast is in the dining room, Dr. Gordon," Eueland offered, "down to your left. But we put some coffee and sweets in your meeting room, if you'd rather have that. It's on the second floor. I can drop you off there on my way to the fourth floor, if you like."

"No, thanks Eueland," Tony responded almost too quickly, having had all the elevator fun he could stand for now, and invisibly shaken by Eueland's choice of "drop you off."

Eueland closed the elevator doors with a nod and Tony paused in the direction of the dining room before taking the stairs to the second floor.

The appointed meeting room on the second floor was not difficult to locate. Tony followed the smell of coffee and the voice of Walker Middleton, and he entered the large conference room at what appeared to be a moment of closing tension.

"What exactly does that mean, Daddy?" Augusta asked before she'd seen Tony in the doorway. By the end of the question, all eyes were turned in Tony's direction, including Augusta's, and the room grew so silent you could hear the elevator climbing the shaft down the hall. A double bad omen, thought Tony.

"Now, my job is to get everybody talking to each other, so don't let me stop a good start!" Tony said, in hopes of cutting the thick tension in the room. Nobody laughed at first. After what seemed like a long elevator ride, Tony was relieved when Walker broke the silence with something other than his pulpit voice.

"Oh hell, Tony, my children were making an honest attempt to decipher the organizational code of the Baptist Church, but you didn't fly two thousand miles to talk about that. We need to get on with your program. We can talk about all this other stuff another time."

"Can I get you a cup of coffee?" Margaret offered from where she was standing, apart from the others by the small coffee maker and large tray of various breakfast sweets. "We've got doughnuts and muffins, too," she continued, busily preparing a plate for someone, maybe Tony.

"Thank you, Mrs. Middleton," Tony replied.

"Margaret. Please call me Margaret," she replied quickly but patiently. Tony had forgotten already his agreement of last night to continue on a first name basis. The oversight wasn't lost on Margaret who began to incorporate the simple error into an emerging, if premature and unspoken, evaluation of Tony's competence. When she wasn't judging a book by its cover, Margaret was often judging a book on the merits espoused by the most recent reviewer she encountered. The oversight wasn't lost on Walker, either. He would have preferred for matters to retain a slightly more formal footing, though he admitted to himself that to be called Mr. Middleton might exaggerate his seniority and Reverend Middleton might blow up in his face with every utterance. In the end he settled for Walker.

"Margaret, yes, thank you," Tony replied. "I'd love a cup of coffee and one of those whole grain muffins would really hit the spot." As he was saying this, Tony moved toward one end of the square table and put his notebook and pad down on the table in front of what appeared to be the head of the table. Once he had committed to that seat, everyone else gravitated toward the remaining chairs and slowly began taking their seats. Everyone except Twinkle, who hadn't arrived yet. Tony took the opportunity to scan the room.

The square table was placed in the middle of the room and was surrounded on three sides by a pair of chairs. Only Tony's side, the side nearest the refreshments, had a single chair. Along three of the walls beyond the table, a pair of chairs had been placed facing one another with a small table in between. The refreshment table was along the fourth wall. Tony was pleased that the room—larger than he'd expected—had been set up almost exactly to his specifications. He'd sent a diagram at the request of the special events coordinator, but he had only half believed—based mostly on the accent of the staff, he admitted—that he would arrive to find the room arranged as he requested. He had anticipated, based on many years of teaching seminars in a university setting, that he would need to assemble the room upon arrival. University staff always seemed to take great pleasure in providing the fewest accommodations possible. This corporate environment was really starting to grow on him, Tony thought to himself, as Margaret put a plate and coffee on the table in front of him.

"Does anyone have any questions before we get started?" Tony asked, choking down his first sip of really strong coffee and looking back at a now fully assembled table of eyes looking back at him. Twinkle had appeared and fallen softly into a chair without the slightest imposition of her arrival on the others. A clear moment of silence followed and Tony began to consider, as if for the first time, how difficult this process might be after all, like opening day of Psych 101, only these were adults hiding—unsuccess-fully, he might add—lots of baggage. He took a second sip, just in case.

"Whose side are you on?" Ben asked, taking Tony by surprise, which was probably his intention. "I guess I'm looking for your angle in all of this, and I've yet to figure that out."

"Great question," Tony replied, "and one that I actually expected, though the anticipation didn't really produce a good answer." He scanned the table and saw, in all but Twinkle and Walker, a polite smile and inter-ested eyes. Twinkle was struggling with a muffin wrapper and Walker was thumbing through the binder that Tony had prepared for each of them and shipped from Los Angeles, along with the room diagram, earlier in the week.

"My participation in this process is funded entirely by Pacific Mergers, so it's fair to assume that my primary allegiance rests with them. That means, more or less, that I'm here to quantify your family culture, to get a feel for the family dynamic—how the members of the family interact with one another within and across generations—and speculate on how that dynamic might manifest itself within your spheres of influence." Tony heard himself saying all the right things, the answer he'd rehearsed many times before leaving Los Angeles. And, as much as it probably sounded like a foreign language to his audience—and their facial expressions gave a nod to that assumption—he felt like the practice had paid off.

"So maybe the part I'm missing," Ben interrupted, "is what's in it for us, if anything. I work for a very large bank that buys and sells banks and businesses all the time, but I've never heard of a consultant working with the sell side. At the end of the day, where's the added value for us?" Ben concluded with a sweeping gesture around the table.

"Ben," his mother said with an impatient smile before Tony had time to respond, "perhaps if we give Tony a chance without asking so many questions . . . ."

"No, Margaret, thank you," Tony replied, trying not to further the tension that was emerging between mother and son, "but Ben's questions are valid ones and asking questions is really at the heart of why I'm here. While Pacific Mergers is paying the bill and there is an obvious motivation on their part, I'm equally as invested in facilitating a conversation between the members of this family. That's the course of action that seems to serve both ends. And I suppose that's why I'm sitting here as opposed to almost anyone else from Pacific Mergers. My background and training is in psychology and family systems theory, not spreadsheets and balance sheets. And while I'd enjoy giving you a summary of the diplomas on my ego wall, that would take away from our valuable and limited time together."

"So you're not really here to talk about the bank?" Walker asked, having joined the conversation when his son's line of questioning had meshed with his own and he sensed his wife's blood pressure rising.

"Yes, and no," Tony replied. "To the extent that it is considered by your family to be a defining asset, yes, I hope we talk about it. The specifics of the daily operation or business itself, no, I don't anticipate it will come up in our conversation this weekend. It is my understanding that your family's involvement in the daily operations have been limited through the years, and that by design, so I doubt that any of us would be prepared to talk extensively about all of that."

Walker sat back in his chair and eased his head to the left to politely make eye contact with his wife. The smile on his face, though still present, was slowly being pushed down his face by his furrowing brow.

"So," Ben chimed in, "what you're saying is that we're working toward a group hug here, and you're grading us on it?"

Everyone chuckled, except Margaret, and even Tony seemed to get a kick out of the perceived purpose of the weekend meeting as distilled by the emerging class clown.

"In a way, I guess you could be right," Tony responded, after some thoughtful reflection. A veteran of undergraduate attempts at oversimplification, Tony offered a different spin. "One of the purposes of this weekend is to facilitate within your family a level of comfort with the dissolution of your controlling interest in the bank. That's the group hug, I suppose. And then there's the job I'm doing for the group who hopes to assume your controlling interest. When you say, though, that I'm grading you, I think you may be overstating my role and even the company's intent. I'm really just observing and facilitating a conversation on this end. At some point next week I'll summarize the events of this weekend in a report and someone with more business expertise will read that report and discuss with me potential implications for the ongoing bank purchase."

He paused to let all of this sink in, having noticed almost all of the brows beginning to furrow, plowing the fields of misunderstanding. Twinkle, alone, remained distant and unaffected. She passed the time by pushing the hotel pencil across the binder and letting it roll back down the incline to her hand. Tony allowed himself a quick mental image of Sisyphus and the boulder in Dante's Inferno, wondering which circle of hell Twinkle felt confined to. She seemed to feel his gaze, though, and as the pause took on a longer form, she stopped and waited for the next directive. The tick of the clock on the credenza beside the breakfast and coffee became clearly audible. The silence at last made Margaret nervous, and she shouldered her firearm and issued the usual "forward" command.

"You kids know that your grandfather thought highly of Pacific Mergers, and he would have wanted us to participate with enthusiasm. This bank has been an important part of this family and this community for many years, and—"

"Margaret," Walker interrupted, "they know all of that. We all know all of that. I think the questions speak more to the structure of the weekend. I believe we've all acknowledged the importance Old Gus would've placed on these proceedings." Walker imagined his father-in-law spinning at the sound of "Old Gus." Some folks had to die before you could get the best of them, but Walker also recognized the old man's potential for reaching out from the grave. He would wait for almost certain payback.

"In answer to that," Tony interjected, trying to cut the tension, "let me say that I am first and foremost a clinician and family therapist."

"So Pacific Mergers assumes we need therapy, some sort of defense against separation anxiety from selling the bank," Ellis, a new voice, entered the fray with his usual lack of comedic timing. As he smiled nonetheless at his quantification of the situation, Augusta moved her hand over on the table and placed it on top of his. They never made eye contact.

"That's right as well," Tony offered in Ellis's defense, "though the assumption is new to them and they offer my services as much for you as for themselves. In all honesty, this is the first time they've tried this, so the benefit to you potentially outweighs whatever Pacific Mergers might learn."

"So we're going to sit around this table and talk for two days?" Ben asked.

"I'm afraid I've structured something far less painful. If you'll open your binders, we'll begin with a review of the schedule," Tony directed, visibly thankful that he hadn't asked if there were any further questions.

Everyone around the table, even Twinkle, opened the binders and looked back at Tony.

"The bulk of Section A is background info on Pacific Mergers. I'll leave that for your review later, but I'll be happy to answer questions down the road if you have them."

Ellis opened his fly and returned most of three cups of coffee to the larger stream of life, noting the older urinals and plumbing lines that adorned the inbound wall of the men's restroom on the second floor of the Planter's Inn. The coffee had gone down smoothly compared to the opening session of a weekend full of meetings he hadn't quite made sense of yet.

But his was not to make sense of it, anyway. This was Augusta's cross to bear. Ellis knew very little, and even that was none of his business. Still, the whole endeavor confused him. As he looked for the identifying stamp on the top of the urinal flush valve—Crane, good stuff back in the day—he caught sight of his brother-in-law approaching the neighboring plumbing.

"What do you think so far?" Ellis asked, staring at the wall and not making eye contact, in observance of unspoken men's room etiquette.

"Beats the shit out of me," Ben replied, punctuating the commentary with a preemptive flush.

He didn't say anything after that, and the extended pause made Ellis initially consider the rules given to sequestered jury members about discussing the case under review outside of the group. He wondered briefly if the same principles might apply in this situation, if the small, individual discussion would in some way detract from the larger group dynamic. Or if, alternatively, alliances would form like they always did on those reality TV shows. If the second were the real situation, where would he want to position his family in the larger tribal council. His business done, though, Ellis decided to flush and run, moving toward the sink to wash and dry without asking any other questions.

"Seems like an awful lot of talking for nothing," Ben said as he flushed a second time. "I know we've got lots of baggage, but I don't see this as the destination for unpacking it all. And none of us has had anything really to do with the bank except Old Gus, so I don't see how it could've defined anybody but him." Ben was now at the sink washing and drying while Ellis shouldered up the wall dividing the sinks from the door.

"I was surprised that you had never spent much time with Old Gus."

"How do you mean?"

"Your response to Tony's question about spending time with Old Gus. You said you never really got to know him, but I was under the impression that you spent a lot of time with him."

"Not really. He seemed to spend all his time at the office or in his study out at the farm. Books weren't my thing and sports never seemed to interest him. I can't remember him without a tie on, even the couple of times he came to my games," Ben said, eyeing himself in the mirror, opening the collar of his golf shirt to emphasize the lack of neckwear, and drying his hands on the small white towel before tossing it in the basket and looking up at Ellis. "Shall we?"

As they walked the short distance back to the meeting room, Ellis couldn't help but venture another question. They had just turned a corner and stood facing a picturesque view of downtown Charleston as he finished the thought and formed the question.

"Didn't you ever get any pressure to come back to work for Old Gus? I think that may have been the point of that spear, or at least that's what I thought when Tony fired it across the table."

"That seemed pretty clear in the question, but I didn't feel compelled to respond. Old Gus used to talk about family and all that an awful lot, but at some point I guess he just stopped talking about it. At least with me. I remember when I was a kid I used to ride my bike down to his office after school. All the employees knew me by name, and I guess they figured one day they'd be working for me. Old Gus had a pair of chairs across from his desk, and I'd sit in one while he finished whatever papers he was working on. Then he'd look up and say, 'Well, Benjamin, what did we learn in school today?' or 'Tell me, Benjamin, would you lend money to a man who wanted to build a factory to make widgets?' I remember that was the first time I'd ever heard 'widgets,' and I spent a lot of time trying to figure out what a widget was. I thought it'd be cool to put one on my bike, like a baseball card in the spokes."

Ben looked at Ellis half expecting to see the silly grin with which he seemed to receive most information, but Ellis was still staring out the window as the morning sun made its way over the rooftops and cast a bright box of light on the hallway carpet.

"I remember the questions and the chairs," Ben continued, "but mostly I remember never having the right answer or never being quick enough with the wrong one. He was a strange old bird. Used to sit in his office after hours and smoke a cigar and drink a small glass of port with an old military revolver on his desk, loaded and facing the door, almost like he expected and even hoped for the opportunity to unload on some thug coming after his money."

"Where'd you hear that?"

"Saw it once when mother couldn't get him on the phone and sent me to the bank to remind him about dinner that night. I think it was his birthday, but I remember thinking it was pretty cool to see that revolver on the desk in that old, dark office of his, with all the books on the shelves and the portraits of all the Guses that came before him.

"Didn't it scare the shit out of you? How old were you?"

"It was another of those times when I rode my bike, so I was probably around twelve. Too young to know what a whacked-out thing it might have been to have a loaded gun in your office. Thought it was pretty cool that he would shoot any bank robbers. At twelve, you don't really think about suicide or anything else an old man might be thinking about there in the dark. It definitely occurred to me later, though, but I always figured Old Gus liked himself too much for that. Or maybe he disliked others too much to leave the helm unattended. Turns out I was right. Guess he disliked these Pacific Mergers people less than the rest of us."

With that punctuation, Ben turned in the direction away from his brother-in-law and made his way back into the conference room. Ellis followed.

The chairs were quickly filled as the first break came to a close and Tony prepared to open the second session. He thought the initial conversation went well and considered continuing the topic into the first set of break-out sessions. The new challenge, though, would be matching personalities to produce fruitful conversations. As he had described in the opening session, Tony hoped to facilitate conversations between each of the family members, but even the first session had demonstrated that such configurations might not be possible. He had taken much of the break to rethink the second session in light of the first. The conversation had been labored, to say the least, defined more by pregnant pauses than by productive revelations. Twinkle hadn't said much of anything, and her body language had suggested that she wasn't likely to alter that stance in the near term. In fact, the in-laws seemed to have established a united, silent front, responding to questions but not expanding thoughts or ideas.

Maybe, Tony thought, the conversation had started too far along in the process. The usual ice breaker activities had fallen short, and the ice was chilling the conversation. Somehow he had to get the entire group talking, and there had to be a funny story shared between them. Every family had a funny story about a cross-country trip or a holiday memory. National Lampoon and Chevy Chase made millions exploiting that fact, and Tony had to find that story. That collective memory would lead the way to the soul of this family. Getting to it, though, was going to be tough if nobody would speak up and lead the way. He looked around the table as everyone settled back in, and one by one their eyes met his and it was show time once again.

"Okay. I want to thank everybody for that opening session. I think it went well, and I want to return to some of those issues later in the day. For right now, though, I want to try something different, shift the focus away from the bank and onto the family in general." There was a slight pause as he considered his next pitch and the other players eyed one another nervously but politely.

"I want you all to think back and uncover some of the defining moments in the family experience. What are some of the crazy things you've done as a family, on trips, on holidays, times when the family was together.

What are some of those stories that get repeated at every Thanksgiving table?"

The other six people at the table moved their eyes between Tony and the ceiling, Tony and the table top, and they eyed the coffee pot on the bureau behind him longingly, despite the full cups staring up from the table in front of them. After a long moment of denial and confusion, Margaret finally broke the silence.

"Tony, I really don't see what this has to do with the bank, and I hate that we might be getting off track. Could you help us understand the point of this session?"

"I understand your confusion, Margaret," Tony replied with a nod of deference, "but if you'll bear with me, I think the purpose will emerge."

Another, even longer pause befell the table, and Tony seemed alone in his comfort with the silence. He was convinced that somebody would break, that the tension would bring forth the fruit. As a rule, he thought, people do not like silence in a conversation, and they will fill the silence rather than bear it out. In the end, about three minutes into the pause, his hunch was rewarded, and he was glad he had waited them out.

"A lot of our childhood memories are more closely tied to Daddy's church community than they are to the bank," Augusta offered thoughtfully. "At least they are for me. I shouldn't speak for Ben. Most of what I remember us doing together involved something with the church. We took some trips during school holidays, too. You know, the usual trips that families take, I suppose. We went skiing in Vail once, and we went to a Baptist convention one year in Orlando when Disney first opened. But most of our vacation energy seems to have been consumed by the mission trips."

Augusta looked over at her father as this last revelation rolled off her tongue, and she could sense the exposed nerve.

"I'm not passing judgment on that, Daddy. I'm just trying to recall what might have been strong collective moments in our family."

"That never seemed to be part of your personal mission," Walker responded. "And we tried to balance family trips with the mission work, though your characterization doesn't include that."

"Let's give air to some of that balance, then," Tony interjected, watching the tension mount between father and daughter. "What other trips or activities do you remember that might define your family experience through the years?"

"Well," Walker replied, "we went to Disney more than once, I recall, and we drove west to see the Grand Canyon one summer."

"That was because you had a conference in Denver," Ben replied without looking up. "And we flew into Denver and rented the car to see the Grand Canyon. The rest of the week we were stuck at that dude ranch resort place with all those weird thumper kids by the pool. Gus had to leave some boyfriend behind, so she was a bitch the whole trip, and I ate nachos and cheese until I puked. And Mom wasn't there because she had some function to organize. Hell of a trip. What else you got?"

Augusta snickered as her father looked confused by the clarity of Ben's recollection. He had described it just as she had remembered it, including the boyfriend, though she couldn't remember if their undying love had outlasted the separation. Ellis looked at his wife as if he were wondering why she had never mentioned that trip.

"Like he said," she replied, "there wasn't much to tell. I had really forgotten all about it. I wouldn't classify that trip as a defining moment for our family," she said to the table as a whole.

"What about the trips to New York?" Walker offered. "We've made a lot of those trips over the years. See some shows, eat some great food. Take in all the sights. Old Gus even arranged that tour of the New York Stock Exchange. That was interesting, you have to admit."

Augusta admitted to herself that those trips had been fun, and she nodded toward her father in agreement. What she didn't say, though, was that she remembered those trips to New York mostly as shopping trips with her mother. Ben usually had a game or some other sports-related commitment, and her father rarely left the pulpit to any of the other preachers on Sunday morning. Both of these put a dent in the family weekend travel, but her father would undoubtedly see it another way, so there seemed little to be gained by pointing it out.

Walker seemed to be particularly challenged by the question of balance in the family vacations, and rubbed his palms together as he often did while either in thought or prayer. His eyes moved around the room without locking in on any one thing. Augusta and Ben watched him and waited. Ellis and Twinkle doodled in the margins of their notebooks. Margaret continued making lists, a habit of hers that emerged when situations diverged from an organized path. The first step along such a path meant, for her, a certain free-fall to chaos, and Margaret suffered fools and chaos with equal disdain. The difficulty, though, was that even she couldn't come up with the defining family trip. Instead, she was making a list of all the service organizations and charitable endeavors they had supported as a family. The Charleston Area Food Bank and the Mission House Shelter and Kitchen had always been favorite holiday traditions for her family. She still received holiday cards from both, even years after the kids had grown and no longer served meals and collected canned goods. She was set to make this point when Tony suggested a new strategy.

"Okay," Tony said with a heightened sense of purpose in his voice, "so maybe the family trips leaned toward the church side of things, a natural consequence of your father's work . . . ." Everyone at the table looked sideways at each other and at Walker with eyebrows raised. "So let's look at how your father's work has and continues to define your family."

"Continues may be a stretch," Ben mumbled under his breath.

"Ben!" Augusta and Margaret trounced at the same time.

"Just correcting the good doctor," Ben shot back at them.

"I'm confused," said Tony, looking at Ben and then Walker. Ben seemed to withdraw back into a shell after dropping the bomb, at once satisfied to have delivered the stinger and aware, after the fact, of the potential for collateral damage. Walker never looked at Ben, only at the binder and pencil on the table in front of him. He spoke softly but clearly, with a tone that suggested he'd clarified his son's words or actions a time or two for people over the years.

"My relationship with the church changed recently," Walker offered.

"Very recently," Augusta added. "That's what we were talking about when you walked in this morning. It was news to us as well." Margaret sighed and looked impatiently at Tony as if to suggest that they were veering off course again. This time he threw her a bone.

"Well," he said, "regardless of the current situation, the church has been a defining force in your family life. So let's look at that and see what we might learn about how things define you as individuals and as a family, and that might help us establish points of connection with the Bank. Let's leave the particulars surrounding Walker's current relationship with the church for a later discussion."

"I don't think it's that easy," Ben said, unable to let it go, rising from his seat at the table. "But I'll let you folks try to work it out while I run to the little banker's room down the hall."

"Benjamin," Margaret said sternly, "we just had a break. Can't it wait?"

"Don't talk to me, Mother. Talk to the coffee. I'm just the conduit."

As Ben walked toward the door, Walker got up and followed him out the door. Tony remained behind, surrounded by women, harboring the thought that the bulk of the conversation had just left the room.

By the time Ben reached the elevator, Walker was in lockstep. When Ben reached out to push the call button for the elevator, Walker put a hand on his arm to stop him, but Ben gave him a sideways glance and pushed the up arrow. Walker pulled his arm back and looked up at the floor indicator to see where the car was coming from.

"Going a long way to find plumbing," he said, though he and Ben still faced the elevator door and something Mancini-ish piped softly through the speaker directly above them. A passerby would have thought them strangers.

"Guess you could say I'm looking for the home-field advantage," Ben replied. "And you?"

"Still trying to make sense of you and your comments."

"I wouldn't waste your time on that, old man. Ain't much to either of them, truth be told." As if on cue, the bell rang and the elevator doors opened to an empty car. Ben stepped in and turned to face Walker, who looked at him quizzically. "Fruit falling from trees and all that," he said as he pushed the floor button and waited for the doors to close.

"Don't hang me on that cross, Sonny Boy. I'm afraid I'm not that complicated."

"I don't know, Pop," Ben replied through closing doors. "Don't underestimate yourself."

Walker watched the doors close and paused as the hallway music shifted to an instrumental version of "Under the Boardwalk." He glanced up at the speaker in the ceiling, turned, and headed back down the hall toward the meeting room.

At about that moment, Ben was sliding his key card into the slot and heading for the bar. Despite Twinkle's mandate to the contrary, he had smuggled a gorgeous bottle of Maker's Mark in his suitcase. Breaking the wax seal almost brought a tear to his eye, and he couldn't help wondering whether or not his parents had always been this insufferable. He lifted the glass from the bathroom counter and held it to the light. Not to worry, he thought. The alcohol would kill any germs left behind by previous guests. As he filled the glass and brought it to his lips, there was a knock at the door. He put the glass on the counter by the sink and moved angrily to answer the door.

"You have got to be kidding me, old man!" he said, pulling the door open with a vengeance.

"Housekeeping?" replied the small voice from behind the pleasant smile and clipboard. "I come back later?"

"No, no," he replied, embarrassed by his outburst. "Come on in. I was just heading out. Have a meeting on the second floor. I guess you could call it that. Doing a little housekeeping of our own, you might say." As he was explaining all this to the maid, he was stuffing the bottle back into hiding and rummaging through his dop kit. At last he found the wintergreen LifeSavers he had been looking for, grabbed his breakfast drink, and headed back to the elevator, leaving the room to housekeeping. As the elevator doors opened, there was Eueland.

"Why, hello Mr. Middleton."

"Right back at you, Eueland." Ben and Eueland had become fast friends the previous evening when, after arriving late, Ben had paid Eueland twenty dollars to take the luggage to their room while he and Twinkle had headed straight to dinner.

"I hope everything in the conference room was to your liking this morning."

"Indeed it was, Eueland, though a stiff Bloody Mary would have saved me a trip." He raised his glass to punctuate the last thought, a gesture that was not lost on Eueland. Not much was lost on Eueland.

"Yes sir, I believe it might've," Eueland replied, making a mental note to deliver a Bloody Mary the following morning.

"Lack of drink and crazy family don't mix, especially early in the morning," Ben replied willing the elevator doors to close as Eueland pressed the button for the second floor and the hotel conference rooms.

"No sir, I expect they don't."

"You got any crazy family, Eueland?" Ben asked to Eueland's reflection in the stainless steel elevator door.

"Not any more, no sir. All my people done gone to their reward. But they was a handful while they was here, though, the whole lot of them."

"A handful, huh?"

"Yes sir, but they wasn't crazy. They was just family."

"Think so?" Ben asked, turning to face Eueland.

"I know so. I seen crazy before. Folks crazy as a runned-over dog. That kind of crazy leaves a mark on a man." The doors opened on the second floor and Ben paused for one last question. Eueland, sensing the pause, stepped off the elevator with him.

"What you reckon our reward looks like once we get there?" Ben asked, not wanting to betray his skepticism or insult Eueland's obvious faith. Eueland smiled and answered quickly.

"Now Mr. Middleton, I don't expect I know any more than what the good book says."

"But you believe it's out there, waiting on us."

"Believe and hope, yes sir," Eueland replied with a thoughtful smile. "And I reckon that's what they call faith."

Ben downed the last of his drink and reached into his pocket for the mints, awkwardly trying to wrestle the empty glass and the roll of mints.

"Can I take that for you, Mr. Middleton?" Eueland asked, again sensing a need and pointing to the empty glass in Ben's hand.

"Don't know what we'd do without you, Eueland."

"Just doing my job," he said with a smile. "Enjoy the rest of your morning." He disappeared down the hallway with Ben's empty glass. Ben walked at a mint-melting pace in the other direction, back toward the conference room and the second circle of hell.

CHAPTER FOUR

Tony was accustomed to patient outbursts in clinical situations, so Ben's abrupt exit from the session didn't come as a complete shock. He had still been in the process of collecting his thoughts when Walker re-entered the conference room without Ben, and as if on cue, Ellis and Twinkle had gotten up to leave the room to make a call. So maybe the shock began to emerge when Tony began to wonder if the entire group was going to leave the room in some form or fashion. Only Margaret and Augusta seemed committed to their chairs. This is where the roles and relationships began to get murky for Tony. He really wasn't there as a therapist, and the family should have felt little to no obligation to offer Tony a therapist's control of the meetings, whatever that might've looked like, so Tony sat back and tried to take it all in.

"My apologies for my son's outburst," Walker said as he walked back into the room without his son. "I can't quite figure what's gotten into him."

"Not to worry," replied Tony, rising to a standing position before Walker returned to his seat. "I think this may be a good time to break out into some early interview sessions."

"All right, then," replied Margaret. "What is the next step in that process?" She began straightening her pencils and binder on the table in front of her, ready to make the transition.

"Very simple," replied Tony. "We've reserved a room on the third floor, very similar to this one, with a smaller table and chairs. And Margaret, since you and Walker appear ready to go, why don't we start with the two of you?"

Margaret looked at Augusta with satisfaction, stood, and made her way toward the door where Walker was already standing.

"Augusta," Tony said, "if you will let the others know when they return, I would anticipate that we will rejoin you in this room within a half hour. Normally I would have exercises for the balance of the group as well, but we'll catch up on those later." With that, Tony left the room with the Middletons in tow.

Ben returned to the conference room to find the door open and Augusta alone at the coffee pot, picking through the muffins. She seemed to catch him out of the corner of her eye and voiced her disapproval.

"What the hell was that all about?" she asked. "Daddy came back in here shaking his head, talking about honoring your mother and father and what might've been several other commandments. What did you say to him?"

"Probably more of what I didn't say to him."

"How's that?"

"Long story," he replied, looking around the table and taking his seat. "Where is everybody?"

"Twinkle went with Ellis to call and check on the girls. They both had soccer games this morning. Ellis likes to give them pep talks before the game, encourage them to sting like a bee rather than float like a butterfly."

"Do they know who Ali is, or was? Is he still alive?"

"Ali is, I think, but the girls don't have a clue. And I think Twinkle was thrilled to have an excuse to get out of this room."

"Imagine that."

"Ellis probably was, too." After a pause she continued. "Everything okay with you two? Not that it's any of my business—"

"But you'll ask anyway?"

"Yep, that's about it. Do I sense trouble in paradise?"

"Who knows," Ben responded, shrugging off the question. "I'm like an itinerant preacher, I guess. Only as good as my last sermon. I go week to week. But speaking of preachers on the edge, where's your father?"

"Our father and our mother have been taken to some room on another floor for their private interviews. We all have that to look forward to, apparently, but your emergency departure a while ago left Tony a little confused, I think. This seemed like a good time to knock one of those interviews out, and Mom was insistent that they go first."

"Imagine that," Ben replied, settling into his chair as if a pressure valve had been opened.

"How long have you been a preacher?" Tony asked, as they were all settling into the chairs in the third-floor conference room.

"A long time," Walker replied, looking around, noting that the details of the room seemed to be identical. "I was working in New York, right out of college. Waiting tables, mostly."

"He was a great waiter," Margaret interjected.

"So you two knew each other then?"

"Oh, yes," they seemed to reply almost together in a way that suggested both rehearsal and reminiscence.

"So tell me more about that time," Tony replied.

"Well, like I said, I was waiting tables at night, working on a novel by day, trying to get some short stories published, you know, the whole starving writer thing."

"Yes," Tony replied, "I know it well."

"I was working at a small publishing house," Margaret offered, "and Walker saw me reading manuscripts at the restaurant, usually while I was waiting on my roommate or a date, if I had one."

"I asked her, finally, if she was an editor or in the publishing business," Walker continued. "She said she was. We made a date for lunch later that week. We shared our stories over chicken salad, our dreams over icebox pie, and we were a couple by the time the check arrived."

"Did it really happen that way, Margaret?"

"I think so. My husband has a tendency to exaggerate, but I remember deciding very early on that I wanted to marry him. Maybe not by the end of the first date, but you know what I mean."

"So when and how did you decide to enter the ministry?"

"Well, I'd like to say that that story was a bit more complicated, but it happened quite simply as well," Walker replied. "I was working on a short story about shelters and soup kitchens. We didn't have those where I grew up in South Georgia, at least as far as I knew. We all just looked out for each other. At least that was what I always thought." He kept looking between Tony and Margaret. The former to make sure he was following. The latter to make sure he was remembering the story the way he'd always told it. "So I'm writing this story about New York City shelters and soup kitchens, trying to get an authentic picture, and I decide to go native, as Margaret Mead would've said."

"I'm familiar with the concept," Tony replied, "and impressed that you are as well."

"That was right after we met," Margaret asserted, not to be left out.

"So I decided to join the homeless for a couple of days," Walker continued. "I slept in the shelters and ate in the soup kitchens. I lived among the down and out, the junkies, the whores, the crazy bums that talked back to the voices in their heads, all with the intent of creating compelling characters in a short story."

This last revelation immediately reproduced, in Tony's mind, the image at the airport Wendy's and his initial analysis of Walker Middleton's sermon to the burger.

"Instead of capturing the details of their lives for use in my story," Walker continued, "I found myself ministering to them, helping them make sense of their lives and situations in a way that only a sympathetic soul could have."

"So you were a believer even then?" Tony asked.

"No, not really. I had given most of that up during college. Spent a lot of time trying to find my inner sinner, I used to say."

"Oh, I see."

"But the Lord tapped me on the shoulder again during those first days in the shelters. Made me see that there was much more to life than a good story, or maybe that His story was the best of all stories and more people needed to hear that story than the one I was writing."

"Wow," Tony replied, "that's one hell of a shoulder tapping."

"Well, He is the Lord, I suppose."

"Yes, I suppose so," Tony said while nodding his head and scratching his chin, thinking that he'd gotten more answer than his original question had warranted.

"So you have time to tell me that long story," Augusta continued, turning her coffee cup around on the table by the handle.

"What story's that?"

"The one you wouldn't tell to your father in the hall a while ago. Probably related to why you keep yanking his chain about all this church stuff. I mean, I get the fact that you're not into the church stuff. Organized religion is the bane of our existence and all that. I get that part. But that has been his life's work, the sermons, the mission trips. All of that. So he wants to retire. What's the big deal?"

"I asked the same question a couple of weeks ago. What's the big deal?"

"Well what did he say?" she replied, leaning forward over her coffee cup.

"I didn't ask him. I asked the DEA."

"What are you talking about?" she asked, slapping her hand on the table and shaking her head, trying to construct another of her younger brother's tales. "Are you talking about the DEA, like the Drug Squad?"

"The very same folks. Met me on the concourse in front of the Financial Center one morning a couple of weeks ago and even knew me by name. Walked up to me in suits like they worked at the bank, except that they had little badges hooked to their belts, right next to their big guns. They showed me both, very discreetly."

"Wait. Hold on for just a minute, cause it sounds to me like you're making this up. Why is any of this what Daddy would've wanted to hear? And are you talking about federal agents, at your office, in Charlotte, who know you by name?" She had advanced in his direction almost to the point of climbing onto the table.

"Yes. Federal agents, on the street in front of my office, calling me by name like we're old fraternity brothers, though that's not very likely." He chuckled at the thought and got up from the table, closed the door, and walked over to the coffee pot only to find it empty. He looked down into the empty pot as if to confirm the void. "Do I need to slow down, professor?"

"They're bringing more," Augusta said, still confused but not losing sight of her hosting gene, and the fact that more coffee was on the way.

"That's good," Ben said, putting the pot back on the tray, "and that's what the agents said they wanted, a cup of coffee. And they invited me to join them. Well, invited might be a stretch."

"Now you're kidding, right? This didn't really happen, right?"

"Nope. Not kidding. It gets better. It gets so much better, in fact, that at some point in the telling you will realize that even I couldn't make this shit up, and I've made up some pretty good shit in my day," Ben replied, all the while moving back into his seat and arranging his binder, pencil, and coffee cup on the table in front of him as if setting the stage for a play.

Augusta sat back into her own chair but never took her eyes off of her brother. Part of her kept waiting for the punch line. She was always suckered into Ben's bullshit stories, only to be the last to see it coming. Another part of her, though, was replaying the tape from years before, searching for any reason why the DEA might've wanted to share a cup of coffee with Ben. She remembered a little dope smoking, and even she had tried it once or twice, but that seemed a bit trivial for the DEA. She continued shaking her head as she ran the tape, but kept the conversation going, still unsure whether or not she was being reeled in.

"So what did they want with you?" she asked. "I thought you stopped all that years ago, right after college, around the time you met Twinkle. Is this part of what she's mad at you about?"

"Well, not all of it, not right after college. And Twinkle," he began, but thought better of it, "well, she's been on my ass about a lot of things, but she doesn't know about my little coffee-club meeting." He let that part settle in before he began the next part. "At any rate, my fears of the DEA were long behind me, or so I thought." He repositioned himself in his chair and lifted his coffee cup to look into the empty bottom. Ben Middleton had a fascination with empty spaces, a feeling or a sense that, upon revisiting, an empty space will have been mysteriously made full. Hole to whole, as it were, though he'd yet to have that little theory proven out.

"So what did all of this have to do with Daddy?" Augusta asked, adopting a new tone that seemed simultaneously critical and nurturing.

"I'm getting to that. It seems that the DEA has been watching Robert Tinsley very closely over the last several years."

"Uncle Robert?" she replied with only half surprise. His image had come to mind as she was replaying the tape only moments before. "I guess I hadn't really thought about him that way, though I always wondered. I mean, he always had money and the people in the village always revered him so, even more than Daddy, and he's a preacher. Or was a preacher. They even called Uncle Robert 'Chief' in that little village. I guess I don't need to wonder any longer."

"I wouldn't if I were you."

They both paused to let it all sink in, and for the first time in a while Augusta took her eyes off of Ben and moved them around the room as if the resolution to all this confusion were secretly written into the paintings or the furniture or the wall paint. Ben moved the players on his small stage around as if cueing up the next act. Coffee cup to downstage left, pencil from top of binder to side. His eyes never left the little stage. When Augusta had resigned her reality to the irreconcilable confusion, she looked back at Ben, searching for clarity.

"But why would the DEA talk to you and not me? Not that I feel left out, but I went on more of those mission trips than you did."

"Unfortunately," Ben replied with more than a hint of irony and hesitation, "our trips often involved different missions."

"What is that supposed to mean? Were you, or are you, somehow involved with Uncle Robert's business? But you were 15 or 16, weren't you, at the oldest? We stopped going after you reached high school age, didn't we?"

"Officially we stopped going at about that time, yes. And I never had any official connection to his business, no." He paused for a moment. "How much of this do you really want to know?"

"How much more is there? And what has this got to do with Daddy? Was he involved?"

"Not really, but you'll need to hear the rest of it to know why." They were both startled by a soft knock at the door as a tray of coffee emerged in the arms of a smallish black woman in a maroon coat and name tag.

"So after seminary you moved back to Charleston? Is that correct?" Tony asked, trying to tie some loose ends together quickly.

"Yes," Margaret responded. "That part was my idea. We had lived in New York through all of that and we had started a family. Augusta was actually born in New York City, much to her grandfather's horror."

"And I had been working with a Manhattan church for a couple of years," Walker continued, "and we felt the need for a change, a return to home or at least close to home. And opportunities were better in Charleston at that time than they were in South Georgia, so that part of the decision was really simple as well."

"Simple decisions seem to be a theme," Tony added.

Walker and Margaret looked at each other, but the strained smiles suggested that things might not have been as simple as they were making them out to be.

"So, Charleston it was," Tony said.

"That's right," Walker concluded. "I hired on with Trinity and have been there ever since. Pretty remarkable, all things considered."

Tony looked confused.

"Remarkable to stay at one church for an entire career," Margaret filled in. "Preachers usually move around to several churches through their professional lives."

"Oh, I see. And to what might you attribute your luck or success?"

"Like everything else, I suppose, I attribute it directly to the Lord. And maybe a little help from a strong tie to the community," Walker added, though he and Margaret did not make eye contact.

"And you have done great things for the community as well," Tony said to Margaret. "At least according to the file they gave me. You've been very active with many of the non-profits and charity boards, the symphony and the museum."

"To those whom much is given, much is expected."

"Yes, I suppose so. Did you ever have day-to-day duties at the bank?"

"Never. Daddy handled all of that until the day he died."

"And neither of your children followed along in the family business?"

"I think my father had hopes for Ben early on, but moving back to Charleston never seemed to appeal to him. I think he has enjoyed banking, though."

"And Augusta?"

"That was never really discussed, and she always seemed happy teaching and working with the parents at her school in Greenville."

"How about you, Walker? Ever get any pressure from your father-in-law to go into the family business?"

Walker chuckled. "I'm not sure what could be farther from the truth," he said. "In fact, Old Gus made it a point at every possible turn to distinguish between family and other. I was other. Thankfully, my children are family, though they do carry the disgrace of my blood."

"Walker," Margaret said, trying to lighten the critical comment, "be serious." Walker said nothing further. That was his story and he was sticking to it.

"Was Old Gus, as you put it, an active member of your congregation?"

"Lord, no," Walker replied. "He was a cradle-to-grave Episcopalian. Never forgave me my Baptist ways, I suppose, even if Margaret and the kids remained active in his church instead of mine." This last thought seemed to take Tony by surprise.

"But I thought Ben was describing his childhood as being characterized by your ministry? Is that not the case?"

"Not really. They went with me on a couple of professional conference trips, I suppose. And they were very active in our mission trips during the summers for a while there. But even that stopped when they got to high school age, I think. Is that about right, Margaret?"

"Sounds right," Margaret replied, "though you know kids have a tendency to remember things differently from their parents."

"Thank you, Mavis," Augusta said, louder than she needed to, catching sight of the name tag on the staff member's maroon coat and looking around for her purse. Ben, catching her line of sight, signaled that he would take care of it, reached into his pocket, and fished a twenty-dollar bill out of his wallet. He gave Mavis the money and thanked her again as she left the room.

"You're mighty generous with that drug money," Augusta said sharply to Ben after the door had closed on them again. "I'm assuming that's part of the story I haven't heard yet."

"I spent that money a long time ago. Been running on bank money since then. But, yes, that's part of the story that neither you nor your father has heard." He got up to fill his coffee cup.

"Well, I'm all ears now, though I'm starting to feel like I'm talking to one of my students who just got caught with beer on a field trip."

"Just like that, only different," Ben replied, thankful to feel a bit of levity re-enter the conversation. This was not Augusta's first rodeo as far as Ben was concerned. He'd stepped in shit more times than not growing up and had relied on her more than he'd liked in navigating the fishbowl of their childhood Charleston.

"No, I think the DEA makes this very different."

"You're probably right," Ben replied. So much for levity, he thought. "But they weren't really after me. At least I don't think they were. I appeared on their radar because of some old surveillance photos. Some down in the village and others at Hampden-Sydney."

"Back when you were in the business?" she replied coldly.

"Back when I sold weed and stolen radar detectors to frat boys across Virginia because my father and grandfather cut me off. Yes, back then. But I was small time and I took care of the security boys on every campus along my route, so nobody really cared about my little operation. Just tried to keep my customers satisfied. Essentially the same shit I do today for the bank and for a lot of the same people."

"So why'd they want to talk to you after all these years?"

"Following trails that led to the Chief, I guess. I stopped selling when I got a job after graduation. The pictures they showed me were from high school and college freshman timeframes. Ancient history. Shots of me and some of Chief's regional boys. The way he explained it to me, if I stayed far enough down the food chain, it was easy money. His way of giving back. He also liked to relive his college days through me, since he hasn't been able to attend one of his own reunions, or anything else in this country for that matter."

"Didn't know that little detail," Augusta said, getting up to refresh her own coffee cup. "How long has that been the case?"

"Shortly after they graduated, I think," though Ben couldn't be sure about his response. He'd never actually heard for certain, but speculation had been fairly strong that Chief Robert Tinsley had been forced to leave the country shortly after graduating from Chapel Hill.

"But he and Daddy were roommates, weren't they?" Augusta asked, trying to work through the confusion of the latest details and shake a sugar packet at the same time. "That was always the story that I heard. So were they both involved with all that, or just Uncle Robert?"

"You have to understand that I never heard any of this from your father," he replied, "so your guess is as good as mine about all that. Chief was always careful to avoid my questions about all that. What I do know is that when they left Chapel Hill in the 60s, one went north to find the Lord and the other went south to become one. Only distinction seems to be the intoxicant."

Augusta's response was interrupted by voices at the door followed closely by Tony ushering in the return of the senior Middletons. Tony went straight for the coffee pot. Walker kept the corner of his eyes on Ben as he skirted the table and told Tony how much he could use another cup. Margaret Middleton made cheerful conversation about the interview process and the benefits thereof, but all the while stared a hole through both of her children whose isolated conversation triggered a paranoia that no amount of caffeine could dissipate. Augusta had pulled out her cell phone to call Ellis, but hung it up as he walked into the room with Twinkle right behind.

"I was just trying to call you," she said. "How were the girls?"

"All is right with the world," Ellis confirmed. "They're all geared up for the game. They wanted to tell Aunt Twinkle about the mascot bears they built at that place at the mall, so that occupied most of the conversation."

"They're so cute," Twinkle said. "I told them we would come down for one of their games in the next couple of weeks."

"They would love that," Augusta said. "They've heard about all of Uncle Ben's soccer games when he was a kid. All knees and feet. I've even showed them an old picture of him in one of his uniforms. Endless giggles."

Ben smiled but chose not to enter the fray. When Twinkle talked to or about the nieces, it rarely worked to his advantage to join the conversation.

"Well," Tony said to no one in particular, "now that we've all gathered once again, why don't we all get a fresh cup of java and begin anew the group discussion." Once this was said, the tension was fog-like to all but Tony. Nobody made eye contact across generations or even across family units. What had been polite conversation became hushed anticipation. There seemed to be a collective effort to count the grain lines in the fake wood table top. All eyes were cast down, waiting for Tony to bring up the next awkward line of discussion. The small quartz clock on the credenza, next to the phone and the small writing pad and pen, marked the slow passage of time like a funeral dirge.

"You've all been a part of this bank and a part of the larger culture surrounding it. The community that helped to define it and was defined by it."

"It really isn't that large a bank," Ben interjected in what was initially thought to be an effort at comic relief. "Really, it's not," he said to the furrowed brows and rolling eyes surrounding the table and him.

"Tell me more about that," Tony replied.

"On a relative scale, I mean. It's tough to imagine that a community could define or be defined by a small bank."

"Ben," his mother said patiently, "our bank has been an important part of this community for several generations. I think that's what Tony is getting at."

"I know that, Mom. But the bank was not defined by the community. It was defined by the Guses. And in the low country and even in Charleston, the bank holds a very small share of the overall market. Other banks have grown considerably faster in the same markets, which to me suggests that Plantation Trust hasn't really been defining communities for a number of years."

All eyes turned to Tony as if this revelation might upset the Pacific Mergers apple cart.

"That's nothing new to Tony's outfit," Ben said. "That's why they want to buy it. It's like you used to say about me when I was in school. The bank is not living up to its potential."

"I don't think you're right about all that," Margaret said. Daddy was a very good businessman, and this bank has always made money. It's provided quite well for all of us through the years."

"There you go, Mom," Ben replied. "You can't take this personally. It's business."

"And it has provided quite well for all the stockholders," Augusta interjected, "not just our family. That has made it a good investment through the years. What Ben is saying is that, as a business, Plantation Trust could be even better than it is now. Could make even more money than it has."

"Well, Good Lord willing, it will keep making money and doing good work in this community," Walker entered the fray with Jesus at the helm.

"Got nothing to do with the Lord, Daddy," Ben replied too quickly. "That's a different business."

"Here we go again," Walker said as he slid back into his chair and turned his head toward the clock and the coffee pot. "It's all about the Lord, son. That's the part you've never understood."

"Daddy," Augusta interjected ahead of Ben, "that may be so, but we need to leave Him out of this for the time being."

"Amen," Ben said with little restraint.

"What's that supposed to mean?" Walker jumped back in.

"I think Augusta's point is valid, Walker," Tony interrupted. "We really need to stick to the subject of the bank and its role in the community."

"Well the Lord Jesus had something to say about banks and their role in the community," Walker continued.

"That may be so, yes, but—"

"Moneychangers at the door of the temple," Walker kept going.

"Holy shit," Ben said under is breath.

"First Tim Chapter Six says money is the root of all evil and Acts Chapter Eight says the power of God is not for sale," Walker continued. "So the Lord is the CEO of every business, the chairman of every board."

The conversation came to a screeching halt as Walker's comments grew into something between a sermon and a really strange response to Tony's original question about community. Margaret watched her husband with a face that suggested patient years of hearing the same rhetoric. Augusta and Ben rolled their eyes at one another. Ellis sketched a detail of the conference room's crown moulding. Twinkle listened intently as Walker continued with fervor.

"And as for defining communities, the church has been building communities for thousands of years. Trinity Church has been a defining pillar of the Charleston community for generations."

"Is it for sale?" Ben asked.

"Of course it's not for sale," Walker replied indignantly with a strong, punctuating furrow of the brow and snap of the chin.

"Then why don't we stick to talking about what is?" Ben replied.

At that, Walker withdrew into his seat back and turned once again to face the coffee pot and the small clock that marked the beat of the fresh awkward silence. Tony waited for someone else to break ranks. Ellis was the first speak.

"Your question was an interesting one, Tony. The one about the community and the bank and possible connections."

"I'm glad you think so," Tony said with a smile.

"And you have to remember that, like Walker said earlier, I am from the 'other' category, not the 'family' category."

"Of course, but you're a part, nonetheless."

Ellis shifted in his seat. The hair on the back of Augusta's neck began to tingle. It always made her nervous when Ellis used that preface, and he used it purposefully if infrequently.

"Remember, also, that Augusta and I are not really a part of this community. We don't live here. So my observations are those of an informed outsider, at best."

"Okay. We'll keep that in mind," Tony replied, curious about what this was leading up to.

"Well, it seems to me that the bank used to swing a big stick in this town. And this may be what Ben was getting at, but for the previous generations, Plantation Trust held quite a bit of social capital. Probably more social than actual capital, truth be told. But there were fewer players in that business then, and the Guses had made good in what was a relatively small town where lots of money could be made. Cotton was king. But now Plantation Trust is old money, and new money has sprung up in other ventures that affords a greater number of people a greater amount of social leverage. Am I right?"

Ellis had drawn everybody, even Walker, back into the conversation brilliantly, and Augusta was the first to respond.

"I agree, yes, and I would even add that our perspective would map fairly readily onto similar situations even in Greenville. It's interesting to see the difference, even, between generations of parents at the school. There is a deference to the old established families on some issues, especially capital campaigns and other fundraisers. People just expect those families to pony up, but not as much as they used to, maybe."

"To whom much is given?" Tony said, with a nod to Margaret.

"Yes, certainly," Augusta continued, "but I think there was a different return on that expectation in the past."

"How's that?" Tony asked, slanting his head like a confused puppy.

"Well, I think there was almost a perceived reverence," Augusta continued, "for those, like the Guses, who held the resources, the promise, the ability to create opportunities. A perception that these men, and a few women, were self-made, magical success stories. The more we look at those stories, though, the more we see that, in many cases, it was the right place at the right time that carried the day, for the Guses and the others."

Margaret sighed and shook her head, but Ben picked up the ball and ran with it.

"That takes nothing away from any of the Guses. They certainly had the smarts and courage to make the most of being at the right place at the right time, and they chose a business that held great promise. Some of their peers did not choose as wisely. And they worked very hard at it. Old Gus was a poster child for the Protestant work ethic." That last remark even got a nod and a chuckle from Walker.

"That reverence that Augusta is talking about," Ellis picked up the ball, "is difficult to sustain across generations within a community. The builders or creators of that community are displaced by those who manage or operate that community."

"Well, you kids are a lot smarter than I am, and for that I am grateful," Margaret said. "And what I think you're saying is that the bank is not as important to the community as it was at one time. Is that what you're trying to say?"

"Sort of," Ellis replied.

"But not exactly," continued Augusta.

"They're trying to say," Ben concluded, "that the principals of Plantation Trust, most of whom are sitting at this table, don't swing as big a social stick as they used to."

"Oh. Well, how about that." With that, Margaret sat back in her chair and nodded her head with eyebrows raised and eyes, conceivably, opened.

CHAPTER FIVE

After a long morning in a closed conference room, the sun appeared much brighter than normal to Augusta Thomason. She squinted and watched the steps carefully as she walked from the quiet hotel lobby to the busy sidewalks of Charleston. The French Market was bustling with tourists, and the Planter's Inn was making good on its promise to be in the center of Old Charleston. Positioned on a busy corner, the Planter's Inn had witnessed the ebb and flow of the cotton trade, the wonder of urban revitalization, and the steady mixture of tourists and college kids and business types through a renewed and vibrant commercial district. And it was into this vibrancy that Augusta was leading Ellis, Ben, and Twinkle. Collectively they were in search of a sandwich shop, though individually they were still trying to make sense of their morning.

"Should I get a cab?" Ellis asked, stepping down to the sidewalk with a similar squint and looking both ways along the busy street.

"No," Ben answered quickly. "There's a joint around the corner that used to make a hell of a cheeseburger."

"A joint, you say?" Augusta snapped back, unable to let go of their earlier conversation.

"Loosen up there, sister," he responded with a laugh. "You can't stay wrapped around that axle forever." They started walking toward the cheeseburger joint with Ben and Augusta in the lead, Ellis and Twinkle following with cell phones to their ears.

"You haven't even finished telling me what axle I'm wrapped around," Augusta replied, turning around to see both her husband and sister-in-law engaged in phone conversations. "Don't even think you're going to get off that easy. Or is that something else the DEA had to say in your little meeting?"

"Not a good time," Ben replied, eyes forward, "but that cheeseburger is going to wash down great with a cold beer."

"Somebody mention a beer?" Ellis said from behind them. Ben looked over at Augusta and smiled as they all crossed the street toward Charleston Place, a mixed-use development of hotel and retail space that provided the commercial anchor for the area.

"So how far are we walking?" Twinkle asked from behind them as they reached the other sidewalk.

"Four of five blocks toward the Battery," Ben answered, eyes forward, anticipating her next thought.

"You go ahead," she said, just as he knew she would. "I'll grab something in here," she continued, pointing at the entrance to the Hotel and Shoppes of Charleston Place. "Ellis, you come with me. Let them talk business while we shop."

Ellis looked at Augusta and shrugged his shoulders. She shrugged back, and Twinkle and Ellis headed into the revolving doors as Augusta and Ben continued down the busy sidewalk toward one hell of a cheeseburger. Ben never turned around completely, never made eye contact with Twinkle, and threw only a cursory glance at Augusta before heading off down the sidewalk toward the Battery.

"I guess you knew that was coming," Augusta said, walking in lockstep with Ben.

"I guess so."

"Is everything okay with you two? There seem to be some issues there."

"Nothing that can't be fixed by a reproduction specialist or a divorce lawyer, I suppose. Or the Good Lord, even. She seems to bring him into the equation more often these days."

"Her father-in-law would be thrilled to hear that."

"Yup. Two peas in a really shallow pod," Ben said, continuing to walk forward, hands in pockets, and never looking at Augusta.

"I didn't know things had gotten that bad."

"I'm not sure things are as bad as they are just married."

"What's that supposed to mean?" Augusta asked, beginning to get curious about how her brother might view her own marriage.

"Unrequited love, failed expectations, irreconcilable perspectives on the important shit. It's real easy to be the right person for each other when you're young and drunk, but once the Joneses grab you by the short hairs, the momentum can work against you."

"Everybody goes through that, I think. Don't you?"

"Sure. But statistics suggest that fewer than half come out the other end."

"And you feel like you're not going to make it?"

"Well," Ben replied, stopping to look at Augusta and make his point, "if the stats are correct, one of the two of us standing here will end up divorced, and you seem a whole lot happier than I do."

"It's not that simple, Ben, you know that."

"The stats or your marriage?"

"Both, probably."

"Well, it is what it is. Nothing more, nothing less."

"Very prophetic."

"Pathetic? You calling my marriage pathetic?" Ben said with exaggerated surprise, yanking his sister's chain.

"Whatever."

They walked in silence for about a block, both looking straight ahead or down at the sidewalk in front of them. Augusta tried to remember the last time she had spent any time with her brother. For so many years she had been her brother's keeper, and it would seem that in recent years she had turned that over to her old friend Twinkle. That had been part of the initial attraction to Twinkle, Augusta thought. Twinkle was someone who could assume responsibility for nurturing her brother, a task that seemed to have evaded Margaret completely and left Augusta with an undue sense of responsibility, especially since she had introduced Twinkle and encouraged their courtship. At this point, though, was it really any of her business to get involved in their marriage? Probably not, she thought. Definitely not. After all, her marriage was far from perfect, so who was she to offer advice? And this was, she thought, probably what Ben was thinking about at that very moment. She would've been surprised, and probably disappointed to learn that Ben was thinking about a cheeseburger. Nothing more, nothing less.

"You never did finish your story," she said as they crossed a third block and, she felt, distanced themselves from other ears.

"What story's that?" he replied, eyes forward, hands in pockets.

"Your coffee-club story."

"Oh, that story."

"Yes, that story. The one your father wouldn't want to hear but is somehow involved in?"

"Yeah, well, I had hoped you had heard all you wanted to hear."

"Not by a long shot," Augusta replied, trying to keep up with Ben's increasing pace. "And, where the hell's the fire?" Ben looked at her with a confused expression and slowed down a touch. He also took his hands out of his pockets, as he tended to talk with his hands, especially when walking.

"So we had coffee a couple of blocks from the bank, at the Dunkin' Donuts there by the Hornets' Stadium." He paused there as if trying to remember what everybody had ordered.

"And?" Augusta insisted impatiently.

"And they showed me all the pictures and we talked about the history of all that, a lot of the same stuff you heard about this morning, and they seemed satisfied with all that. And then they asked what I knew about the mission program."

"The mission program?"

"Yeah, the whole project, going back to when Dad first started going down there and taking folks from the church to work in the village."

"What did they want to know that for?"

"I'm getting to that," Ben said, patiently, as they waited for the lights to turn so they could cross the street. "There's the hamburger joint." He pointed to the middle of the next block, and Augusta looked in that general direction. She also caught sight of the graveyard and gothic structures of St. Phillip's Episcopal Church in the distance, thinking to herself how she'd missed this little diner through all the years of going to church right down the street. She had never even heard of it. The lights changed and they started across. As they started across, Ben's memory returned to the Dunkin' Donuts to pull the details in real time.

"So how old were you when they first started this mission work?" the larger agent asked from over his steamy cup of coffee, stirring in the cream and sugar.

"I think the mission thing started before I was born," Ben replied, blowing across his cup to cool the contents. "And I don't think we even started going down there until I was about 11 or 12."

"And how did you good Christian folks happen to pick that village?" asked the same agent.

"I never asked my father, but I always assumed it was because he and Robert Tinsley were old friends. I never asked Robert about it either. I was a teenager. I didn't give a shit. It was all fun to me."

"When you say old friends, what do you mean?" asked the other, smaller agent who had said very little to that point."

"They were roommates at Chapel Hill," Ben replied, beginning to feel the conversation turning away from him, and even away from Uncle Robert, and toward his father. He focused his attention on saying as little as possible, unsure of where the questions were headed.

"When you were meeting with Robert Tinsley while on your mission trips, did he ever mention the work your father's group was doing?" the agent continued, "or if he was ever involved in the mission process at all, in any way?"

"Not that I remember."

"Never really saw him hammering nails or raising walls or any of that?"

Not that I remember," Ben repeated.

"So how was Robert Tinsley involved in the process?"

"I don't think he was directly involved. Each year we went down there, he had a different project identified—a hospital, a church, a house— and we would work on those projects in that little village and the doctors would do the medical stuff and we'd have church services and all that. Robert used to have the volunteers to his house at the end of the week for a dinner to thank them for their work, but that's all I remember him doing."

"So how did your father's church raise the money for all this mission work? Bake sales and car washes?" This last remark brought a smile to the faces of the DEA, and Ben cracked a grin as well, but he was beginning to see the trail ahead.

"The youth groups did the car washes," he replied. "I remember those. The older girls in bikini tops was quite a sight."

"I bet," the agents replied almost in unison.

"But I don't remember if that covered the whole nut. Like I said, I was a teenager. The business side of mission trips to me was making sure we had access to beer," Ben continued with a shrug and a laugh.

"I'm assuming Robert Tinsley made that available," the smaller agent said without a smile.

"The beer? Oh, who the hell knows. We were in the middle of nowhere." Ben scratched his head and tried to steer the conversation away from wherever it was going.

"So, as you remember it, Robert Tinsley didn't have anything to do with the mission projects, other than the dinner at the end. That sound right?"

"As far as I remember it, that sounds about right."

The smaller agent paused to flip open a small notebook and make some notes. The larger agent was eyeing the donuts behind the counter from across the room. Ben moved his eyes back and forth between the two, waiting for the next question, feeling certain he'd said too much already. A loud voice called out from behind the counter.

"Y'all want some more coffee?" the voice said with a smile. "Cause you keep staring at them donuts like that, you liable to get thirsty." Ben smiled at the voice, though he never turned in its direction. He kept his eyes moving between the two agents.

"No, thank you," said the larger agent.

"Okay, then," replied the voice behind the counter. "Let me know if y'all need anything." The Dunkin' Donuts had only the three customers at that moment, and for that Ben was grateful. While he was never one to shirk his social responsibilities, he began to wonder how he might introduce his new friends to any colleagues that might wander in for their morning caffeine fix.

"So you say you began going at 11 or 12," the smaller agent returned to the conversation. "But the mission trips began before you were born."

"That's right, "Ben replied, trying to figure out why they kept returning to the same details.

"So Robert Tinsley could've been more active in the earlier years. Fair statement?"

"Beats me," Ben replied. "I guess anything is possible. You should ask him." Anything to point the trail ahead away from his father, if that's where they were headed.

"Well, if anything is possible, would it also be possible that Robert Tinsley funded most of that mission work?"

"Like I said, I don't really—"

"I mean," interjected the smaller agent, "they were old friends, college roommates. Your father's church sets up shop, coincidentally, in Robert Tinsley's village in the middle of nowhere."

Ben listened as all the words he had used to answer the agent's questions now got thrown back at him with new inferences, new possibilities, new fingers pointing at his father, and his own fingers went cold around his hot paper cup of coffee. He tried to respond without changing his facial expression, but he failed.

"I suppose that's possible, but I doubt it played out that way."

"And why is that?" the smaller agent replied.

"Well, he's a preacher, first of all, and I don't think preachers would, you know . . . ."

"Let's pretend I don't know," replied the larger agent, "because I've seen preachers do a lot of things that might surprise you."

"What's that supposed to mean?" Ben replied, squinting and raising his jaw at the agent in response to the perceived threat.

"Let's focus on this preacher," said the smaller agent. "Don't worry about the ones he's talking about." He seemed to love setting the hook on the good-cop/bad-cop routine. It just never seemed to get old. Ben looked back at the smaller agent and the agent reeled him in. "What you're saying is that your father the preacher wouldn't knowingly take drug money and do the Lord's work with it. That sound about right?"

"Damn right," Ben replied, throwing a glance at the larger agent.

"But you can't say for sure where the money came from that did all of the Lord's work," continued the agent, "especially in those early years."

"No, I can't, but I bet my father could. Why don't you just ask him?"

"Probably should," replied the smaller agent, closing his notebook and downing the remaining coffee from his cup.

With that image, Ben returned to the streets of Charleston, or a small window table of the diner where he and Augusta had settled as he was finishing his description of the DEA encounter almost as an out-of-body experience.

"So they think Daddy was involved with Uncle Robert?" Augusta asked, incredulous and wide-eyed.

"That certainly seems to be the case," Ben replied, pulling the menu from its perch between the salt and pepper shakers and the sugar dispenser. He eyed the menu, decompressing from the memory of the DEA encounter, as Augusta shook her head in disbelief.

Margaret busied herself with the organization of her space as Tony and Walker talked through the local lunch options. She assumed, perhaps rightfully, that Walker's culinary preferences were more closely aligned with Tony's than hers would have been. She felt the morning session had been a success and looked forward to getting Walker's opinion at some point, but she felt an obligation to entertain Tony, to take him to lunch and tell him all about downtown, to ensure that he felt at all times that Charleston was the center of the universe. On the other hand, Tony had made it fairly clear that he needed to take care of some e-mails and prepare for the afternoon session. He had planned, he said, to grab a quick sandwich somewhere with a Wi-Fi connection. It was at that point that Walker, whose knowledge of local Wi-Fi hotspots was admittedly limited, launched into the litany of local eateries and their characteristic and often idiosyncratic fare. Margaret rarely ate downtown, so she didn't really have an opinion. She was, however, ready to leave the small conference room and even the hotel. She needed some fresh air and a break from the discussion. The last comment had thrown her. She recognized that Charleston, indeed the world, was changing, but she didn't agree that prominent families, especially hers, were not as vital a part of the social fabric as they had always been. If she had conceded that point, she felt, she would leave herself open to criticism. Her father might protest that her generation had fallen asleep at the wheel, slumbered while the reins of power had been usurped by the great unwashed, the very masses that had been the beneficiaries of the Camber determination and work ethic.

"Margaret," she heard in the distance as she saw her father's face behind his desk at the bank. "Margaret!" She looked up from her binder and pencil to see Tony and Walker standing at the door of the conference room looking back at her with eyebrows raised in question.

"You ready to go?" Walker asked, shrugging his shoulders and gesturing toward the hall.

"Yes, yes. I'm sorry," she said. "Trying to take all of this excitement in. Will Tony be joining us?" she said, standing and smiling toward Tony.

"No, no," Tony replied. "I'm heading up to the room to grab my laptop and then over to the shops across the street. Walker thinks there might be a sandwich shop over there that suits my purpose."

"You sure?" Margaret said, walking toward the door.

"Very sure, thank you."

"Suit yourself," Walker said, reaching out to take his wife's arm and lead her out into the hall. "Margaret and I are heading down to a little diner I frequent, right there in the shadows of her church, a couple of blocks up the street. Their chicken salad has folks dancing in the street, though, truth be told, it's not chicken. Turkey. But don't tell anybody."

"I hate to miss that," Tony repeated, "but duty calls." He walked the Middletons to the elevator. He pushed the up arrow for himself, the down for them. A lounge version of "Georgia on My Mind" played through the speaker above them, though the irony was lost on all but Tony. The down car arrived first, they said their goodbyes, and Tony began to hum along with the speaker as he waited for the elevator to return on its way northward.

After retrieving his laptop, Tony set out to discover both Charleston and Wi-Fi. Out of the hotel lobby, he took a couple of right turns and walked along the commercial storefronts and unknowingly toward the College of Charleston, as if gravity or some force of nature were pulling him back to the ivory tower. He began to notice the demographic shift from older business and tourist types to coeds and frat boys, running shorts and flip flops, and his pulse seemed to settle. He was like a den animal finding comfort in the presence of known walls. In fairly short order he stumbled into a small sandwich shop with the Wi-Fi decal in the window. Cafe Brigitte, they called themselves, and Tony would learn later from the barista and waiter with tattoos and dreadlocks that Brigitte was among the original European madams to set up shop in the newly-founded Charleston, and it was rumored that King Charles himself had been one of her early clients, before she departed for the new world. Fascinating story, thought Tony, even if absolutely none of it was true. But George, the decorated barista and waiter, was able to convince him that Brigitte's coffee was potentially as good as sex in a brothel, though he placed a lot of trust in the word "potentially." Tony's love life was in such a state of shambles that he was in no position to disagree.

"Do I need to do anything special to pick up the signal?" Tony asked as George was walking away to get the coffee. "No" was the reply, and Tony exhaled deeply, settled into his chair, and opened his laptop to begin his characterization of the morning session. Michael Kelly, his boss of almost a month now, had not specifically requested twice daily updates, but there had been a sense of urgency because the Plantation Trust deal was set to close in the next 90 days, and Tony's report was considered a significant part of their due diligence. All of these thoughts ran through Tony's mind as he waited for his email program to boot and retrieve e-mails. He was having a tough time wrapping his mind around exactly what he would say. He got some guidance from his boss, though, and just in time. There was an e-mail from Michael Kelly waiting for Tony in his inbox.

Tony—

Got your early thoughts and find them helpful. Keep the conversation focused as much as possible on the dead grandfather and the parents. I don't think the next generation can tell us anything useful. I'll be in the office most of the day.

Michael

Tony considered the e-mail and used it as a springboard for his reply.

Michael—

You may be right about the next generation, at least as far as direct data collection. They haven't been involved at all in the business and, quite frankly, have little interest in the process. For that matter, the parents seem to have little interest in the process, except that Margaret seems intent on showing me all that Charleston has to offer. They continue to wonder what my role in the process might be, though we expected that. As I mentioned to you very early on, the therapeutic may not meld naturally with the capitalistic. There is a hesitance to drill too deeply on any topic related to the bank, though they seem to roam pretty freely over the impact of Walker's church work on the family. The morning sessions did not yield much, but I hope to approach the same points from new ground this afternoon. Augusta, the daughter, seems to understand a great deal about the larger family dynamic, and I hope to work with her individually this afternoon. Ben, the son, carries quite a chip on his shoulder. There is a lot of tension between father and son, though, that seems to have nothing to do with the bank. I get the feeling, though, that somehow all of these things are connected. Maybe that's just the hopeful therapist. Progress is slower than I expected, but time remains. If you have further specific ideas about lines to follow, they are welcome.

Tony

He closed the lid of the laptop as George returned with coffee and a lunch menu. Instead of spending too much time on the menu, Tony hoped for advice.

"So what would the Lady Brigitte have recommended for lunch?" he asked George.

"Initially, she would have argued the Lady title," George responded, keeping the myth of Brigitte alive in dialogue, "but then she would have suggested that, for the discerning traveler, we have a white bean soup and a grilled ham and cheese."

"I'll have that."

"Very well, indeed," George replied, exaggerating the language of the response. He returned to the kitchen, leaving Tony to explore the view of Charleston from the coffee shop. As he waited, and as the sidewalks of Charleston rolled past the window like the moving sidewalks at the airport, Tony almost struggled to see the legs and feet of the passersby. He leaned left and right, but neither position offered him a view of the ground level. Consequently, everybody seemed to be floating by. Some looked in the window toward him. Others didn't. Those who did made the sight even stranger. They were floating by without looking where the conveyor belt was taking them. Tony began to imagine the window as a painting or a photograph, an artistic expression of constant motion. But who were the players on this little stage? There was the coed with the too-tight t-shirt who glances knowingly into the window long enough to make eye contact with Tony. There was the young suit passing in the opposite direction, looking not in the window but back over his own shoulder at the coed. What a difference a couple of years make, which Tony guessed was all that separated the two. And still the younger coed had seemed more comfortable in her own skin than had the suit. From across the street, an older woman in a large red hat crossed while waving to someone outside the frame. Very few cars passed through the scene, and Tony thought this odd. There always seemed to be a car in the picture in L.A. There were also fewer people of color than Tony had expected, based on his conversations with his colleagues, some of whom were not convinced that slavery had actually ended in the South. Most of the black kids seemed to be college kids with book bags and headphones, pausing in the frame to greet each other from beneath baseball caps worn askew in South Central style, only this was South Central Charleston.

"Taking it all in?" asked George, holding a cup of soup toward the window.

"Looks a lot like a lot of other cities, I suppose."

"Maybe so. What other city are you from?"

"L.A."

"And you think that," George said, pointing out the window, "looks like L.A?"

"Well, fewer cars, fewer people, older buildings, and narrower streets, I guess," Tony replied in jest. "Other than that, though . . . ."

"Right. Sandwich on the way, Galileo."

Tony chuckled and turned his attention back to the window just in time to see Ellis and Twinkle moving through the frame, looking into but avoiding eye contact with Brigitte. Finally they stopped about mid-frame, recognized Tony, and circled back toward the door of the shop.

"Well, what do we have here?" Ellis said. You can't escape the Middletons, can you, Professor?"

"Making no attempt to do so, Ellis, let me assure you. If anyone should be hesitant to engage, it should be the two of you. From what I can gather, being an in-law to the Middletons is no walk in the park."

"Far from it," Ellis agreed. Twinkle nodded in affirmation but said nothing. "Are we interrupting a working lunch?" Ellis continued, pointing to the laptop.

"Not at all. Just trying to stay current on e-mails. There never seems to be enough time for technology, and I thought it was supposed to make our lives easier."

"Amen to that," Ellis replied.

"Please join me if you care to," Tony offered. "Madam Brigitte is very accommodating, according to the legend." The reference and story were lost on the other two, and Tony chose not to elaborate.

"Hate to intrude when you're off the clock."

"No such thing this weekend. Have a seat and let's see if a menu can be found, unless you've already eaten."

"Not yet. We were walking through the shops and found ourselves back on the street and still hungry. Can you recommend something?"

Tony could only follow George's suggestions, but those appealed to both Ellis and Twinkle, so soup and sandwiches were ordered for all. Tony decided to make use of the time.

"Twinkle, you've been very quiet this morning," Tony said, heading back into the fray. "Is that normal for you or am I doing a poor job of engaging you in the discussion?"

There was a pause as Ellis and Twinkle, at first, looked only at the table, not at each other. At some point they made eye contact and knowing smiles came across their faces. Ellis was the first to speak.

"I wouldn't describe her as quiet," he said, looking back at Tony, "but I would say you're doing an admirable job of herding cats."

"No, I'm not normally quiet," Twinkle continued, "but I don't think all of this is any of my—our—business. I really don't have anything to add, so I figure the best bet is just to keep quiet."

"That certainly sounds reasonable," Tony replied, and they all exchanged nods in agreement. "But your perspectives would add value to the process, even if the decisions are not yours to make."

"But what if," Twinkle continued after a short pause, "what if we don't really have an opinion on all this bank stuff? I mean, I don't think it affects me one way or the other."

"I guess we're really saying the same things," Tony said, "but I think I should be saying it differently. I'm not really interested in your perspectives on the bank, only the family. And since, like me, you both arrived at this family from the outside, you tend to view things objectively, on a relative scale. You have some of the history, but not all, and sometimes that can make a difference."

"Oh. Well I never really knew the grandfather, except through all the stories," Twinkle replied, trying to connect the current conversation with the morning session. "He was never really a part of the family gatherings and command performances."

"Command performances?"

"You know. All the mandatory things that we have to attend. Margaret stays very active in a lot of things and expects us to be supportive."

"Even from Charlotte?"

"Even from Charlotte."

"Even from Greenville," Ellis interjected, "though we have gotten better at saying no. Or Augusta has gotten better at saying no. I've never been one to really say yes."

"Old Gus never cared much for those things either, I guess, Twinkle continued, "because we never saw him at many of those events. He was in his 80s by that point anyway, so we rarely saw him at all. Or I didn't see him. I think Ben made the effort more often at his parents' insistence."

"How about you, Ellis?"

"More of the same really. I spent more time around him, but I can't say I ever really knew him. I remember little things, like the button under the dining room table."

"Yeah, I remember that too," Twinkle said.

"What about that is memorable?" Tony asked.

"It was a call button," Ellis said, "for the help. It rang in the kitchen, very quietly, when Old Gus was ready for the next course or needed another drink."

"Really?"

"Yep. And I didn't know it was there for the longest time. I always thought it was remarkable how the staff could almost anticipate his thoughts like that. I mean, they were on it. And then Augusta told me about the button. I had never seen one of those features, and I had been a practicing architect for several years by that point."

"Sounds like a nice feature."

"One of the remarkable things about Old Gus, I suppose," Ellis continued. He'd let go of a nickel only to get a better grip, but a staff was not optional. He always had a cook and a maid, as far as I remember."

"A tradition I assume you've continued?"

"Hardly."

"What about the parents? Walker and Margaret have a staff?" Tony recognized the need to tread lightly, but he opted against it, choosing instead to forge ahead into new territory. "They seem like fairly strong-willed individuals. Augusta had said in our calls over the last couple of weeks trying to arrange travel and such that I should prepare myself, that communication within the family, and especially the two of them, left a lot of room for improvement. Would you agree with that assessment?"

Twinkle looked at Ellis as if to say that she would follow his lead. Ellis looked at his newly arrived sweet tea, watched a sweat bubble trickle down the side of the glass onto the napkin and considered the question, an open door of sorts.

"I'm not sure there is such a thing as a normal family anymore," he said finally. "I think dysfunction is the new norm. So I wouldn't throw stones at that glass house."

"I'm not asking you to throw stones, though I can see how it might look that way. There are obviously positive things about your extended family, so feel free to focus on those. I'm just a stranger trying to start a conversation. Nothing more. Nothing less."

"I would hardly consider that an accurate description of your role here." They both nodded in acknowledgement and were both surprised by Twinkle's interjection.

"They don't seem to talk a whole lot," Twinkle said a little too loudly and without the luxury of segue or contextual connection. Tony and Ellis both looked at her, but Twinkle's eyes never left the table that anchored her iced tea, even as she continued. "I mean, they never seem to say anything to each other, you know, like normal married people do. Especially married as long as they've been."

"Maybe that's the issue," Tony replied. "Maybe time has revealed to them a way of communicating that younger married couples wouldn't recognize."

"I could see that," Ellis said, "since Augusta and I fall somewhere in the middle of the timeline, between the two Middletons."

They let that sink in, though Twinkle didn't seem to buy it. Tony noticed the hesitation, and he also noticed music for the first time. The Eagles were preaching about a peaceful, easy feeling, reminding Tony of Sweet Home California as George brought some tea refills and soup bowls and Twinkle shook her head slowly. By the time George was walking away, her thoughts had coalesced.

"I understand what you both are saying, and I recognize that time may be a factor, but there's more to it than that. There's a disconnect that seems almost unnatural. Almost like they carry on conversations using third parties, saying very little face to face. Very little of any substance, anyway."

"Tell me more about that," Tony said, blowing on his soup to cool it down a bit. Twinkle looked up at Ellis before continuing, then returned her gaze to her own bowl of soup.

"I don't know. I guess I'm looking at their marriage and comparing it to mine."

"That's completely natural," Tony confirmed, feeling a gear shift somewhere as he slid into therapist mode.

"But even when I'm completely pissed off at Ben, which is most of the time lately, we might hit a bump and not talk at all for days, but eventually we work our way back into conversation. Otherwise I guess we'd just go ahead and get divorced. But the Middletons just seem to exist in that state. They prop up a happy public face, I'll give them that."

The three of them ate soup and considered the new-trodden ground behind them. When Twinkle didn't continue, Tony hit the spurs.

"And I'm assuming this behavior affects the larger family in a number of ways," Tony offered, trying to connect the dots drawn by Pacific Mergers, some connection between family behavior and the world around them. "Is that the case?"

"It frustrates the hell out of my wife," Ellis interjected. "I can tell you that."

"I can imagine. And she led me to believe that was the case fairly early on. But can you think of specific ways, specific instances where this sort of thing has had unusually difficult results?"

"Sure," Twinkle replied, "an easy one. How about this weekend and this family meeting of yours?"

"Okay."

"Well, every couple of days or so, as we were finalizing the details," Twinkle continued, "I'd get a call from Margaret. I suppose she got tired of trying to work it through Ben. He never returned her calls, so she said. But she would call and say, 'Walker thinks we should . . . .' You can plug in any idea you want. Dinner here, lunch there, stay at this hotel over that one, have a cocktail party for Tony, whatever. It's all the same. So I'd call Augusta to confirm the plan and she'd go through the roof because Walker had never had such a thought. But Walker would never go back and correct Margaret, not that it would do any good anyway. He would set the record straight with Augusta who would call me and I'd tell Ben and the whole crazy cast of characters would act out whatever we were supposed to do, and never would there be a conversation between the Middletons. That's what I mean by third-party conversations. Walker does the same thing, I suppose, but he tends to use actions instead of words."

"How's that?"

"He just seems to disappear, I guess. Maybe it's a guy thing. But Ben doesn't do it, as far as I can tell. He likes the confrontation, at least with me. But Walker seems to shy away from the confrontation with Margaret, as far as I can see. I mean, Ellis, is it a guy thing or what?" She turned to Ellis to confirm.

"I don't know whether it's a guy thing or not, but I would agree that Walker is good at it. Something will come up at the church and he'll have to be there to turn on the heat or turn out the lights or comfort the sick, even when nobody's sick. It's like he's in perpetual motion, like only through constant activity can we prove our worth. It's really strange, but maybe it's part of the whole Protestant work ethic."

"It probably helps," Tony speculated, "that the rest of the family attends a different church. Reinforces the escape hatch, in a way."

"Probably so."

"But why do you suppose he needs the escape hatch at all?" Tony asked the loaded question. "It could be part of his wiring or it could be a coping mechanism he's developed through all the years of marriage." Tony could tell from their facial expressions that he had crossed some line. His, theirs, somebody's. He had drilled too deep into sensitive teeth and he knew it.

"You're the therapist," Ellis said with a welcome chuckle. "I have a tough enough time keeping my own marriage between the ditches, so I'm in no position to analyze somebody else's."

They paused as an ambulance approached and passed in front of Brigitte's, weaving slowly among the shoppers and college kids who seemed to accept the intrusion as part of the charm of urban living. The fading siren was followed by the dulled ring of a cell phone. Ellis fished his phone out of his pocket, checked the caller ID, and flipped the phone open to answer the call.

"Hello, dear," Ellis said into the phone as a matter of habit, and then talked in broken responses to Augusta on the other end of the line. "Oh. Damn. Yeah, I think it just passed by here. Okay, I'm on the way." He ended the call, took a deep breath, and looked between Twinkle and Tony. "Walker has collapsed on the sidewalk. Margaret got one of the store clerks to call an ambulance, probably the one that just passed."

"Is he okay?" Twinkle asked. "How did they find Augusta?" Ellis was getting out of his chair and taking a last drag on his sweet tea.

"It happened across the street from the little diner with the killer cheeseburger. Augusta noticed the commotion and recognized the players. Anyway, Walker is back among the living, it seems. Even told Margaret he 'didn't need the damn ambulance,' apparently."

"So he's okay?" Tony repeated Twinkle's concern.

"Seems so. I'm heading that way."

"Hold on," Twinkle said. "I'll go too." They both looked at Tony and down at the table.

"I've got this. No worries," he said to them both. "Please go and be with your family. Don't worry about me."

So Ellis and Twinkle walked hurriedly out the door and down the street, leaving Tony alone with Brigitte and thinking that the weekend was certainly not going as planned.

CHAPTER SIX

The waiting room at Medical Center Hospital looked like a cross between an erector set and a fishbowl. The walls were a darker than standard shade of gray and sections of the large room were walled off by what appeared to be bulletproof glass. The floor was a scored and stained concrete variation with a contemporary pattern and palette of colors, mostly grays and beiges with a prominent black section every six feet or so. Across the top of this stone pattern, perpendicular in most cases, were set a series of benches with arm rests, very clean lines and very bright colors. Porsche-red support bars and sleek black arm rests, perforated seats and stabilizer bars made the benches look both contemporary and industrial, cool but trendy, subject to change with the next fashion wave. And it appeared to Ellis that they were already behind a wave or two. He began redesigning the space in his mind, starting with achieving some sense of symmetry, at least with the benches.

"Do you think this is the original furniture for this space?" Ellis asked, leaning over toward Twinkle, who had chosen the seat next to him when Ben had gone to find Margaret and Augusta, who had arrived with Walker in the ambulance.

"How the hell would I know, Ellis?"

"Just curious," he said, defensively, as he returned to his survey of the room layout. He had only a fleeting idea of how long they'd been waiting in the poorly designed space, and his coping mechanism for boredom and collective indecision was design. He sketched on church bulletins and wedding programs, PTA agendas and business plans, redesigning houses, offices, interiors, exteriors. And sometimes even waiting rooms like this one in which the registration window was across the benches akimbo. It was, he thought, an ironic feature of the room, a small, unassuming glass box with aluminum speaking portals that served as the gatekeeper for the frenzy of ER activity beyond. A single staff member—would it be a nurse?—held court behind the glass, entering essential information into a computer and then directing the infirm to take a seat until they were called back. Next to the registration window were a couple of doors with obvious two-way glass in the center, as if doctors and nurses looked into the sea of desperate faces in the waiting room to determine, anonymously, who would be the next to be called back, the next winner of what was behind curtain number three in the healthcare lottery. Ellis found that to be disconcerting, almost as much as the series of metal detectors that adorned the room. Not just one at the main entry, but others at transition points throughout the room. This was a far cry from his suburban Greenville hospital, and Ellis was reminded that Medical Center Hospital served downtown Charleston and its decidedly urban residents. He imagined a rough and tumble Saturday night when the metal detectors screened guns and knives and implements of all types. Even on a relatively slow Saturday afternoon, the detector's buzzers beat the time of a slow metronome, accompanied by several televisions mounted high on three of the four walls, all playing different shows. And then there was the music streaming softly from several ceiling speakers. Ellis felt on the verge of sensory overload and wondered if the architect had thought through all of this, noting the various changes he would make.

"Victoria Covington?" came the voice from the patient entry room, and a large woman pulled herself up from a much-relieved chair and made her way through the two-way glass into the beyond. Just before the door closed behind her, Ben pulled it open and emerged from the beyond, presumably with news from the other side. Ellis and Twinkle both stood up as Ben walked toward them. Ellis was the first to speak.

"So, how's he doing?"

"Stable, the doc says, which is probably not something anybody's said about him in years."

"Ben," Twinkle corrected, turning as if to take her seat, or maybe just to look away from him.

"And more than they're saying about Mother," he continued. "I think they've medicated her as well."

"Ben!" Twinkle said a little louder.

"And not a minute too soon," he finished, looking at Twinkle to punctuate the comment.

"So what are they saying," Ellis asked, trying to move the conversation forward. "Heart attack? Stroke? What?"

"Heart attack," he replied, almost too quickly. "Small one, though, on a relative scale. Could've been worse, considering the pressure he's been under."

"Pressure?"

"And they haven't ruled out stroke, as far as I know, but the doc says that the fact that he was talking on the ambulance ride decreases the likelihood of that."

A television caught his eye and Ben paused. Twinkle sat back in her seat and pulled her purse up from the floor to her lap, rummaging through it for paper and pen. Ellis eyed the two-way glass as if Augusta would emerge with the next opening. The door opened and closed several times. No Augusta.

"Do you need me to call anybody?" Twinkle asked, holding the paper and pen at the ready.

"Not that I can think of," Ben replied without taking his eyes off the television. "Mother already called the guy at the church, so he should be here soon. That ought to liven things up a bit. And I'm sure he's got one of those Christian phone chains set up, so the Pope should be calling any minute now. Who knows? Maybe even the Lord himself."

Twinkle rolled her eyes in disgust and shoved the paper and pen back into her purse, wondering to herself how she could've married such an insensitive asshole. Then she looked at her watch and wondered how much longer they would be at the hospital. Twinkle didn't like hospitals, had never liked hospitals. But her dislike had been exacerbated as of late by Mimi Boucher, a surgical nurse at Carolina Medical Center in Charlotte. Mimi had been one of the attending nurses during Ben's emergency appendectomy the previous year, a nurse so committed to Ben's care that she had scheduled frequent follow-up visits at her apartment over the subsequent seven months, usually during lunch or in the early evening. When she confronted Ben with the discovery, brought to her third-hand by a member of her tennis group, Twinkle had been outraged by his response. If you want the tractor to run, he had said, you better bring it out of the barn more than once a month. Or something to that effect. She couldn't remember it exactly, though she had written it down exactly in her journal, feeling certain that it would come in handy one day. But that day had not come yet. Rather than divorce him immediately, as had been her initial thought, Twinkle had resolved to lock his tractor in the barn while she interviewed second husbands, hoping to settle on one who could actually get her pregnant. She was prepared, despite her loudly ticking biological clock, to take her time with the interview process and, as such, hadn't actually identified any strong prospects, a task further complicated by the daunting ratio of women to men in Charlotte. She also had difficulty reconciling her mission with her reluctance to be a home wrecker, though she was quick to admit to herself that the man she was looking for was currently married, albeit unhappily, and wished always to be married. She also had to admit to herself, though, that this qualifier further cut the prospect list, and dramatically so. But, she felt, it would be worth the wait, not having to break another one in, so to say. Oh, and she also required that the new husband be a born-again Christian, a characteristic that would ensure, in her mind, domestic happiness. She kept her search for this needle a secret from the entire haystack, even her closest friends. Even her tennis group, though they had suggested just such a strategy.

"Is he ready for visitors?" Ellis asked, trying to draw Ben's attention back from the television.

"I guess so," he replied, "though they have him sedated to a point where I don't know if he'd even notice."

"Well, I should probably go back and check on Gus, anyway," he replied, though Ben had looked back to the television and the golf tournament underway. Ellis walked toward the two-way glass and, as if by magic, the door opened and several people emerged. He held the door for them and filled the void created by their departure, looking back to see Twinkle on her cell phone and Ben moving closer to the television, as he moved into the beyond, through an initial maze of rooms and curtains, and into a hallway where Augusta was standing and talking on her cell phone.

"Well, here's Daddy, so let me catch up with him and I'll check on you guys later," Augusta said into the phone as he approached. "Love you, too. Bye."

"How are the grandchildren?" Ellis asked, making the connection. "And how did they take the news?"

"They're fine, but I didn't tell them about all this. They were on their way to a movie, and I figured this news could wait until we knew more."

"Probably a good idea," Ellis said, rubbing her shoulder and nodding in the direction of what he assumed to be the room. "What's the latest? Ben said they had him sedated."

"Really sedated," she replied with a sigh. "Something about balancing blood pressure and heart strength."

"So he had a heart attack?"

"That's what they're thinking so far, but they're not ruling out anything." They paused as nurses made their way by them and into the room pushing carts with computers and instruments on them.

"Wow," Ellis said. "Fancy."

"The miracle of technology," Augusta replied, "though I wouldn't mention that around Daddy just now."

"Why's that?"

"He's hung up on miracles right now. Even more than usual. It's a miracle he lived. A miracle it happened across the street from where we were. A miracle to be so close to the hospital. All of that. He preached quite a sermon there on the sidewalk waiting for the ambulance, was in rare form even when we got there. Said the wondrous and mighty Lord had opened the door but closed it at the last minute, sending him back into the game for more. He had already tried to stand up before we got across the street. Mother was beside herself."

"I remember that part," he said as a gentle reminder.

"Oh yeah. Sorry. Just trying to play the tape back and make sense of it, of all that he was saying."

"So how was he on the ambulance ride?"

"Same thing, really. He asked the EMT guy twice if he knew the Lord, had welcomed him into his heart as his personal Lord and Saviour. I think the guy sedated him after the second time. Daddy wasn't giving up."

"Wow."

"Yeah, wow. It was driving Mother crazy. She kept telling him, 'Walker, don't go getting all worked up.' And then she'd look turn to me expecting me to do something. All I could do was shake my head. So surreal."

"Sounds like it."

"And then I overheard the EMT guy tell one of the nurses, 'This one's a real thumper.' I didn't know whether to laugh or cry."

Ellis hugged her with a consoling chuckle. Augusta put her head in the crook of his neck and opened the tap on a little stress. Not crying, really. More like recognition of emotion under the bridge, giving the moment its due. As he lightly rubbed Augusta's back, looking over the top of her head and down the hall, Ellis noticed Margaret making her way out into the hall, looking both ways, confused until she saw Augusta and Ellis and made her way toward them. Ellis squeezed Augusta's shoulders to alert her, and she pulled away, rubbing her eyes and turning her head toward her father's room.

"Is there a problem?" she asked as her mother approached.

"No. Just wondering where everybody got off to."

There was an awkward silence as Margaret entered the moment, probably one of the most intimate Ellis and Augusta had shared in quite a while. Augusta continued to collect herself, wishing her mother could care for herself, if only this once, while recognizing how difficult it would be if roles were reversed, and feeling guilty for being anything but wholly consumed by her mother's situation, which, of course, she recognized was exactly what Margaret would have expected.

"So, have the doctors said anything else?" Ellis asked.

"Not yet," Margaret answered, continually looking up and down the hall. "They ran a number of tests, though, and we haven't heard results from any of those." Another pause. For people so practiced at cocktail conversation, Ellis thought to himself, they have a hard time sustaining a real conversation. In fifteen years of marriage, Ellis had never known Augusta's mother to be at a loss for words, a trait that seemed to have conditioned her daughter to be guarded when offering them.

"Ellis," Margaret broke the silence, "would you be a dear and go find Benjamin for me and send him back here?"

"Sure. I think he's in the waiting room."

"I suppose we should call a family meeting of our own to talk through some of this. Thank you. Just send him back here when you find him."

Ellis left to find Ben, cognizant of his mother-in-law's distinction of family, but unfazed by it. Part of his own conditioning, he thought, as he turned the last corner and looked out at the waiting room through the two-way glass. There he saw the scene much as he had left it, only now there was a new face in the crowd.

"Ben," he said as he pushed through the door, "your mother needs you back here." He held the door as Ben reluctantly left the televised golf and made his way past Ellis. They exchanged glances but no words.

As Ellis approached Twinkle and the strange new face, he struggled but failed to place the face in the larger Middleton collection. That is until he noticed the small Bible in the stranger's hands, leading to the correct conclusion that the preacher had arrived.

"Buddy Hill," the face said, rising to shake Ellis's hand. "I work with Walker down at Trinity Baptist."

"Nice to meet you," Ellis replied. "Heard a lot about you. Thanks for coming." The middle part was a lie, Ellis thought to himself in the pause that followed the introductions, but one of those social lies that seem to be expected in certain circles. Ellis had never heard of Buddy Hill and knew nothing about him.

"Everything okay back there?" Twinkle asked.

"Yeah. No changes. Walker's still under pretty heavy sedation and they're waiting for some test results," Ellis answered, looking at Buddy Hill as much as Twinkle, who still had a quizzical look on her face. "Margaret sent me back out to get him. She wanted a chance to talk to them together, while there was a lull in the action."

"Family meeting?" Twinkle asked with a sideways glance, also conditioned by Margaret's distinctions of family and other, and also happy to be included in the other category.

"You know how she likes a theme," he replied, cementing the conspiratorial bond that in-laws often share, but also noticing the effect on Buddy Hill, who was not a part of the conspiracy. His expression betrayed his confusion at the comments, and Ellis stepped in to clarify.

"It seems to be my role in this family," he said, "to offer inappropriate humor in times of crisis." Buddy smiled and nodded as if equilibrium had been restored.

"Well, I was just telling Twinkle that our entire church family is praying for Walker," Buddy said. "We've let the Guild know and the Men's Prayer Group leaders, and they'll let everyone know the situation."

"Like a phone chain?" Ellis said, looking at Twinkle out of the corner of his eye. She caught his glance but looked away.

"Of sorts, yes. But the whole church will want to know. I think the Men's Group is organizing a prayer vigil for tonight."

"A vigil," Ellis queried, "really?"

"Down in the fellowship hall, yes sir."

"But not in the sanctuary?"

"No," Buddy replied with a demure smile, aware that he was being played. "We really try to reserve that space for worship. And we like Walker, think the world of him, but I don't think we're ready to worship, if you know what I mean."

"I do, yes. A vigil. Humph. That's extraordinary."

"That's the power of prayer," Buddy said with remarkable certainty. "We're blessed to have Walker among us, and we'd like to keep it that way."

Ellis was fascinated to say the least. He had never really been a religious person, though not for any specific reasons. He harbored no convictions for or against religion. It had simply never been a real part of his life. Even through all the years of marriage to a preacher's daughter, the family trips, the holiday dinners, and even the face time with Walker, Ellis had never really given it a whole lot of thought. He and Augusta had always been members of a church, just as he had as a child, but only because it had been important to her, just as it had been important to his mother. He hadn't cared one way or the other, even when he had served on the Vestry and headed up the various building projects through the years. He had actually found the Episcopal Church to be very elastic in that regard, comfortable with his ambivalence. The flip side, though, was that he had never held church concepts—prayer, for example—with any passion. It was all just part of what a community did, on Sundays and holidays. Faced with a prayer vigil, though, Ellis didn't know whether to be awed or amused. The passion with which Buddy Hill seemed to be advocating on behalf of his mentor and colleague, Ellis thought, was admirable and delusional at the same time.

"How long have you worked with Walker?" Twinkle asked.

"Several years now. I moved here shortly after my wife died unexpectedly."

"I'm so sorry."

"Don't be, please. The Lord has helped me from that really dark room and into the light, and Walker had a strong hand in that as well."

"Still, it must be tough," she continued.

"Miss her every hour of every day, truth be told, but life goes on," he responded. And Trinity Church has been my life, and a good life at that."

Have you always been a preacher?" Ellis asked, taking the seat on the other side of Buddy and forcing him into a volley of conversation.

"Actually no," he responded, looking left at Ellis and then right at Twinkle, not wanting to exclude either. "I was a stock broker right out of college, really up until the time Heather and I married. But I think I always felt a pull, and then the Lord tapped me on the shoulder, and I've been working for him ever since."

"That's such a great story," Twinkle said. "The Lord tapped you on the shoulder. Nice way to put that."

"I think he taps us all now and then. He just offered me a job in the process. And part of that job is to comfort the sick and grieving, or however you would describe your current situation. In other words, less about me and more about what I can do to be of help to you." In saying this, Buddy's eyes were drawn to the two-way glass and the family beyond. Ellis followed his eyes.

"You think you should do the preacher thing and visit the sick?" Ellis asked. "I mean, you've got more experience with this than we do."

"Unless there's something further I can do for the two of you."

"All we can do is sit and wait," Ellis replied, "and you're welcome to join us for that, but . . . ."

"Well, you're probably right," Buddy said. "Not much work for me out here, so I better go back and check on the others. Shall we pray together first?" Ellis was considering the question thoughtfully when Twinkle answered with enthusiasm.

"Yes, of course. That would be great. Thanks." So the three bowed their heads and the Reverend Buddy Hill took them to the Lord in prayer.

"Gracious and loving God," he began, "we just come to you with prayer and thanksgiving, trusting you in your infinite wisdom to look after those in need. And Lord, we just pray that you'll keep Ellis and Twinkle in your heart as they face the days and decisions ahead. And Lord, we just look to you and your son for comfort, to heal the sick and to help us, Lord, to know you better. And Lord, we just ask these things in the name of your Son, our Saviour, Jesus Christ, amen."

"Amen," Twinkle said, again with enthusiasm, as she opened her eyes slowly and refocused them again on Buddy Hill for the first time. And she liked what she saw.

Ellis, who hadn't closed his eyes during the prayer, had never really understood the point of that exercise, had instead watched as a brown liquid crept slowly along the floor beneath his chair, moving from back to front, originating somewhere among the perforated seats behind him, and beginning to threaten his own shoes. Without thinking, he punctuated the Reverend Hill's prayer not with "amen" but with "I've got to move" as he rose quickly and seated himself across from the other two, on a bench that was not quite parallel with his original seat, a flaw he noticed right away. He also noticed quickly that the source of the brown liquid was a crushed plastic cup beneath a vacant seat. He shook his head and shook the hand of the Reverend Buddy Hill who left the waiting room and headed back into the ER.

"But that's not what the doctor said, is it?" Augusta's voice was beginning to show her frustration at having to say the same things several times for her mother to understand. She looked to her brother for assistance and found him staring blankly at a series of photographs hung on the wall behind her, as if he was staring through her. Either way, she thought, he was of absolutely no use.

"You want to add something here?" she said to him anyway.

"I don't have a dog in this fight," he said with a shrug of his shoulders. "In fact, I don't think any of us do just yet." With that, Ben looked at his sister and then his mother as if that comment should've ended the discussion the two of them had been having since he had walked back into the ER and found them huddled around a small table in what appeared to be a nurse's break room. Their expressions suggested that the discussion was far from over, so Ben shrugged his shoulders and went back to staring at the series of photographs depicting, as far as he could tell, coastal scenes with beach houses and fog.

"I'm just suggesting," Margaret said in a soft, patronizing voice that drilled like a root canal procedure into Augusta's head, "that we need to start thinking in that direction."

"He's been sedated, Mother. Not euthanized."

"I know that, Augusta."

"Then stop trying to bury him while he's still breathing! The doctors are still doing tests, and we don't even know for sure what the hell happened to him."

At this comment the tensions seemed to settle, if only a little. At least nobody spoke for a short while. The two women seemed to reflect on the possibilities and probabilities, and Augusta's breathing returned to normal. Ben seemed content to tease out the various nuances of foggy coastal scenes and beach houses.

"Well, I can tell you it was not a simple heart attack," Margaret said softly but defiantly.

"And you know this based on what, Mother?" Augusta said, rolling her eyes with frustration.

Margaret got up from her seat at the small table and walked toward the window that looked out over the roof below and Charleston beyond. She looked for friendly landmarks but her eyes settled on St. Phillip's instead. Somewhere in that small churchyard, she thought, Augustus Camber was getting uneasy in his grave.

"Have the doctors said something that you're not sharing?" When Augusta finished the sentence, she looked at Ben and noticed that his attention was now focused on Margaret. Finally, she thought, the prodigal son joins the party.

"No, nothing like that," Margaret answered calmly.

"Okay. What then?"

Margaret turned around slowly and leaned back against the window sill, folding her arms across her chest, trying to keep the words from coming out, and looking at the tile pattern on the floor between the window and the table.

"He was saying crazy things," she said at last, "while we were walking to the diner."

Ben and Augusta looked at each other as if to say, in the loving way conditioned into adult children, that this was getting interesting.

"What do you mean by 'strange?'" Augusta asked.

"About the church, mostly," she replied, "and the meetings he had yesterday in Atlanta."

They eyed each other again. This was getting really interesting.

"Well, he had asked me several weeks ago if I thought it might be a good time to retire, and I was in a hurry, and we never got back around to talking about it." She unfolded her arms and began walking back to the table to take her seat. "And next thing I knew, Walker was saying that Buddy was going to take on more responsibilities, so I just assumed he had made his decision. So we never really talked about it. But he was saying this afternoon as we walked to lunch that he had been asked to step down, officially, by the powers-that-be in Atlanta, and that Buddy was his replacement.

Margaret, by this point, looked at her children's faces for the shock and confusion that would mirror her own, but found none. Her children had long since given up playing dumb, and while they may not have known all the details, they seemed to know where this story was heading. The lack of response in their faces didn't seem to faze Margaret, though, and she continued with her recounting of the events leading up to Walker's collapse.

"So apparently he got fired yesterday, if that's what you would call it after 40-plus years of service, and this was the first I had heard about any of it." She got up and walked back to the window, hoping to catch sight of the sidewalk where she had heard the news as she continued trying to tell the story and make sense of it at the same time. "So, I asked him as calmly as I could to please explain what he was talking about."

"I've been replaced, Margaret. I'm no longer a preacher," Walker had said, entering into Margaret's story as she told it.

"I understand that part," she said. "I don't understand why you were replaced and why so quickly. You haven't told me that part."

"Your old friend Robert Tinsley, that's why."

"Robert Tinsley? What can he possibly have to do with this?" They paused to wait for lights to change and traffic to allow them to cross. Margaret was looking at Walker, but he was just staring straight ahead, willing the light to change and the traffic to stop, needing to tell this story but wanting it to pass through their lives unnoticed.

"Drugs."

"So what's that got to do with you?" she asked, looking around to make sure there were no listening ears.

"They think I've been laundering drug money," he said as the light changed and he stepped off the curb and started across. Margaret tried to keep up with a confused look on her face.

"Have you been laundering drug money?"

"Of course not," Walker replied without even slowing down.

"Then why did they fire you, or retire you, or whatever it is that they did?

"I was eligible for retirement and I retired, at their request."

"Why would they suspect you in the first place? I mean, you are a preacher, after all. All because you know Robert Tinsley? There has to be more than that, I would think."

"The DEA seemed to think there was plenty more."

"The DEA? Good Lord, Walker. How were they involved?"

"Something about the mission trips down to Robert's over the years."

"Oh."

"There is no 'Oh,'" he replied. We never laundered money or did anything out of the ordinary. So don't climb aboard the train to Paranoia, for God's sake."

"Okay. But you still lost your job, so there must have been something."

"Look," Walker said with exasperation, "the committee said that the DEA approached them last month."

"Okay."

"The DEA told them that my name had shown up on some documents they had collected. They're apparently trying to build a case against Robert after all these years."

"Okay."

"Would you please stop saying 'okay.'"

She was silent.

"The documents were all related to the mission trips, obviously, and the DEA was obviously not interested in me. They approached the committee as a courtesy, really, to let them know that their investigation had uncovered this connection, between me and Robert—"

"Robert and me," Margaret said without thinking but with immediate regret.

"—and that they, the committee, might want to reel me in or cut me loose before any of this was made public."

"I'm confused, though. It was mission work. You were there doing the Lord's work. If anything they should be applauding your work, not giving you the boot."

"Unfortunately, that's not the way the DEA saw it. At least that's not the way they explained it to me."

"So the DEA was in the meeting as well?"

"No. I met with them after the committee was done with me, which really didn't take long. Their position was that even if I was completely innocent of everything that might be suggested, the committee had a responsibility to protect the larger Church. My relationship with Robert Tinsley made me a liability, despite the good works we did in the Lord's name over those years."

"So how did the DEA see things?"

"Let's just say they weren't all that concerned with the Lord's work. They talked about forensic accounting and the money Robert gave us for materials and such, even as far back as the first year we went down there."

"I thought you raised all that money here in Charleston!"

"We did. Most of it anyway. But Robert wanted to help out as well; I mean, even beyond finding the village and the various projects, he saw it as his way of giving back. So he filled in the gaps through the years. That's why we never had to do bake sales or car washes to make the numbers work."

"Oh, Walker. But you had to know where the money was coming from. Or you should've known, or at least asked to be sure."

"I never gave it much thought, I guess. As I told the DEA boys, Robert never asked for anything, there were never any indications that the money had any strings attached at all, legal or otherwise. He just made it happen, and we made that primitive village a better place for it." This last point he made with certainty and passion.

"With drug money."

"No, damn it, Margaret, you're not listening to what I'm saying."

"Yes, I am. But I'm also listening to what the DEA was saying, and they were saying that you were doing the Lord's work with drug money. And I'm still confused why they wouldn't applaud your efforts."

"Applaud my efforts? What the hell are you talking about? Why would the DEA applaud my efforts? They—"

"No. The committee," she interjected, though he didn't hear and continued on his rant.

"They just wanted to know more about my relationship with Robert," he said, confused and beginning to walk more slowly and deliberately. "I told them we were college roommates and there wasn't much else to tell, but they kept pushing and pushing." He had come to a complete stop by now and looked disoriented.

"And then he collapsed," Margaret said, returning the conversation to the small break room and turning from the window back to the small table. Augusta looked at Ben who diverted his eyes from the series of beach photos to hers, though not fully, as if to confirm that she had just heard the rest of the story he had begun earlier. There was a long silence, and just as Augusta moved to break it, there was a knock at the door and a doctor making his way into the small room.

"Mrs. Middleton?" he said, looking at Margaret who nodded and made her way to him.

"Yes. Margaret," she said, extending her hand.

"I'm Dr. Bupta," he said, shaking her hand and acknowledging Augusta and Ben, who also stood to greet him. "I am the cardiologist assigned to your husband's case. I believe you spoke with my colleague earlier, when you first arrived here at the hospital.

"Yes. Dr. McRae. Tom McRae." Margaret was thankful she had made the call. She was convinced that having a friend on the inside at a hospital enhanced the level of care significantly.

"Yes, well, I was brought in because of the initial diagnosis of cardiac arrest."

"They said he appeared to have had a small heart attack."

"Yes, and that is true. He probably suffered a minor heart attack, but I'm afraid there is more." Margaret looked at Ben and Augusta as if to say, "I told you so." "The MRI revealed an aortic aneurysm, a weak spot in the artery wall where it leaves the heart and carries blood to the lower body."

"A weak spot?" Margaret asked.

"Yes. The weakness in the artery wall causes a swelling or a bubble to form as the blood pressure increases."

"But you have him sedated?" Augusta asked, making a connection between the aneurysm and the need to balance blood pressure and heart rate.

"Yes, and we have regulated his blood pressure to reduce the risk of rupture, and the aneurysm is reparable with surgery."

"You mean like open heart surgery? Augusta continued asking questions as her mother assimilated the news.

"Like that, yes. This is a thoracic aortic aneurysm, meaning it is located above the heart where the aorta forms a horseshoe shape and turns downward to service the lower body. We would enter the chest cavity and repair the weak spot with a man-made graft to strengthen the area."

Here, even Augusta had to pause. Dr. Bupta was obviously well-trained and very polite, but his Indian accent seemed to struggle with words like "horseshoe" and "reparable." She looked at the others while forming her next question. Margaret beat her to the punch.

"So, you're saying he needs this surgery and he needs it fairly quickly."

"We must weigh the risks of surgery against the risk of rupture, but my response to your question is 'yes.' He is quite lucky to be alive at this point. Most aneurysms of this type go undetected until the damage is done. But his has been detected and we have a tested strategy for treatment. So, yes."

"And without the surgery?" Margaret asked just to be clear.

"Once we have located an aneurysm, if it is accessible, there really are no alternatives. The weakened artery will eventually fail if left untreated. It becomes a function of time and pressure, and neither of these are on his side."

"When would you operate?"

"As soon as possible, of course, but that will be up to the surgeon. Given the urgency of this case, it will be given scheduling priority, but the surgeon will need to review the case to make that determination. Some prefer, for example, to allow time for the dye we used to find the weakness to dissipate completely before surgery."

Again, Augusta caught herself struggling to follow Dr. Bupta's explanation through words like "accessible" and "dissipate," but she was understanding the central idea that her father was going to need surgery as soon as possible. She watched the doctor's mouth carefully trying to gather every nuance, fishing for prognosis and certainty of success. None was forthcoming, and she figured if her mother didn't ask, some things were better left unsaid.

"Can I answer any questions before I go back? I will have the nurses gather the papers for your review and signature, and I will be in and out checking on Mr. Middleton as we move toward the surgery. Okay? No questions? Okay. The nurses can always find me if you need me. Okay?"

And with that Dr. Bupta left the break room and took all the oxygen with him. It took a while for Augusta and Margaret to catch their breath, or at least to collect their thoughts and share them with one another. Ben, on the other hand, considered the doctor's visit and surgical recommendation a sort of punctuation on the discussion they had been having, closure for the family meeting that had originally brought him back through the ER. He assimilated the information—and the absence of necessary decision—more rapidly than the women in the room. So while they continued to consider the impending surgery, Ben rose from his chair and made his way toward the door, catching the questioning glance from his sister as he did.

"I'm going to go check on Pops."

"Oh," Augusta said, looking at Margaret, who seemed hesitant to leave, as if she had a little more to say. "Okay. We'll be right there."

When Ben reached the door of his father's room, he found Buddy Hill standing near the head of the bed, Bible open, reading quietly. Ben stood just outside the room and listened for a moment. He recognized the Psalms, the walking through the shadow of death, the comforting rod and staff, the still waters. When Buddy reached a pause, Ben stepped into the room, catching Buddy off guard.

"He has always been a sucker for the Psalms," Ben said.

"He taught me early on to find comfort there," Buddy replied, closing the Bible and stepping back to join Ben at the foot of the bed.

"He tried the same with me, but it never stuck."

"We all have to find the passages that speak to us."

Ben let that last comment drop, a move that didn't go unnoticed by Buddy, who decided not to press the issue.

"Have the tests come back?"

"Yep. Aortic aneurysm. They're trying to schedule surgery right now."

"Lord have mercy. Have they given any prognosis or expectations?"

"You mean is he going to make it?" Ben asked without looking up. Buddy offered no response. "No, they haven't. But the doc says the procedure is fairly common. Tested, I think he called it. So I'm thinking the odds are pretty good."

They both let that sink in as the heart monitor beeped a quiet, steady rhythm. Just outside the door the hustle and commotion of the ER continued. Nurses and technicians moved from room to room, space to space, taking and giving life in various degrees, while Walker Middleton rested with his head slightly elevated and lit by an overhead fluorescent fixture, wires and tubes sprouting from all the usual places, sleeping the sleep of the would-be dead, as two men of roughly the same age stood at the foot of the bed, struggled to make conversation, and probably wondered to themselves which was closer to the son that Walker would've envisioned. Though neither would have recognized or admitted to the tension, it stood between them as surely as a weak artery stood between Walker and his next heartbeat.

"He is a man of strong faith," Buddy said at last, "and his God will reward him for that. He is surely blessed to have his family here to support him in the face of this."

"I admire the strength of your faith."

"It was your father who helped me develop that strength."

"But I wonder: what does that say for the others?"

"What do you mean?"

"The others who are here, in this ER, or will be later tonight, with or without family support. Are they not blessed?"

"I'm not sure what you're asking," Buddy replied, turning to look at Ben in hopes of better understanding the question.

"It's like that Bible College over in Tennessee that got hit by a tornado a couple of years ago."

"Uh huh. I remember. Can't think of the name of the school, though."

"Doesn't matter. I just remember the students and faculty that were interviewed the next day, and the fact that the tornado really hit one dorm pretty hard and did no damage to the one next to it."

"Yep. Remember that too."

"And the students interviewed from the untouched dorm kept saying that they were blessed to have survived, blessed that the tornado missed their dorm."

"Indeed they were."

"But what does that say about the poor little Christian kids who were praying and sleeping in the dorm next door, the one the tornado hammered? Does that say that they were not blessed, that God didn't like them as much, or at all for that matter?"

"No, of course, not at all," Buddy responded quickly. "God loves us all."

"So what does it mean to be blessed, then, if we are all equally blessed? I've never understood that distinction."

Buddy was considering his response when Margaret and Augusta walked in. Buddy was the first to see them and his face lit up as he moved toward them to offer a hug.

"Hello, Buddy," Margaret said as she hugged him and looked past him to Ben and Walker beyond. "How's the patient?"

"Ben tells me they want to operate," Buddy replied.

"And soon," Margaret replied, walking around the foot of the bed to stand near Walker's shoulder. "A weak spot in his heart, they say."

"Well, the whole church is praying for him," Buddy replied, looking from Margaret back to Ben who did not return the glance.

"That's a great comfort, Buddy," she replied. "Please thank them for us." She would never tell Buddy this, but the idea of her family being beholden to Baptist prayers for Walker's successful surgery and recovery was ludicrous. Baptist had always been what Walker did for a living. She had never really known many of his congregation socially. Baptists and Episcopalians always held each other with mutual condescension, and Cambers were cradle-to-grave Episcopalians.

"I will. Is there anything else we can do?" Buddy looked at everyone, including Ben, but got no immediate response. Augusta, who had said nothing since entering the room, filled the void.

"I don't think so, not right now. We'll call when we know something, but thanks for coming by. And please thank your congregation for us as well, for the prayers."

Buddy Hill could sense that his normal exit strategy, coming together in prayer with the family, was probably not a good idea. He had already offered his prayers over Walker before Ben had arrived, so Buddy felt comfortable saying his goodbyes and leaving Walker's family at his bedside.

CHAPTER SEVEN

Ben strolled purposefully into the bar at the Planter's Inn, opening his eyes widely to adjust for the change in light, but navigating without effort to the same barstool he'd held the night before. He might have thought to himself that he was a creature of comfort, but his thoughts were focused steadfastly on the under-lit shelves of whiskey on the wall behind the bar.

"Ah. The prodigal son returns," came the voice from across the empty dining room. Ben recognized it immediately but didn't turn to acknowledge it.

"Two nights in a row, you workaholic," he said over his shoulder to Jim Taylor, the old friend and new bartender.

"Well, it ain't exactly night yet," Jim responded. "More like about three-thirty, last I checked."

"Always five o'clock somewhere in the world," Ben replied anxiously, "and some of us are thirsty."

Jim moved behind the bar and poured Ben a Jack and water without asking any questions. Ben accepted it gladly.

"You've got a great memory and a bright future in this business," he said, raising his glass having reached the bottom in his first sip, and offering the glass back to Jim for a refill.

"You really are thirsty," Jim said, mixing a fresh drink. "Family re-union going that well, is it?"

"I wouldn't go that far," Ben replied more slowly. The first drink had already taken the edge off. "But I can tell you that it hasn't gone according to anybody's plan."

"Nobody's plan?" Jim said, looking Ben in the eyes.

"Oh shit," Ben said after a pause. "Not you, too."

Jim shrugged slightly but held his gaze on Ben's eyes.

"Meetings and everything?"

Jim offered no response but held the Jack Daniel's bottle ready to pour the next drink.

"Well, if you're inclined to tell me that your God had a plan for all this, you better tell him that either he's got some explaining to do or he's got a fucked-up sense of humor."

"That bad? No way."

"You wouldn't believe me if I told you, which I'm not leaning toward doing anyway. Suffice it to say that your God and hero has a fallen soldier in ICU over at Medical Center Hospital."

"Oh yeah? Who's that?"

"Benjamin Walker Middleton, Sr., Man of God, bathed in the blood, and victim of some weak plumbing somewhere around his heart, some-thing your God overlooked, I suppose."

"Damn."

"We agree, then."

"Sorry to hear that," Jim offered. "It happened today?"

"Around lunchtime, though you know my sense of time," he said with a smirk.

Jim let all of that sink in. He got a glass, filled it with ice, and used the fountain dispenser to pour himself a Coke, without the Jack.

"Damn." It was all he could think to say.

"The docs think they can fix it, but I don't know what kind of odds they're giving." Ben said all this to no one in particular, and Jim was a good enough bartender to recognize that. He took another sip of Coke and then kept his mouth shut as Ben worked through the issues.

"It's got the women all in a tizzy, I can tell you that." Ben took another long drink and considered the last comment. "I guess that's what they do, though. Give them an axle and they'll find a reason to get wrapped around it." He swirled the small straws around in practiced fashion, looking into the crystal balls of ice among the brown water, wondering what the future would hold. Jim used the pause to ease down to the other end of the bar to continue his preparations for the dinner crowd.

"Hey, uh, let me ask you something," Ben said without looking up from his drink.

"Fire away," Jim replied from his cutting board of lemons and limes.

"You remember Robert Tinsley?"

Jim put down the small paring knife he was using, wiped his hands on the small black apron around his waist, and walked slowly back down the bar as he responded.

"Sure. Why do you ask?"

"Just curious."

"Strange sort of curious to bring that name up out of the blue. Gotta be a reason."

"Not really. You have anything to do with him after we finished the mission shit down there?"

"Like what?"

"I don't know," Ben said, still looking into his cocktail glass. "Anything, really."

"You mean, did the DEA boys buy me some coffee and ask me a lot of questions recently? Something like that?"

"Yeah, something like that, I guess," Ben said, nodding his head and smiling without really looking up.

"Something like that might've happened, I guess. Can't really remember."

"Vague recollection for me as well," Ben said, and they let their shared experience sink in as Jim fixed a new drink for Ben and topped off his own.

"Even if something like that had happened," Jim continued, "wasn't much I could tell them."

"How long were you part of the system?"

"Never, really. I never did the distribution thing."

"Then why would the DEA boys want to buy you coffee?"

"That's a little more complicated," Jim said, turning and heading down the bar toward the uncut citrus.

"Complicated? What the hell is that supposed to mean?" Ben said, looking up and following his friend with his eyes. "The connection to me was fairly simple, and they found me. Why was yours complicated? How was there even a connection, other than from the mission trips?"

"Robert and I kept in touch after the mission trips," Jim said after a long pause, "but I was never a good candidate for the distribution side. I liked it too much to objectify it for others. Kind of like I had to stop drinking to make a living selling it to others, but those other demons held tight."

Ben returned his eyes to his glass as if reconciled to Jim's non-answer. He didn't really give a shit anyway, so he damn sure wasn't going to pry it out of him, especially since Jim's story was starting to sound an awful lot like a 12-step meeting. He was aware that Jim continued to talk, but Ben stopped listening, choosing instead to stir his drink thoroughly and forget that he had asked the initial question. Then a single turn of phrase brought him immediately back to the conversation.

"Robert and I were together, off and on, for seven years."

If Jim had wanted a reaction, he would've been pleased with the result. But he didn't see the reaction. He never looked up from the cutting board. Ben looked at him from down the bar.

"When you say 'together,' what does that mean?"

"Probably what you think it means."

"Damn, that is complicated," Ben said, looking back into his drink.

There passed between them an awkward pause, as Ben tried to reconcile the two Robert Tinsleys in his mind. Jim fixed him another drink and slid it in front of him.

"Bet you didn't see that one coming," Jim said, trying to lighten the moment.

"You're right about that. I really didn't. But how did the DEA boys . . . ."

"Surveillance pictures from a long time ago. You?"

"Same. Bet yours were more interesting than mine."

"Doubt it," Jim said, cutting the thought of lewd images off at the pass. "I was already in the system from a buy bust from college. Like I said, though, and like I told them, I was not involved in the business. I think they were talking to everybody with a possible connection, but I don't think anything will come of it."

"Maybe not, but they make it sound like a real shit storm is brewing."

"Yeah, but—"

"Walker lost his job over it," Ben said, regretting it almost immediately, succumbing to the urge to trump Jim's revelation, but knowing it fell short.

"What?"

"The government boys went to the mother church in Atlanta and told them to set my people free, and they did."

Jim's initial reaction betrayed that he was stunned. A little too stunned, in fact. Stunned and maybe even a little guilty, as if something he told the drug czars had led them to Walker. Jim was in the process of recounting the conversation, re-tracing his steps to make sure he hadn't mistakenly stepped into that bucket of shit, as Ben stacked and mixed Biblical metaphors trying to get his mind around the absurdity of it all.

"Robert was a moneychanger, they say, and Old Walker turned the other cheek there in the Temple trying to turn loaves into fishes for the village poor while Robert was trying to shove a camel through the eye of a shared needle."

The shared needle comment jolted Jim back into the conversation. He looked at Ben as if to say "What the fuck are you talking about," and Ben shrugged his shoulders as if he didn't really know how to answer that question. They let the moment pass all but forgotten in trademark male fashion, each retreating to collect his own thoughts and position himself to renew the conversation.

"Sorry to hear about your dad's job," Jim began. "When did he find out about that?"

"Yesterday."

"Damn, it has been a weekend."

"Enough to make a man very thirsty," Ben said, after draining his glass and rattling the ice cubes.

"How's your mother doing with all of this going on? I mean, aren't you guys in the middle of some family stuff, too? The guy you ate dinner with last night looked to be from out of town."

"He was," Ben said, eyeing Jim as he edged toward asking too many questions. "California. But Margaret Camber Middleton will weather this series of storms with characteristic grace and charm. She and my sister will Batman-and-Robin-up, and all the world will stand in awe and wonder at the efficiency and apparently effortless resolution of it all," Ben continued, the alcohol beginning to loosen his mind and mouth to their own peak efficiency. This combined with the receptive ears and an empty bar was all the impetus Ben needed to begin to unpack the baggage as he stirred the next drink.

"Different worlds," he began, to himself, to Jim, to nobody at all. "That's all I can think to say. I feel like either I'm a shallow little shit, or the relationship with him is, or was, shallow, or something like that. I mean, I love him as a son loves a father, I guess, but there's not much to that. You know what I mean?" This last line he said to Jim who, practiced at the interested non-response, said nothing. Ben didn't wait for an answer anyway.

"We just seem to live in different worlds," he continued. "We occupy completely different realities. There's got to be more to it than just the God thing, but that's a big piece.

"How's that?" Jim asked to fill the pause.

"It's kind of like DNA," Ben said, building the story and point in his mind as he went. "I was watching this bullshit show on Court TV or Discovery or somewhere, and the use of DNA testing was the deal breaker. The narrator was giving the background on DNA testing and said that DNA was discovered or figured out in, like, 1953. You know, the spiral staircase thing we learned about in biology?"

"Yep. Remember it well. The church had a spiral fire escape when we were in high school. That's how I remembered it. We used to fire up on those steps."

"That's right. I had forgotten about that. Makes this story even better, then. So, it was discovered in '53, and it was probably standard fare in textbooks by the early 60s. And it occurred to me that Walker had completely missed that wave, forced to surf the same old post-war bullshit since he graduated in 1951, I think. Same thing with technology, I guess, since he doesn't really use or understand the Internet or e-mail. It's almost like he lives on a different planet, especially when he starts in with the God shit. And I have long since given up trying to talk to him about it. That doesn't do a damn bit of good."

Jim let the dust settle on the bar before venturing a question. He had never really been at odds with his parents, though his preferences through the years had stretched the family fabric a bit and neither of his parents had faced a serious health threat, which he recognized as the driving force behind Ben's struggle.

"How does the rest of your family feel about all that 'God shit,' as you put it?"

"Obviously more tolerant than I am," Ben replied, looking up from his glass and catching his reflection in the mirrored bottle shelf behind the bar. "My mother is an Episcopalian, which allows her great flexibility. My sister is probably the same, but she's in the game mostly for the kids, I think. God eventually dissolves like Santa Claus. That sort of thing."

"And your wife?"

"Ate up. Absolutely. Been drinking the Kool-Aid for several years now. May be why the marriage has fallen apart."

"Blaming an awful lot on the Almighty, don't you think?"

"Spare me the witnessing, please," Ben chided. "I think we've established a disconnect between our worldviews, me and Twinkle. That's all I'm saying."

"I can see that."

"And that ain't all that's been disconnected."

"I got that feeling as well. Is she back at the hospital with your mother and sister?"

"I doubt it. I left her there when she started talking about going to some kind of prayer meeting tonight at Walker's church."

"Oh."

"Like I said, ate up. Convinced that she can't write a check that the Holy Spirit won't cash. So I just let go so she could let God. It is what it is."

As the Reverend Buddy Hill made his way into the fellowship hall, he was aware of a potentially life-altering force around him. He immediately attributed the feeling to the presence of the Holy Spirit and was thankful for such a palpable manifestation, though palpable was not a word Buddy was prone to tossing about in thought or conversation. His was a simpler vernacular, borne on the wings of a bachelor's degree in physical education and several misspent years dialing for dollars before the Biblical teachings and commentaries restricted and defined both his topics of conversation and the limits of his curiosity. So, as he walked into the prayer vigil for his mentor and former boss, he did so on the wind of the Holy Spirit, a force that had altered his life so many times before.

He arrived to a large crowd and worked his way into the room, shaking hands and nodding, answering questions and concerns, making his way to the small oak podium at the front of the room. The word of Walker's collapse had spread rapidly through the prayer network, as had the update about the impending surgery. The news had come so quickly, and the decision to hold a vigil as well, that the fellowship hall was only partially configured, chairs spread in a loose fashion around the room and too few in number to seat the prayerfully assembled. Buddy looked out over the group from behind the podium, mapping out in his mind what a prayer vigil - this prayer vigil - should look like. After all, this was Walker Middleton they were praying about, and he would need every ounce of prayer they could muster.

"Brothers and sisters," he said as the group grew quiet and awaited instruction, "as you know, one of us has fallen, stumbled under the weight of human imperfection. We gather tonight to offer up to the Lord Almighty our prayers and thanksgiving, asking the Lord to shine His face upon our brother Walker as he faces this test of the physical body, knowing that his faith and his love for the Lord will sustain him through all trials and tribulations."

Buddy was fervently trying to make eye contact to gauge the impact of his opening remarks. Speaking to large groups without prepared notes had never been a strength of his, and while he usually trusted the Holy Spirit to move through him, he didn't seem to be gathering the usual momentum.

"I left Margaret and the family a little while ago, and they send their thanks to all of you for your thoughts and prayers. They will let me know as things progress and surgery is scheduled, probably in the next 24 hours. So let's circle up the chairs and join hands and go to the Lord in prayer."

There was the sound of folding chairs being moved and the murmur of those wanting greater detail, about both the illness and the concept of collective intercessory prayer, but the room still remained fairly quiet. As the chairs were almost circled and everyone positioned as if preparing for a game of musical chairs, the familiar squeak of the fellowship hall door was punctuated by the muffled click of the lock, and all eyes turned to see Twinkle Middleton standing at the door, purse and Bible in hand, eyes wide like she'd arrived for a mani/pedi at an unfamiliar nail salon. At that point the room fell completely silent, as Buddy recognized her and made haste to greet her quietly. She recognized him and her face softened immediately.

"Twinkle, what are you doing here?" he asked with a confused smile. "I had no idea you were interested in joining us this evening."

"I hope it's alright," she said demurely, looking around the room as if asking the question of the entire group.

"Of course it is," he replied, taking her arm and turning to face the group. "We're just about to start. Have a seat over this way." A path emerged and seats were found for Twinkle and Buddy as the group circled up and stood in front of their chairs, joined hands, and went to the Lord in prayer, once again.

"Lord, we just come to you now, friends and family of our brother Walker," Buddy said, giving Twinkle's hand a squeeze as he passed over the family part, "and we just ask your guidance, Lord, as we stand vigil tonight. Help us, Lord God, find the right words, the words most pleasing in your sight, that you might know, Lord, the depth of our love and faith in you; that you might find it in your heart of hearts, Lord, to direct your angels to be with Walker tonight and tomorrow to see him through the earthly trials of human medicine and on to the wonders of divine regeneration."

There was, sporadically through Buddy's prayer, a pronounced "amen" as the group both followed Buddy's words and began launching into their own silent pleas.

"Lord, we just ask that you keep Walker's family in your heart tonight," again a squeeze, "assure them of your plan, your love, and your mercy. And we just ask, Lord, that you keep them free of doubt as you steady the surgeon's hand and focus the nurse's precision and compassion. Light the way, Lord, that we who are gathered before you this night might invoke your Holy Spirit to descend upon us and lift our voices to your ears, and to Walker's ears as well, that you both might know our steadfast love and devotion. All of this, Lord, we just ask in the name of your Son, our Saviour, Jesus Christ, with whom, with thee and the Holy Spirit, be all honor and glory, world without end, amen."

"Amen," the group said in unison, all eyes re-opened and turned toward Buddy.

"Please be seated," he said, taking his seat after Twinkle. The circle of chairs filled and a handful of folks stood behind the chairs, some by choice, some by default.

"Thank you all again for coming. We don't normally have this big a group for our prayer vigils, but then this is no ordinary prayer vigil, and I know Walker will benefit from our efforts. For those who don't know," he said, turning to Twinkle, "this is Twinkle Middleton, Walker's daughter-in-law, and we'll be praying with her and for her tonight."

Twinkle's eyes left Buddy's momentarily to scan the circle with a smile of appreciation, but they quickly returned to Buddy to await the next step. This was her first prayer vigil, and while she was torn by Walker's need for surgery and the odds that the surgery would prove successful, she was thrilled to see Christians in action, ready to see the power of prayer and the benevolent force of the God she had only recently gotten to know, the healing power of her personal Lord and Saviour. And she admitted to herself that her heart beat a little faster because Buddy Hill, an attractive, young, family-loving, Christian widower was leading this, her first active prayer session, and that her heart had skipped a beat when he had held her hand in prayer. And what pangs of guilt she should've felt, she thought, were hammered into submission by the loud ticking of her biological clock. Let us pray together, she thought, as she listened to the Reverend Buddy Hill explain a prayer vigil.

"So we pray silently and individually, joining hands to lift our prayers collectively, if you're comfortable with that. If you prefer, the sanctuary is open. Whatever works for you. The object is to pool our prayers, create a critical mass of intercession on Walker's behalf."

Twinkle listened patiently as he explained the timeframe, the flexibility to move in and out of the circle, the coffee pot in the corner, and the intent to pray together as long as two remained. She had never really been one to pray, so the structure, she figured, would be a good exercise. In the interest of full disclosure, though, Twinkle had prayed quite a bit, especially lately, but without training or instruction had never felt comfortable that she was getting it right. In Buddy, she was beginning to see both the instruction and answer to her prayers.

"So, let's bow our heads, join our hearts and our hands, and let's go to the Lord in prayer," Buddy said, at last taking her hand again and giving her a quick smile as they bowed their heads.

As the group began to pray silently, Twinkle closed her eyes tightly, took a deep breath, exhaled slowly, and began to pray to herself, silently, making a conscious effort to ignore the other sounds in the room. The ice maker in the adjoining kitchen dropping frozen cubes, the hum of the air conditioner blowing through the ceiling registers, the whispers of those who stretched the concept of silent prayer, the squeak of folding chairs moved by the passionate rocking of the prayerful. Even those small sounds became cacophonous distractions as Twinkle struggled with the beginning of her prayer.

"Dear God," she began, "I'm not very good at this, but you know that. But here's the thing: Walker has been a good and loyal preacher of your gospel for a long time, and I think a good man as well, probably even a good father, all things considered." Twinkle paused here. She wanted to qualify the statement by saying that she sometimes thought she saw in Walker's eyes the look that had long since left Ben's eyes, but she figured God didn't need to hear that. She then opened her eyes slightly and looked around the circle to make sure nobody was looking at her like they had just heard that last part, it being a group prayer and all. Everybody seemed to be busy praying, so she closed her eyes and returned to action.

"Please, Lord," she continued to herself, "help Walker come through the surgery and back home to a family that loves and needs him." But here she paused again, trying to figure out what she was going to say next and beginning to wonder how she was going to keep this up for—how long did Buddy say?—several hours. She opened her eyes ever so slightly again and turned her head to squint at Buddy. Her eyes travelled from their joined hands up his arm, across his broad shoulders, up the collar of his blue dress shirt, around the ear and the close-cropped hair, across the closed eyes and down his nose to his soft lips that moved as he spoke his prayer silently but fervently. And it occurred to Twinkle that she hadn't had sex in a really long time. And with that thought she closed her eyes tightly and tried to get back to the business of praying for her father-in-law, the former leader of that very church, who was at that moment being queued up for surgery. Her thoughts returned to Walker, but as she began to convert those thoughts into prayers, her mind drifted back to Buddy and what his wife had been like, what their short marriage had been like, the circumstances of her death, and the details of the path his life had taken in the years since. She opened her eyes to squint again, this time looking down at his shoes, modern versions of dress shoes with squared toes and bright silver buckles. Very metropolitan, she thought, as her mind drifted ever further into his closet. Where did he like to buy his suits? Did he space his pants and shirts evenly along the closet rod? Boxers or briefs? Twinkle shut her eyes tightly again as that last thought crossed her mind. She was embarrassed to find herself in Buddy's pants again. In fact, she was becoming strangely aroused. But this was a prayer vigil for Walker, and she needed to return to the work at hand. It was her Christian duty. Luckily, at that very moment, one of the vigilant broke into audible prayer, which the participants had been encouraged to do as the Spirit moved them. Still, the voice took Twinkle by surprise and she jumped slightly and opened her eyes. She looked quickly at Buddy who smiled reassuringly in response to the jump and then closed his eyes again. Twinkle looked around the circle. Some of the vigilant were nodding in affirmation at the spoken prayer; some were rocking back and forth in their chairs; some had their hands raised in the air; still others held their hands over their hearts while they gazed heavenward with expressions of great anguish. All in all, it was more than Twinkle had experienced before, her grip on Christianity being relatively new, and this combined with her inability to sustain a prayer on Walker's behalf left her feeling a bit overwhelmed. All at once she resolved to leave the circle and the vigil, and she set about to do so as inconspicuously as possible. She squeezed Buddy's hand to signal the departure, gathered her purse and Bible, stood up and walked quietly—in heels across a linoleum floor in a cavernous cafegymnatorium—until her departure was punctuated by the same doors that had announced her arrival. Once outside, she took a deep breath, her first since standing up, and began making her way around the outside of the building to where she had parked. As she turned the corner and caught sight of her car, she heard Buddy's voice calling from behind her.

"Twinkle," he said, closing the distance between them. "Just a second."

Twinkle continued to walk toward her car while fishing the keys out of her purse. She didn't know the exact and complete cause of the emerging awkwardness she felt around Buddy, but she recognized it was there. He caught up to her as she was opening her car door.

"I just wanted to thank you for joining us," Buddy said. "It meant a lot to me and to our prayer group, and I hope it was helpful to you as well," he continued, extending an arm to Twinkle's shoulder. "And I know it will help Walker as he—."

Buddy was interrupted by Twinkle's urgent kiss, an embrace that took him by surprise, but in a good way, awakening emotions previously locked away in a Bible somewhere. But the kiss was over as suddenly as it began, punctuated by only brief eye contact and no words, as Twinkle got in her car and drove out of the lot. Buddy watched her drive away and only then turned to walk back to the prayer vigil, noting thankfully the lack of windows on the parking lot wall of the fellowship hall.

Ellis had redesigned the waiting room a thousand different ways by the time Augusta emerged from the secret, two-way glass door. He had decided to leave that feature in most of his designs because it added some mystery to the whole enterprise, at least for those in the waiting room. Maybe a sense of privacy for those on the other side. Augusta walked from the doors to the row of chairs where Ellis was sitting shaking her head confusedly. He stood as she approached.

"You could've come back there."

"Well, you know how Margaret is about the line between family and other. Easier to stay out here with all the other outlaws. What did the doctor have to say?"

"Aneurysm somewhere around his heart," she replied, letting the Margaret comment fall by the wayside but looking around the room almost nervously. "They're trying to schedule surgery as soon as they think he's ready." She continued to look around him instead of at him.

"You okay?"

"Yeah. But I really need some air. Can we go now? There's nothing we can do here. He'll be out of it until they schedule the surgery. Trying to keep his heart rate stabilized. Mom said she would be staying with him. So can we leave now? I really need some air."

"Sure. Where do you want to go?"

"I don't care, Ellis. I just want to get the hell out of here. So can we go?"

"Sure. Okay. Let's go," he said as he led them out of the waiting room and back into the streets of Charleston.

"Should I get a cab?"

Augusta never stopped to answer the question. Once she saw the light of day, she turned and headed back toward the hotel without looking at or even waiting for Ellis. He followed behind for several steps and finally caught her as they crossed the first street. She had to wait for the traffic. Otherwise he'd have never caught her in the first block. From his experience, Ellis knew that she'd let off whatever steam had, for whatever reason, reached a boiling point, and he knew the best strategy was not to ask too many questions. Sometimes it was a student or a particularly unreasonable parent, or maybe the reverse, but usually it had something to do with her mother. Augusta had gotten progressively better at handling Margaret who was, as it usually happens, getting progressively worse. The tea kettle began to whistle mid-way through the next block.

"That is the strangest damn woman I've ever encountered," Augusta said to nobody and anybody who was listening. "I mean, what the fuck? Are you kidding me? You really think this is something I needed to know, and that I needed to know it right now, right before he goes under the knife, not knowing if he's going to make it or not? This is not information that could've waited?"

At this point they were walking side by side, but Augusta neither knew nor cared that Ellis was beside her. She kept her head down and walked quickly and would have appeared, to the passersby, to be dressing down her husband for another of his shortfalls. Except for the fact that the husband, Ellis, seemed not to bear the weight of the emotional tirade as the beleaguered husband would have. Instead, Ellis just let her keep talking until, he assumed, she worked through it or asked his opinion.

"And the bitch of it is, I can't figure out how she's using this revelation to her advantage. But I know she is, somehow. Otherwise she would never have brought it up. And the man is on what might be his deathbed, for God's sake. I mean, give it a fucking rest, would you?" Augusta continued her tirade to no one in particular, her fists clenched tightly at the ends of arms held tightly to her sides. She would punctuate her points by slowing or stopping as if she were considering her frustration anew. The two of them, Augusta with Ellis trailing, covered a block or more in this fashion, searching for both resolution and composure. As they reached the next corner, two blocks from the hospital and probably eight or ten from the hotel, Ellis eased up beside her and put a calming, experienced hand on her shoulder, an invitation to unload and assimilate, encouragement to take a deep breath, reassurance that her mother was crazy, not her, and that the rest of the world recognized that—all of this clearly unspoken with the touch of his hand on her shoulder. She turned with anger, fear, and tears in her eyes, and continued the conversation, from that point forward with him rather than beside him.

"I know, I know," she said wiping her eyes and pointing to her head, "all that stuff Dr. What's-his-name would be telling me right now. I know. You don't have to remind me. He's kicking around up there right now." She walked over to the vacant storefront on the corner and checked her reflection in the dark glass, shaking her head and trying to focus on the strategies the therapist had recommended.

"There's a deli across the street," Ellis asked. "Did you get a chance to eat anything? Are you hungry?"

"I can't sit down right now," she replied, "so let's just keep walking until I can get this—shit!—out of my head." They crossed the street and continued making their way back toward the Planter's Inn.

"Dare I ask what it was that lit you up?" Ellis asked, treading lightly.

"She was talking nonsense, really, but you know in her reality it probably makes complete sense."

"Like what?"

"Well, when you went to get Ben, we went into this small break room so she could have her 'family meeting,' and I thought that she had some important issues to talk about like living will or health insurance or something the doctors had told her that she needed to break to us about some condition that Daddy had or something like that."

"Okay."

"But she didn't. Nothing like that. She wanted to talk about how Daddy had been acting funny lately, saying strange things while they were walking to lunch today, that kind of stuff.

"Okay." Ellis tried to stay immersed in the conversation, but found himself distracted, as always, by the architecture of downtown Charleston. His eyes caught glimpses of details and millwork and iron work that warranted further investigation, but he tried to stay focused on Augusta, despite the fact that this was not his first rodeo on the Margaret bull.

"And then she started in to all this stuff about the church and Daddy's mission trips and how the church had asked him to retire because the DEA was about to expose his old college friend down there, who, as it turns out, is also a drug lord, that helped set up all the mission work in the little village down there."

"And Walker was saying all of this on the way to lunch?"

"That's what she was saying."

"Well, it makes a great story, but do we think any of it is true?"

"Every bit of it. The DEA talked to Ben as well. But that's another story."

"Wow. This family gets more complex every minute."

"It gets better," Augusta said with frustration. "Still glad you married me?"

"So far. What else you got."

"So Ben and I listened to all this, and the doctor came in and told us about the aneurysm and the surgery and all that. And Ben checks out, leaves the break room and heads back to Daddy's room, and I started to do the same, but that's when she drops the bomb."

"What's that?"

"After Ben has walked out, I'm turning to leave, and she says, 'I knew Robert would get back at me.' I turned around to look at her and she seemed on the verge of hateful tears." Augusta stopped mid-block and was drawn back into the break room.

"What is that supposed to mean?"

Margaret just shook her head and shrugged her shoulders.

"What is that supposed to mean, Mom? Get you back for what? Are you talking about Robert Tinsley, still?"

"Oh, sugar, it was a long time ago."

"What the hell are you talking about?"

"When we first met, your father and I, in New York. He was a struggling writer waiting tables and trying to catch a break, and I was a young editing clerk at a publishing house. I used to go to the little cafe where he worked, Arianna's, after work until he finally asked me out."

"I know the story, Mom. Heard it a thousand times. And Daddy and Uncle Robert were roommates. Cheap wine, struggling artists, the whole 60s thing. I get it."

"We were such friends. But there was more to it than that," Margaret said almost with a sigh. "When I met your father and Robert, I was so naive. We all were, really. But I never took the time to understand relationships, I suppose. Certainly not ours, the three of us, or my part in all of it. I mean, I knew early on that they were more than just roommates, I guess you would say. But it just seemed like a passing fancy to me, something they would grow out of with the right motivation."

Margaret looked up to find Augusta looking at her with a furrowed brow and a confused squint across her eyes, her head cocked sideways, trying to make sense of what Margaret was saying.

"Oh, Augusta. You're an adult now. You have to expect some twists and turns."

"And you considered yourself the right motivation? Am I getting this right? You're saying that my father and his drug lord college roommate were lovers until you sashayed up with the goods to turn one from the other? That sounding about right, Mom?"

"Don't be so melodramatic. It's certainly not the first time something like that has happened. I mean, even in your own life. Haven't you ever looked at Ellis and wondered?"

"What?" Ellis asked, bringing Augusta back to the mid-block spot in the current moment. "Wondered what?"

"Whether or not you were gay, I guess."

"What? She really asked you that?"

"She really asked me that." They stood there mid-block, looking at one another in amazement.

"What did you say?"

"Nothing, I just left the room and went to check on Daddy. And then I came out to get you. And here we are."

They started to walk again, both trying to formulate the next statement. They didn't speak, though, as they passed the storefronts and coffee shops and antique stores that populated the next block or two. Augusta's explosive interactions with Margaret always seemed to be punctuated by these moments of silence, time for Ellis to assimilate the new discovery and catalog it among the seemingly insurmountable feats of strange parenting he'd encountered over the course of his relationship with Augusta. He loved his in-laws, of this there could be no doubt. They were generous souls with effervescent character who kept life afloat in wonder and curiosity, but he had to admit with equal certainty that they did the damnedest things, things that were often difficult to reconcile with his own models for parenting and living.

"Strange woman."

"Don't go there," Augusta said as they paused at another crosswalk. "Where you usually go."

"I'm not going anywhere."

"It's not about you," she said, pushing the crossing signal button and looking up at the sign as if willing it to change immediately. "And it's not about me."

"I agree, though I assume that one day it will be about you and about me."

"Probably. And our kids will be walking along some street somewhere having this same conversation, trying to figure out how we got so fucked up, when we seemed so normal."

"Someday. But for now, you and your gay husband need to circle the pink wagons and try not to scratch each other's eyes out. Something like that?" he said with a hint of a smile.

"Something like that."

"You calming down, now?"

"Working on it."

"Good," he said as they started across the street. "I called the kids and let them know that Walker was sick and was going to need surgery, and that you may need to stay here for a while, but that I would be back tomorrow."

"That sounds good. Thanks for doing that." Augusta had slowed her pace and they seemed to be walking together now as opposed to simply adjacent to one another. "You're going to kill me when I bring this up," she said after a pause, "and especially right now, at this moment, with the insanity still so close at hand, but—"

"You want to move back here."

"Well—"

"Your father's going to need some recovery time, and your mother's ill-suited to such a task, and the two of them would be more likely to kill each other than escape the whole recovery process cleanly."

"In a nutshell, yes. But—"

"And they're getting older, and somebody's got to look after them, and—"

"You going to let me talk?"

"It happens. When the illnesses start to complicate the aging process, the natural instinct is for the child caregiver to feel the call or pull back to the nest. Nothing unusual here. Very predictable. You may have some new reasons swimming around in there, but the big paddleboat is guilt."

"Got it all figured out, do you?"

"Doesn't make it a good idea. Might be the right thing to do, but that doesn't make it a good idea."

"But somebody's going to have to look after things."

"There's that paddleboat. Toot the horn!"

"Asshole."

"Just being honest," he replied, pausing in front of a small coffee shop and turning to look at his wife. "We've chased this horse around the paddock before, and it has never been the right horse. I know why you would want to saddle it up again right now. Anybody would. Your father's in the ICU, your mother's facing a long road, your only sibling offers little hope of assistance. I see the same picture, but it still doesn't make it the right choice. You hungry yet?"

"What?"

"Hungry, for food. I'm starving, and we're standing in front of what appears to be a reputable establishment complete with tables, chairs, and menus."

"Oh. Sure. Sounds good. But we need to talk about this. I think it's a new issue, but I hear what you're saying."

"Well nothing says new issue like a chicken salad sandwich," he said, opening the door and waving her in.

CHAPTER
EIGHT

Tony Gordon had never really seen such charm in a city, though charm wasn't his word. His word was more like age, or character, or useful disrepair. He couldn't imagine the number of buildings that, at first glance, appeared to be falling down despite the fact that a bar or a coffee shop or a bookstore or an antique shop was operating within its crooked walls. Hell, the whole city seemed to be an antique, much older than even the oldest buildings in California, his only real point of reference. He had walked the streets with his tourist map in hand for several hours that afternoon, avoiding the hospital where his presence was certainly unnecessary, and making his way toward the Central Business District, directed by Michael Kelly, his boss at Pacific Mergers. They would reschedule the meeting, Michael said, but Tony might as well see a bit of Charleston while he was there, including the Plantation Trust offices. He had even gone so far as to recommend a couple of dinner spots. So Tony was seeing a bit of Charleston, trying to assimilate the real with the imagined. He stood on the Battery, looking out across Charleston Harbor to Fort Sumter and Fort Moultrie, the twin peaks of the American Civil War, at least according to the tourist brochure. The order to fire on federal troops barricaded on Fort Sumter, wired from the cradle of the confederacy in Montgomery, Alabama, had been the opening blow of the "War of Northern Aggression." The simple brochure in his hands held all Tony really knew about that war. He had probably read about it as an undergrad, in an American history survey class, but it had held little relevance for him until now. And even now it was barely more than quaint, though he felt like it ought to be more, that there ought to be more of a sentimental pull, a recognition of the country's great inner struggle. The Civil War had even been used metaphorically in the realm of family systems theory, the notion of a house divided against itself, and Tony was supposed to be a specialist in family systems. The trouble was, he couldn't remember any Civil War battles that were fought along Hollywood Boulevard or any great naval campaigns off the Santa Monica Pier. But here he was, a West Coast American standing on the shores of the East Coast, viewing history in the flesh and trying to connect with people whose forbears probably stood along this same sidewalk and watched as their husbands and sons ushered their national family into years of bloody conflict.

"Funny thing about war," the voice had said from the other side of the bench. Tony had not noticed anyone sitting there.

"Pardon?" Tony replied to the strange figure seated across from him, a neatly dressed bum, it would appear, whose eyes continued to gaze out across the water.

"It all seems like such a good idea at the time," the man continued, "fighting for God and country, for honor and civility, at least as we define those things."

Tony couldn't take his eyes off this guy, a vagabond with what appeared initially to be an extraordinary grip on reality. Tony tried to remember if that would be a paradox or an oxymoron. He couldn't remember if either of these would apply, or if maybe it was a term that was out of his reach, but Tony watched in awe as this older man, snappily dressed in very dated clothing from the 70s section of a second-hand rack somewhere, held forth on war in an articulate manner. The man stroked the remnants of a gray beard as he spoke, keeping his eyes on the harbor as if transfixed.

"What are these if not human constructs, including the God one?" he continued. "Worth fighting one another and killing over? Probably not, but we seem to enjoy it, I guess. We keep doing it anyway."

"I don't mean to interrupt," Tony said with a confused expression, "but you seem to have appeared from nowhere."

The old man nodded quickly to the bench before turning back to the harbor to form the next treatise. Tony looked down to the bench and then through the tiny wooden slats to the ground below, where there appeared to be a covering of some sort, a pallet of the everyday trash of Charleston to house the human refuse.

"It was the fart that did it," the old man said sharply.

"Pardon?"

"You woke me up when you farted a while back. I would guess black bean soup for lunch, but I have a heightened sense for that sort of thing."

"I see. I do apologize for waking you."

"It happens. Quite impressive, I thought. For a while there I wondered if you might've soiled your linens."

"Thank you, and no."

"Very well. Back to the point, though, we seem to set up scarecrows so we can shoot them down with automatic weapons and steal their oil. That sound about right to you?"

"I don't know. I've never really thought about it in those terms, I guess."

"Better start thinking, Sonny Boy. They're watching us right now. Probably got sound as well."

"Who is 'they?' Do you mean the government in some way?"

"No, I mean the fucking sea turtles. Of course I mean the government. See, now you're thinking, though slowly, I must admit."

Tony chuckled and began to stand, deciding it was best to give the crazy man his space.

"Hit a nerve with that needle, did I?"

"No," Tony replied quickly, trying to be polite. "I've got to meet some people pretty soon, so . . . ."

"Bullshit. You're a tourist or maybe a suit whose afternoon just got shot to hell, leaving you with nothing to do but wander down to the shore and look out over the history you've never taken the time to know. That sound about right, sonny boy?"

"What gives you that idea?"

"Heightened sense of that, I suppose."

"Is that right?"

"Yup," the old man continued, never taking his eyes off the harbor. "That and the fact that you're dressed for a casual meeting, and you're not from around here. The dialect is decidedly West Coast. We don't get many of your kind off the cruise ships. You got your own water out that way, I hear. But you're holding a map of the historic Civil War sites and you ain't in any hurry to meet anybody. If you were, you'd have looked at your watch by now. Like I said, heightened sense of that."

The two sat on opposite ends of the same bench looking out over the harbor, one stroking his gray beard in affirmation and the other nodding in surprise. When he was through nodding, Tony flashed back to his introduction to Walker, in the Atlanta Airport, wondering if he was a magnet for the apparently disturbed, or if he just had a heightened sense of that. He also wondered if he'd be reintroduced to this man in his real context, perhaps as the mayor of Charleston, just as Walker had progressed from clinical case study to client. Either way, Tony shifted into therapist gear.

"Okay, so maybe it's you I was supposed to meet. Call it fate."

"Didn't think you folks on the West Coast knew anything about Presbyterian determinism."

"Whatever you want to call it. You seem to have all the words at your disposal. Tell me your story. Why is an otherwise articulate, snappy dresser like you preaching sermons on a park bench?"

"Oh, hell no," the old man said. "I know the game you're playing, Sonny Boy. You probably work for them. Probably wearing a wire and everything. I'm not that stupid." The old man looked around the park as if expecting to see guys in blue blazers and black shoes talking into their watches while watching him from behind the standard issue aviator sunglasses.

"But you assume that I am that stupid. I find the man we've been looking for, hidden in a blanket of newsprint under a bench, and the first thing I do is fart on him. That sound about right, old man? Standard operating procedure for us government types, right?" Tony had to chuckle at the series of thoughts he'd just expressed. The old man just eyed him with suspicion before turning back to the water and continuing his story.

"I'm not preaching from a park bench, and I'd be the last to deliver a sermon of any type. Strictly a humanist. Always have been."

"Really?"

"Tough row to hoe in these parts, let me assure you."

"I can imagine."

"Can you now," the old man replied, still suspicious.

"Coming from the West Coast, I mean," Tony said quickly and reassuringly. "We don't have as much God on our side of the world."

"Oh. Yes, you're right about that. I studied the evolution of world religions as an undergraduate. Senior thesis on the deism of the founding fathers."

"Sounds fascinating. What college might that have been?"

"Harvard, '53, AB in American history."

"No kidding?"

"Is this a diploma check?"

"Well, you have to admit that such a revelation is a bit incongruous, given the present circumstances. I can't remember the last time I farted on a Harvard man."

"Well, we can't all work on Wall Street."

"I suppose not, but you're probably one of the very few Harvard grads living under a park bench. Tell me more about that."

"It's all about the authenticity, sonny boy."

"The authenticity?"

"Living life deliberately, as Thoreau was fond of saying. Life as a tactile experience, embracing the rough edges that our culture tends to groom away in pursuit of homogeneity."

"Under a park bench," Tony asked, forming any number of Harvard jokes in his mind as he listened to the old man. Even if he didn't go to Harvard, this was a great story.

"Wherever life takes you, I suppose. Your life brought you to the same bench."

"But I'm not planning to sleep here."

"Opting, instead, for some luxury hotel on the company expense account and further separation from the elements that make you human."

"I'm confused as to how that makes me less human. Shelter is, after all, a basic need, along with food and water. How does my use of shelter make my life less authentic? Your argument starts to sound a lot like a sermon on the camel and the eye of the needle. That sound about right? The homeless inherit the earth?"

The old man crossed his arms across his chest and stared out into Charleston Harbor. Tony couldn't decide if he was locked up or simply formulating his next response, but either way it seemed like a good time to leave him to his own devices. His own work with the psychologically unsound had led Tony to consider it unnecessary to apologize for holding patients' feet to the fire, so he rose to leave and left the old man with a parting thought.

"I think you're right about one thing, though. The founding fathers were probably deists at best." As he turned to leave, he saw a small grin creep across the mouth of the old man. An authentically unapologetic apology. Tiptoeing through the tulips of mental disorder. Tony just shook his head and walked back toward the large houses of the Battery. As he made his way onto the sidewalk and down the block, a voice called out to him from the porch of a large, attractive, yellow brick house.

"I hope he wasn't bothering you," the voice said. Tony stopped and followed the voice to find a petite, 50-something woman sitting in a rocking chair along the shadowed rail of the porch. He was taken by both the size of the house and the size of the woman, looking up and down and attempting to reconcile the two as responded.

"Pardon?"

"My father," she said as she pointed with a small hand toward the bench in the park. "I hope he wasn't bothering you."

"Your father," Tony replied, further confused, "under the bench?"

"I'm afraid so."

"No. Of course not. No bother at all."

"That's good to know. He can be quite a nuisance when there are more people in the park. When the cruise ships come in or when the local historical society is doing a tour of the harbor. He likes to correct the docents on fact and fiction." She smiled as she said this last part.

"I can see that," Tony said, looking back at the bench to see the old man hadn't moved. "Fascinating man, though. Did he really go to Harvard and all that?"

"Class of 1953," she replied with a proud but humble grin. "May I offer you a glass of lemonade?"

"No, thanks. I've really got to meet some people."

"No trouble. I've got some right here," she replied, pointing to a chilled pitcher of lemonade on the table between two white wicker chairs. "I'd love to hear what else the two of you had to talk about. He seemed to have taken a liking to you."

"Really? How can you tell?"

"He let you win the argument," she replied. She poured him a glass of lemonade and offered it in his direction with one hand while pointing to the empty chair with the other. She had her father's gift for drawing people into conversations.

"Let me win, you say? Well, that's an interesting perspective. And I wouldn't call it an argument, necessarily."

"Rhetorically."

"Oh, well yes. That I'll concede," Tony said taking his seat and looking back toward the park bench. "But I don't think he let me win."

"But you'd still be sitting on the bench if he hadn't."

"What makes you say that?"

"I have a heightened sense of that, I suppose."

Tony felt as if he'd been pulled into a vacuum of sorts when she used her father's exact turn of phrase, as if the dementia was creeping up the porch like a rising tide, threatening to raise all boats, including his. As much as he loved the challenge of the mental labyrinth and the thrill of diagnosis, he was also aware of his own limitations, and the walls of the porch began, ever so slightly, to close in on him.

"Was he holding forth on conspiracy theories or reliving the War of Northern Aggression?"

"A little of both, I guess. I think I might've stepped on his toes a bit."

"Good for you. He needs that. Most folks just back away from him, smiling and nodding and that sort of thing. I think it helps him to face a worthy adversary now and then." She spoke about her father in a very clinical but loving fashion, looking out over the street and park as she sipped her lemonade. Just another day on the porch.

"I know this is none of my business," Tony asked, "but how long has he been living under the bench, so to say?"

"Oh, he doesn't live there," she replied with the same knowing grin. "He lives here. Has for nearly fifty years. He spends the day in the park and comes in the house for supper and sleep, then he's back under the bench at first light."

"So much for living authentically, I guess," Tony said almost under his breath.

"Oh, I see he made the case for authenticity," she replied. "He was re-reading Thoreau last month but watching Tony Robbins infomercials at the same time."

"Really."

"Indeed. Interesting combination when you think about it."

"I'd rather not. So how long has the bench been the daytime destination?"

"Since he retired, really, about eight years ago," she replied without having to think to hard about it. "At first I think it was a way to go to the office, once he no longer had an office to go to. He would put on his suit and tie and take his paper and sit on the bench. Then, almost like reverse evolution, he went from taking short naps on the bench to spending the day under the bench."

"From what did he retire?"

"Banking. He worked for the same bank for almost fifty years."

"That's impressive. Quite a career."

"Well, Plantation Trust was quite a bank."

"Plantation Trust?" Tony asked to clarify, thinking that surely he hadn't just stumbled across a career employee of Augustus Camber.

"Yes. It's a local bank, family owned. Have you heard of it?"

"I might have, but I'm not from Charleston."

"No, I didn't think you were. Somewhere out west, I'm assuming from your accent. California?"

"Exactly. You're very good."

"Thank you."

"But, I'm curious. What was it like for him to work for the same company for so long? That seems almost unheard of today."

"More like a fixture, really, than a company, but—"

"How's that? A fixture?"

"An establishment, I guess you could say," she continued. "The same family has owned the bank from the beginning, several generations I think. The Cambers."

"Old family?"

"In a city known for having old families, yes."

"Was your family originally from this area?" Tony asked, trying to keep the woman from seeing the focal point of his questioning.

"No. My mother, rest her soul, was from New York, and my father," she said nodding in the direction of the park, "was from Michigan originally. We ended up here when Daddy started working for the Cambers."

"What did he do at the bank?"

"A little of everything through the years, I think," she replied as she continued to watch her father in the park. "I don't think the bank was very big at that point, so he did a little of everything. Eventually he worked directly under Old Gus. That's what they called Mr. Camber."

"Really?"

"But not to his face, mind you."

"Tough customer?"

"Let's just say Old Gus had expectations," she said with a chuckle. "I don't remember Daddy ever leaving this house wearing anything other than a suit. Even on the weekends. I don't think he owns any casual clothes."

"Sounds like Old Gus ran a tight ship. Whatever happened to him?"

"They carried him out of the office in a box."

"Humph."

"And I mean in a box, not on a stretcher. Daddy was the one who found him. Before he called the ambulance, Daddy called Old Gus's personal physician, and by the time the ambulance arrived, Dr. Goddard had already pronounced him dead. So Daddy was able to call the funeral home, and they showed up with the simple pine box Old Gus had stipulated in his will."

"No kidding."

"He told Daddy for years that he expected to be carried out of his office in a pine box, and by damn he was. Told Daddy that if he didn't make that happen he'd haunt him until his dying day."

"Wow!"

"Sure did. But looking at Daddy these days I wonder if he doesn't haunt him just the same." Her face adopted a look of resignation as she steadily eyed the park bench.

"What makes you say that?" Tony was trying, unsuccessfully he thought, to conceal his training in asking evocative questions to draw information out of patients.

"He spends his days in a suit under a park bench, soliciting the opinions of strangers if only to disagree with them."

"Well, there is that, I suppose. But you can't lay that at the feet of Old Gus, can you?"

"Not unless you know the whole story."

"You mean there's more?"

"This is Charleston. There's always more." Her face tightened as she said this, and Tony could see that she was weighing the merits of continuing the story, telling the rest to a complete stranger from California, or leaving well enough alone and changing the subject. The pause was long and deliberate.

"My mother was, for many years, Mr. Camber's mistress," she said without taking her eyes off of her father.

She paused, though Tony couldn't tell if it was for his benefit or her own. He didn't turn to follow her eyes toward her father. Instead he continued to look through her into the story she seemed to want to tell despite

- or perhaps because of - the perceived and relative anonymity of the audience. Tony was doubly fascinated by the revelations and felt the rush of the double agent, the giddiness of the child who has found the Santa stash in the top of the closet, the feeling at the moment just before secretly opening the packages to discover the contents but well before the letdown of the surprise-less morning that ushers in adulthood all too quickly. He couldn't take his eyes off the train wreck.

"He won her in a chess game," she continued with nonchalance, "though I never heard that from either of them. And even if that was the way it began, something stronger must've been at work there."

"Must've been a hell of a chess game," Tony said after a short pause, both to relieve the tension and stir the pot. She looked at him and took the bait.

"Both famous and famously secret. A chess board built into the floor of the giant foyer of the Camber Plantation just outside of town. Old Gus lived there all his life, I think. The floor is black and white marble squares arranged in a square pattern, and the stairs rise to a fork and wrap around both sides. Reminds me of the Von Trapp stairs in The Sound of Music. From the top of the stairs on either end, the floor looks like a chess board, and Old Gus played chess like other men play poker, I guess."

"High stakes?"

"Considering the man under the park bench out there and the wife he lost when she swallowed her pride along with two bottles of sleeping pills, I would have to agree with you on that one." She let the weight of that sink in before continuing. "Must've been a sight to see, though."

"How's that?"

"The chess board all set up with human pieces."

"Human pieces?"

"Yep, so I've been told. All in costumes to match."

"You mean like horses and castles?"

"And little nigger children as pawns."

"Really."

"Yep, with some of Charleston's finest sitting in as kings and queens. It was considered quite an honor, I've heard. Rivaled the debutante balls for prestige, though nobody on the outside knew anything about it."

"And the players?"

"Old Gus invited folks for dinner," she continued, her eyes moving off to a point in the trees somewhere as she continued the story, "sometimes for business, sometimes for pleasure. Though it is hard to imagine Old Gus taking pleasure in much except business. They say as the drinks flowed and the meal came and went, Old Gus would introduce the concept of a game along with a friendly wager."

"Like some amount of money?"

"No, never money. He was too fond of money to place it in harm's way, even though he was apparently very good at chess. So the wagers never included money."

"Apparently they weren't all that friendly, either," Tony said looking down at the nearly empty glass of lemonade in his hand.

She seemed to chuckle at that, or raised her eyebrows at least. Tony wondered if the telling of this story was, in any way, cathartic for this woman whose life had been so dramatically altered by one man.

"Some nights there were no takers, especially as the wagers grew legendary. It went from bottles of wine to cars and paintings pretty quickly. Most nights somebody would take the bait, though, and that's when the party really started." She put her own lemonade down on the table and began using her hands to describe the scene. "The players would face each other from the stairway above the foyer as the pieces were costumed and placed on the board."

"Even the pawns?"

"Locals. Their folks probably worked the place in some capacity. Easiest five bucks those pickaninnies ever made."

"Fascinating."

"The dinner guests were all in costume on the board somewhere," she continued, "and they could participate in the game."

"How do you mean?"

"Except for the pawns, who never said a word, the game pieces could offer up advice to their player, sort of a board-level view of the game. And they had a stake in the game as well. The winning king got the losing queen for desert, they say. So you had all these voices and ideas rising from the floor of the foyer to the player at the rail above who was on the clock."

"They played on the clock?"

"Yep. Old Gus required a wager and a clock. He said that both created a requisite sense of urgency. His words, not mine."

"And one night," Tony said tentatively with a nod toward the park bench, "your father was the player looking at Old Gus from across the foyer?"

"That's right," she said, withdrawing back into her contemplative self. "Bank folks only, though. Management retreat, I was told. I think the whole thing was a loyalty test. Old Gus was big on those. For a man with so much he seemed awfully insecure. So the wager was my mother."

"And Old Gus won?"

"Almost always."

"And your mother took her own life because she felt she was leveraged to ensure your father's job?"

"Not exactly," she said with the same expression that had hid the most recent part of the story. "She didn't make that call until I was 'leveraged,' as you say, some twenty years later."

CHAPTER NINE

Augusta stood in the door of her mother's closet, chin in hand, trying to figure out what change of clothes her mother would want her to bring to the hospital, and beginning to realize the full distance that had grown between them. She stared at the clothes hanging on double racks as if they belonged to a stranger. She didn't remember her mother wearing any of the outfits, some of which still had the tags hanging from the sleeves. At least that part made sense. Margaret really hadn't worn some of the outfits before. Her closet wall took on the shape and color of a display window at Neiman's or a St. John boutique. It was an awkward moment compounded by the fact that Augusta had strongly encouraged her mother to leave the hospital for the night, that there was really nothing she could do for Walker, and she would be more comfortable with a good night's rest and a change of clothes of her own choosing. Seldom and few are the rational thoughts among the laymen in an ICU, though, and Augusta had been dispatched to the house with a stern look of expectation and a list.

"Boo!" came the loud voice close behind her. Augusta shrieked and jumped, turning to find her brother standing behind her with a big grin on his face and a half-full bottle of Maker's Mark in his hand.

"Damn it, Ben," she scolded as she slapped his arm with all the strength she muster, "you scared the shit out of me. I didn't hear you come in."

"Neither have the parents for years now. Practice makes perfect, they say. You want a drink?"

"You got any left in that bottle?" she replied, eyeing the bottle scornfully.

"If not, there's plenty more where this came from," he said, nodding down the hall toward the liquor cabinet. "Practice makes perfect."

"Okay, but make it a light one," she replied, turning back to face the closet, "not that toxic waste you drink."

"I prefer the term weapons-grade, but I'll lace yours with the estrogen you demand."

"Smart ass," she said under her breath.

"Guilty as charged," he said over his shoulder, walking down the hallway toward the kitchen and the bar. "Mom give you a list?"

"What do you think?"

"I think you'll bring her the wrong outfit," he called from the kitchen, "the wrong shoes, and you'll prove yourself inadequate as a daughter once again, but that's just one opinion." He walked back into the room with her drink to punctuate the thought, and she knew he was probably right. "Predictability becomes our only defense as they get older. I think Dr. Phil said that."

"You listen to Dr. Phil."

"Fuck, no. My wife does, though. And it's like second-hand smoke. Kills you just the same." Ben made his way across the well-appointed bedroom to the sitting area with the bay window looking out into the small courtyard garden. He plopped down in a thickly-upholstered chair that threatened to completely envelope him. He let his head fall back as if he could easily drift off to sleep.

"Speaking of your wife," Augusta said, taking a sip of her drink but continuing her search through the clothes, "did you abandon her at the hotel?"

"Not a chance," he said without opening his eyes. "She never came back to the hotel, as far as I know. At least not to the bar."

"Aren't you the least bit concerned?"

"Nope. I've got my eyes out."

"What's that supposed to mean?"

"Only that I see everything. Part of that omniscience thing I've been working on."

"You're so full of shit."

"Maybe so. How's that weapons-grade drink of yours?"

"Hits the spot," she replied, sliding hangers across chrome pipes without much success. "I'd ask your opinion, but I already know your response."

"You know me too well."

Augusta gave up on the closet and crossed the room to sit in the chair opposite Ben. She threw her feet up on the ottoman and surveyed the room.

"You think they ever sit in these chairs?"

"Not for very long, unless they plan to sleep here," Ben said without lifting his head.

"I'm serious. I've never seen either one of them sit in these chairs." She turned to glance at the bookshelf behind the chairs. Family pictures were scattered among the beach fiction and religious treatises. Prominent among the books was a small photo of her grandfather and namesake, sitting behind his desk, face framed by a small scowl and a big cigar. His eyes threatened the photographer with bodily harm and his right hand held a fountain pen ready to seal a loan or a contract of some sort. Over his hand, on the bookshelf in the background behind her grandfather, a second photo caught her eye. It was a picture of a woman in a dress and hat, smiling as posed, eyes less threatening but demanding nonetheless. Augusta couldn't remember ever seeing that picture in her grandfather's office.

"Is that Grandmother in the picture behind Old Gus?"

Ben opened one eye and tilted his head to take the picture into his field of view. He let his eye focus, studied the picture, and then returned to his relaxed position.

"Beats the shit out of me. I never knew her. Hell, you never knew her. Your mother's played sort of fast and loose with the whole Grandmother story. Again, that's only one opinion. You don't have to agree."

"What do you think she was like," Augusta said, ignoring much of what Ben was saying and looking in vain for more pictures of her grandmother on the shelves behind her.

"Had to be strong woman to put up with him, even if it killed her in the end."

"It was cancer, Ben."

"Liver cancer's what Walker told me. He said that's why your mother's never been much of a drinker."

"MY mother?"

"You're the one asking all the fucking questions. I'm just trying to retain my distance and objectivity," he said with a grin creeping over his face.

"That doesn't mean she drank herself to death."

"You're absolutely right," Ben said, "but it's in the gene pool somewhere." He raised his glass to emphasize the sentiment.

"Must've been tough to be married to a man who was married to a family business and an almost psychotic work ethic."

"Twinkle seems to get by okay," Ben said, tongue in cheek.

"No, I mean, look at him. He looks like a bitter old man."

"I think he was a bitter old man. Plus, I don't think people smiled for pictures back then. The Great Depression beat the smiles all out of them."

Augusta studied the picture without listening to any of what Ben was saying. She had developed a keen ability to turn the volume down on her brother's commentary, the result of watching his years as the would-be prodigal son who never really left home to make his return in disgrace, choosing instead to tread water in a continuing downward spiral of disappointment. Looking at her grandfather's face, she wondered how anyone could choose to get trapped into such an apparently unhappy life and, further, what it had been like to be Old Gus's only child and daughter. The adjacent photograph on the shelf was of Margaret and Old Gus on her wedding day, and Augusta eyed it sentimentally.

"It couldn't have been easy to be her," she said to Ben and to nobody in particular, "growing up with that face, those expectations, without a mother's nurturing to balance it out, isolated from the soul of the man and the work that haunted him."

"What the hell are you talking about?" Ben said, raising his head finally to bring his sister into focus, her face and her words. "He looks more haunting than haunted, and he's done quite a number on your mother."

"And probably disappointment that he never had a son, that she was the only child and the wrong gender. And then she married a Baptist."

"What?"

"Maybe that's why she's always favored you over me, expected more of me than you, turned a blind eye to your indiscretions. Boys will be boys, after all." Augusta was talking through the issues with her mother, or her mother held captive by the photograph, an unwilling but available audience she'd never really been in the flesh. Augusta kept her eyes on her mother's as she continued with Ben. "Inattention breeds insecurity, especially in young girls fighting for the approval of their fathers. We see it every day at school, girls acting out to get their fathers' attention. Of course, their mothers do the same thing, wearing the little tennis outfits and yoga tights trying desperately to recapture the attention of their husbands. It's a vicious cycle."

"Are you listening to yourself," Ben asked the ceiling, unsuccessful in his attempt to keep his head upright through the conversation. "I knew I should've fixed that drink a lot stronger."

"You wouldn't understand. It's mothers and daughters."

"Yeah, fathers and sons have it made. Peas and carrots. Ball games and titty bars. The fun never stops with my old man."

Ben chuckled to himself at the absurdity of the last comment, but then the room fell silent. He had expected a comeback from his sister, but none was forthcoming. He closed his eyes and awaited the inevitable, the question that always cropped up when Old Gus crept into the conversation.

"Why didn't you come back here to work?"

"Same reason you didn't," he said quickly, trying to make this line of questioning retreat as quickly as it had advanced.

"I was never asked. You were. Repeatedly."

"Too easy to throw that on me. Would you have worked for Old Gus if he had asked?"

"Tough to say," Augusta replied. "I'm not a banker."

"Same old cop out line. You should be weary of it by now, along with this whole conversation. How many times have we been through this?"

"That was then. Things are different now. The bank has never been on the verge of a sale before."

"Family businesses are sold every day. It's just never been our family's business."

"Exactly," she said, turning to face him, chair to chair.

"Exactly, what?"

"It shouldn't be ours this time either."

Ben raised his head to look sideways at his sister through furrowed brow as he tried to reconcile her logic. As her face came into clear focus, her eyes were clearly focused. Scary focused, he thought. He felt like the kid across the desk from the headmaster about to be punished for an honor-code violation. He tugged and scratched on his left ear, sat up in the chair, and propped his chin on his empty hand, all without leaving her gaze. He had an uneasy feeling that his sister had an idea that would likely claw him out of his comfort zone.

"Okay," he said finally, "help me out here, because I really don't know what you're talking about."

"Of course you do, Ben. You're drunk, not stupid."

"I'm sobering quickly, against my will and better judgment."

"Don't tell me you haven't thought about it."

"The romantic notion of saving the family business usually comes to a screeching halt when I remember that your mother is the majority shareholder. At that point I try to count the money. The offer is a cash sale, if you'll remember, which is both inefficient and liberating at the same time. We get taxed on the zero basis but we get to walk away. Literally. Walk away. Live the life you imagine. All that new age shit."

"She's our mother and she'll do what you say. We both know that."

"Even with a mandate from Old Gus to sell the bank? You think she's gonna walk out on that limb? Talk about a haunting. She'd never sleep again."

"I don't think she sleeps much now, and yes I think she'd follow you out on that limb. Gladly, even. The only reason to turn her back on Old Gus is to save her baby from what appears to everyone around him as a downward spiral into marital despair, vocational impropriety, and social obscurity."

"Damn. I'm really starting to sober up now."

"Stay with me, Ben."

"Throw me a rope with one of those life saver rings on it. Maybe I can hang myself with it."

"We're talking about the bank, Ben."

"I know what we're talking about, Augusta." He never called her Augusta, and she raised her eyebrows when it came out. Must've struck a nerve, she thought. The danger, she recognized, was withdrawal and passive capitulation, two of Ben's trademark maneuvers. He would simply wrap himself in a perception of Protestant work ethic and wait out the storms of commitment and expectation in his own safe harbor of busy inactivity.

"Is this something we have to talk about right now?

Buddy Hill was immensely pleased with the turnout for the prayer vigil, and the dedicated followers had remained in almost full force until shortly after nine o'clock, when the tendency to glance at watches became almost epidemic. Buddy understood. These were family men and women with responsibilities of their own waiting for them at home. He assured them that Walker understood as well, and would no doubt tell them so as soon as his recovery allowed. Their prayers and supplications to the Lord Jesus on behalf of Walker would not go unheard but would pass unhindered to the ears of the Lord and Walker both. He assured his followers of this as well, and they seemed pleased as they made their way out of the fellowship hall and into the night. Even Buddy felt the post-prayer lightness of being, the euphoria associated with letting go and letting God, as he climbed into his Buick sedan, preferred by Baptist preachers almost five to one it seems, and turned the key to let the engine idle as he straight-armed the steering wheel and stared at the gauges on the dashboard, tension beginning to crawl up his shoulders as his mind played back the evening tape. At last he shrugged his shoulders and shook his head. Twinkle was obviously distraught about Walker and maybe even struggling with her own marriage, he thought. Some of the pastoral care textbooks even suggested that these types of encounters would manifest themselves with all men of God, and especially the ones who could form the strongest bonds with individuals within the congregation. It was a matter of projection, he remembered from the text, an outlet whereby the minister, through the word and grace of God, was able to connect dysfunctional parts of the person's life, and the person, unable to reach out to a physical God, would project that emotional release through the minister. The text advised, further, that ministers must necessarily recognize the intended target of that emotional release, must objectify the experience and render it wholesale to the Lord, on behalf of and in witness of the sender. Twinkle's reaction was textbook, it seemed to him, and Buddy Hill was prepared to render her emotions to the Lord, just as soon as his erection subsided.

In the meantime, Buddy backed his car out of the still unfamiliar space reserved for the Senior Pastor and pulled out of the parking lot headed for home. Traffic was light but heavy enough that he didn't notice the Volvo wagon pull in a couple of cars behind him. He rolled the windows down to enjoy the evening air and turned the volume of the radio up. He never failed to glean some sermon and prayer ideas from Faith Radio, and he had even been a guest preacher on a couple of occasions. Tonight was different, though, and as he listened to the conversation between the host and guest, a Christian physicist who seemed reluctant to apply a literal interpretation of the Genesis account of creation to age the earth at 6,000 years old, Buddy found his creationist ire beginning to rise.

"Genesis 1-12, pal," he said to the radio and to passing motorists who might've been the beneficiaries of his zeal, "it's the foundation, the very Word of God. You can't ignore it or write it off as a good story. The Word is the Word." Buddy felt the tension begin to relax in his shoulders, and elsewhere as well, as his blood began to flow in support of the argument he was making with the unsuspecting Delco radio in the dash. Nothing like righteousness, he thought, to shake the dust off the central principles and focus our attention on the roots of our crosses. He began looking around the front seat and center console for the small digital recorder he kept for capturing sermon ideas on the road. He felt strongly that a hard look at foundational texts would be timely for his congregation right now, but he was unable to find the recorder. He made a mental note and rejoined the conversation.

"You're missing the point, whatever your name is," he said to the radio guest. "The inerrant word of God. He said it. I believe it. That's it. You can't go picking and choosing, tempted by a better version or a more convenient outcome. Seven days is seven days. Eve tempted by Satan, Adam tempted by Eve, original sin. That's the burden we bear. We are not perfect. We are all sinners, up to our necks in sin. But the Lord Jesus has bathed us in His blood, saved us from ourselves, and we are born again! Can I get an 'amen?'" He said this last part so emphatically that he hadn't seen the small car full of teenagers pull up beside him at the traffic light. He looked out of his window in their direction in response to their question.

"Man, who the fuck are you talking to?" the boy in the passenger seat asked very calmly, hat cocked sideways, several faces from around the small car framing his bullet-proof expression of teenage confidence.

"Brother, I'm talking to the Lord. Have you talked to him lately?"

The car erupted in laughter, though the expression on the questioner never changed. He just continued to stare at Buddy quizzically. As the cross street light turned yellow and with almost impeccable timing, the kid offered his last thought.

"I ain't your fucking brother," he said, and the car took off like a street racer anticipating the green light, three laughing faces turned back through the rear window.

Buddy accelerated slowly through the intersection and chuckled at the reaction of the kids to his sermon on the dash. He reached down and selected a different preset button on the radio, and began to tap his thumbs on the steering wheel as Wang Chung brought the 80s hits into the Buick. He looked in the rearview mirror out of reflex more than anything else, embarrassed without really being embarrassed, more conscious of the potential need to be embarrassed.

Watching from the industry-standard safety of her Volvo wagon several cars back, Twinkle hadn't made out what was said, but she was certain that there had been an exchange between Buddy Hill and the small car next to him. This is crazy, she said to herself, though she really wasn't listening. You're stalking a preacher, she continued. You've done some stupid things through the years, but this is crazy, crazy, crazy. Her lecture to herself was interrupted by the ring of her cell phone.

"Hello," she said without looking at caller ID.

"Twinkle, sweetie, Grace returning your call from earlier. Sorry I missed you but we were finishing the girls night outing at the club. We missed you. Could've used your backhand. I just couldn't find my rhythm. How's Charleston?"

"Grace!" Twinkle said loudly into the phone, "listen to me. I'm doing something stupid, I think, and I need somebody else to tell me so." She had stopped at a stop sign and looked both directions, phone to her ear, and proceeded through the intersection crouched over the steering wheel like she was about to sell nuclear secrets to the axis of evil, all the while trying not to lose sight of the Buick.

"Oh, pray tell," Grace said as if huddling the other women in Twinkle's tennis group tightly around the table filled with stemware and bottles of pinot. "Is something the matter? Is Ben up to his old tricks? Did you catch him again? Have you got a gun or a dull, rusty knife?"

"Grace," Twinkle said with frustration, "shut up and listen to me."

"Okay. I'm listening."

"I'm following a preacher, stalking him really, and I think he's heading home. At least I hope so.

"Wait. Back up, sweetie. Did you say a preacher?

"Yes, but he's not married."

"He is to God, but that's not why I'm asking. I'm wanting to know why you're stalking a preacher. You got some unanswered Bible-study questions or something?"

"No, listen to me. I met him in the Emergency Room this afternoon and kissed him and got all hot and choked up."

"You kissed a preacher in the Emergency Room?"

"No, at a prayer vigil?"

"A what? Who were you praying for?"

"Walker, my father-in-law. He's had a stroke or something, they're not sure."

"And that's why you were in the Emergency Room?"

"Yes, but Buddy is actually Walker's replacement."

"Who's Buddy?"

"He's the preacher I'm stalking. Following. This is crazy."

"Twinkle, honey, I'm confused. I'm handing the phone to Weezie."

"No, wait!" Twinkle shouted to no avail.

"Twinkle?" the new voice asked. "Mary Louise. I'm walking outside so I can hear you better. What's all this about sex with a preacher in the emergency room?"

It occurred to Twinkle, probably too late, that even her tennis group was not equipped to offer advice on something this crazy, despite their good counsel in the recent past. Thinking surprisingly quick on her feet, Twinkle chose to throw dirt quickly into the hole she'd just dug.

"Hey, Weezie," she said with a hint of secrecy, "I was just yanking Grace's chain, but don't let on that you know. I was just calling to let y'all know that Ben's daddy had some sort of stroke, and I probably won't make it back to play in Monday's round-robin. I don't know when we'll be leaving here."

"But what about the, you know—"

"Made all that up, Mary Louise. You know how Grace likes a bit of juicy gossip."

"Oh, you got her good, girl. She's looking at me through the window right now trying to read my lips. We'll have fun with this. Sorry to hear about Ben's father. Should've been his son that got struck down. Is he going to be okay?"

"They don't know yet, but the doctor just walked in, so let me go. I'll call you later." Hanging up the phone, Twinkle saw the Buick's brake lights up ahead along with a left turn signal. She slowly pulled to the curb about a block from the driveway where Buddy parked the Buick. She anxiously watched him get out of the car and walk to his front door, even lowering herself in her seat as a car passed her Volvo, drove to the end of the block and turned left.

Jason Herbert turned left and circled the block and, killing the head-lights, pulled the small pickup to a stop under a tree that afforded him an unobstructed view of both the Volvo wagon and the subject's residence. He took another bite of the Milky Way that he'd started while parked across from the church parking lot, but pulled up the Coke can from the console to find it empty, again. Chewing on the candy bar, he readied the digital camera that he kept on the passenger seat, a Nikon professional grade with a telephoto lens adequate to the task of capturing both light and persons of interest, the latter usually in the throes of activities suspected by his clients, husbands and wives whose domestic bliss has been tainted by the infidelity or inattention of those same persons of interest. Nothing compared to his military training, the work had grown all but routine to Jason. People, he had begun to conclude, were predictable in their stupidity. But while the hours were not, the money was good, and there was still a little rush at the moment when the person about to do the stupid act actually commits to it. Jason had gotten to where he felt like he could talk them, even will them into the breach. He often found himself saying to the perp and himself, "Wait for it, wait for it," and pulling the trigger on the cam-era at just the right moment, resulting in a clean shot for the lawyers, the primary players in his referral network.

Twinkle Middleton had been a hard case, and he had informed her husband, his client, of that fact at every possible turn. Other than tennis, he'd said, she doesn't seem to have much of a life. He hated taking Mr. Middleton's money, even though he seemed to have plenty of it to go around. She had been what Jason described as a frigid jailer, a seemingly asexual woman whose faint libido found satisfaction only through the painful celibacy of her adulterous husband. He'd coined the term on his own wife before going into business, after the divorce, with the PI that she'd hired to document his own infidelity. But today stood to be a new day for Twinkle. Jason had been shocked and ill-prepared earlier that evening when she'd left the church hall, and he'd completely failed to capture the unexpected kiss on film. Then in consolation, he'd rationalized that the kiss was only an innocent gesture. But when Twinkle returned to the church and waited, Jason had a hunch he'd get a second chance. He did enough research to conclude that the man in his pictures was the same man listed on the church website as Lead Pastor of Trinity Baptist Charleston, a man by the name of Buddy Hill. When the parking lot began to clear around 9:00 and then she began to tail him, Jason began to construct a new characterization of Twinkle, one that probably wouldn't include frigid.

When the door of the Volvo opened, Jason started snapping shots. Twinkle shone like the star she was going to be, he thought, and he began talking his talk.

"Don't do it," he said. "Look both ways before you cross. Safety first!"

He chuckled as he narrated the story that unfolded in predictable fashion. He rolled the window down slightly and began listening for neighborhood dogs. Hearing none, he took another bite of the Milky Way and watched as Twinkle crossed the street and then back to the Volvo again in indecision.

"Come on, sweetheart," Jason whispered. "Make up your mind. Step across the line or step back. One or the other."

She crossed the street again and began walking toward the house. As she was walking away from him, Jason felt comfortable stepping out of the dark shadow of the truck and tree, camera under his jacket, and walking across the street to get a better angle. Once she crossed the street the last time, Twinkle appeared to be committed, and Jason wanted to make sure he captured the moment.

Twinkle approached the house and rang the bell, oblivious to the almost silent shutter sounds of the camera half a block away. Jason watched and narrated as the Reverend Hill answered the door with a look of surprise. They exchanged words, he invited her in, and then he looked both ways before following her into his house. Jason made his way back to the truck. To supplement the big camera, he armed himself with a special model, one with remote and flexible periscope-type optics better suited for close-up and clandestine shots. Jason liked the word clandestine and tried unsuccessfully to incorporate it into his everyday speech. Then he made his way down the sidewalk and past Buddy's residence checking for access and visibility. He ducked behind a tree and pulled up the camera just in time to capture a moving embrace, emotionally and physically. Locked in the sudden release of pent-up passion, Twinkle and Buddy were making their way from the entry hall and living area into what Jason suspected was the rear of the house. He remembered noting an alleyway that cut the block down the middle for water meters and trash collection. Tucking the camera, he continued down the block nonchalantly, trying not to raise the suspicions of the neighbors or their dogs. Once in the alleyway, Jason hit pay dirt. The Reverend Hill had not secured his gate when taking out the trash most recently, leaving Jason an opportunity to approach the rear of the house undetected. Using the flexible optics from the bushes beneath what he assumed to be the master bedroom, Jason was able to capture both stills and video of the Reverend Hill and Mrs. Middleton engaged in inappropriate sexual congress. The lighting was poor, but the images and activities were clearly discernible. As he watched the scene unfold on the tiny screen from the bushes, Jason pulled out his Blackberry and sent a text message to his client.

"Yes, this is something we have to talk about right now, Ben," Augusta said, her tone suggesting her frustration with her brother. "And can't you let it ring?"

"Just a text from a buddy on a fishing trip," Ben replied calmly before putting his phone away. "Says he's got a fish on."

"That's great. I'm happy for him, but we have a family situation here, so can we stay focused on that? Please?"

"You bet," Ben replied, rubbing his eyes and sitting up straight as multiple family issues swarmed his rapidly sobering mind. "What have you got in mind? I mean, let's say you, or I, talk your mother into holding onto the bank. Then what? You going to run it? You've said yourself you're not a banker. And let's face it, I'm a banker in name only, in a downward spiral it seems."

"I don't know, but there has to be an answer to that question. After all, Pacific Mergers seems to think it's worth buying, so part of me thinks it must be worth holding onto."

"It's worth it to them because they can grow it or lever it up or bolt it onto an existing financial services entity they hold. That or break it up, but that wouldn't make sense. There aren't enough pieces. At the bottom, it's just a balance sheet. It's always just a balance sheet."

"Not when you look into his eyes," she said nodding back over her shoulder to the picture of Old Gus.

"Yep. For him it was also terminal constipation, so let's jump ahead to the good part of holding onto this thing."

"There's got to be something. I mean, we could keep it going, the two of us, working as a team, couldn't we?"

"Funny thing about business and stocks. Treading water doesn't pay. If all we did was keep it going, it would never really be worth more than it is right now, and we have an offer on the table. You have to grow it, buy low and sell high, expand up and out."

"I know all of that, Ben."

"Then you're wrapped around the axle of this thing because you've secretly always wanted to be a banker? You want to get back at Old Gus for not giving your mother an opportunity, a connection to her father, a piece of the family pie? You want to move back to Charleston and need a good reason to make that happen? What?"

"No. None of that, but maybe all of that."

"Ah, the siren song of home fires and maternal insanity. You need the tension of being the inadequate daughter. Or will the move home give you that burst of nurturing that you seem to think skipped a generation a while back," he said facetiously as he fished his cell phone out of his front pocket and saw his mother's name on the caller ID. "And speak of the devil," he showed Augusta the number and then answered the call.

"Hello, Mother. Yep, she's here. Right now? We're getting your—. Sure thing. We're on the way. Be right there." He ended the call and lowered his head to the back of the chair.

"Bad news?" she asked, her eyes beginning to tear.

"She didn't say, but it didn't sound good."

The ride to the hospital was a strange blur for Augusta. They passed familiar landmarks from the neighborhoods of her youth, through the center of Old Charleston, and even past the cemetery at St. Phillip's where her grandfather probably awaited his son-in-law. Old Gus was going to be chapped, she thought, if Walker arrived in the family plot before Margaret. The only solace he might have was the place cards. In testament to her efficiency and organization, when Margaret had made the arrangements for Old Gus, she had directed the funeral home to bury the vaults and erect the headstones for herself and Walker, putting hers between the two men in her life. Augusta remembered the awkwardness of her grandfather's funeral with her parents' headstones already in place, and she also remembered Walker's outrage at the premature reminder of his own mortality. From that point on, Walker had made if fairly clear that his wishes were to be cremated. His ashes were to be cast to the wind from the edge of the Sea of

Galilee, a site he'd always hoped to visit but hadn't seen. If he was dead, Augusta thought, holes would be dug but no airline tickets would be bought.

They arrived in the waiting room of the ICU to find Margaret talking with Father Bennett, the Rector of St. Phillip's. Augusta offered tentative hugs to both and Ben shook the priest's hand with a nod.

"Well," Margaret began, foregoing the usual pleasantries, "the doctors were hopeful, but the aneurysm burst a short while ago and your father had what they've described as a massive stroke."

"And?" Augusta asked tearfully.

"And," she continued, "he's on a ventilator, but all brain activity has stopped."

"So he's gone," Augusta said, looking between her Mother and the Father. They both nodded, Margaret's face softening in light of Augusta's tears. Ben had resigned himself to the idea on the drive over, if not before.

"They're waiting for you two to visit with Walker, if you'd like to, before they retire the ventilator," Father Bennett said. "And then we'll serve last rites, of sorts, to usher Walker into the Kingdom of Heaven."

"Do Episcopalians typically receive last rites?" Ben asked, surprised by the procedure.

"The Prayer Book refers to it as a ministration, but the concept is the same. A way of commending Walker to the care of his Lord and Savior."

"But he was a Baptist," Ben continued.

"Jesus, Ben," Margaret whispered with enthusiasm, "do you really want to argue about this right now?"

"Sorry," Ben said, wide-eyed. "Just curious. Apparently there are some steps in here we have to get right. Just trying to understand."

"Perfectly natural, Ben," Father Bennett said in his calming voice. "The Baptists are on board with this. It's a common practice among most Christians. I've placed a call to Buddy Hill's office. I was hoping he could join us for this. I'm afraid I haven't updated my contact list, though, and I don't have his home or cell number."

"I do," Ben said, fishing a business card out of his left pocket and offering to dial. "Should I give him a call?" He dialed the cell number and then looked back up as everyone eyed him in surprise. "He gave me his card this afternoon in the waiting room, in case I needed to talk." He let the phone ring until the voice mail started to pick up.

"Voice mail," Ben said ending the call and putting his phone back into his pocket and handing Buddy's card to the priest.

"That's alright," Father Bennett said, taking the card. "I'll follow up with him later this evening or first thing in the morning. Would the two of you like to join us for the Commendatory Prayer?"

The four of them circled the foot of the bed as the nurse removed the intubation apparatus and turned off the breathing machine, suggesting that he would now simply fade away and that the doctor would be right in to pronounce. Augusta watched her father's face and sobbed quietly as the other three watched the heart monitor flatline. Father Bennett then opened his prayer book and offered the prescribed prayer.

"Into your hands, O merciful Savior, we commend your servant Walker Middleton. Acknowledge, we humbly beseech you, a sheep of your own fold, a lamb of your own flock, a sinner of your own redeeming. Receive him into the arms of your mercy, into the blessed rest of everlasting peace, and into the glorious company of the saints in light. Amen."

CHAPTER TEN

The air was cooler, crisper than he had anticipated, and Tony opened the front windows of the rental car to let the fall breeze wash the recycled air of the long flight from his lungs. As he made his way out of the Charlotte Airport and onto I-85 South, Tony could see the city skyline in the distance, glass buildings bunched together like a small version of Los Angeles. As he crossed under Billy Graham Parkway, though, he realized that there were also some dramatic differences, and he shook his head and asked himself what could possibly have been worth a return trip. Maybe he'd made a mistake in coming back to talk to these folks on a hunch, a whim really. He'd even had a hard time explaining it to Michael Kelly, his boss at Pacific Mergers.

"It's tough to explain," he'd said two weeks before, having just returned from the abbreviated meeting in Charleston, "but I have a feeling that there's a lot more to this story than the family wants to talk about."

"Based on?" Michael replied, thumbing through a preliminary report and case file on the Plantation Trust acquisition.

"Nothing more than a hunch, really. I don't even know if the stories I've been told are true, but if they are, they manifest a strange corporate culture that would rival anything I've read in the news lately."

"And you got this information from this woman on the porch, the daughter of the homeless guy who wasn't actually homeless. That right? Because it's not in the report or file anywhere."

"I didn't put it in yet because it was too damn strange to believe. That's the part I need to confirm before I put it in writing where someone might make decisions because it's in the report. I'd hate to look stupid or make the firm look stupid, but I think there may be something to it."

"And the story?"

"I'd rather not say, at least until I've had a chance to vet it out."

Michael Kelly was curious, but he weighed his curiosity against his need to bring this deal in on time and under budget. Chasing a cast of characters like the ones Tony was describing stretched Michael's interest in this new strategy for underwriting the family when buying a family business. He was all about it, he tried to admit to himself, until the qualitative began to compromise the quantitative. At that point it began to look an awful lot like a waste of money.

"But you also view this as a replay of the meeting in Charleston that killed the preacher? Is that fair to say?"

"That's fair to say about the meeting," Tony chuckled, "but I don't remember a smoking gun in the conference room. But, yes, I would hope to follow up with the family. The children more so than the mother."

"Why's that? I thought the mother was the key to the whole thing."

"Very loyal to the good memories, if you know what I mean. Hesitant to stray too far off message, so I didn't see a whole lot of possible traction there. Plus, with the death of her husband at the hands of a murderous meeting, it doesn't seem like the right time, even if it is just business."

"Well, I don't see you getting much traction with the kids, either. They're stockholders, but they don't seem like stakeholders to me. But you're the highly-skilled psychologist in this equation, not me," he said, closing the folder and handing it back to Tony. "And lucky for you we have deep pockets as a lead investor on this deal who specifically said to spare no expense on the due diligence. So follow your hunch and let's see if you can find the ghosts in the machine."

With that, Tony was back in the Carolinas looking for ghosts, victims of the all-terrain machine of capitalism, souls cast aside by Plantation Trust. Or simply ghosts of a tight Charleston social order, impenetrable to all but the old guard and their progeny, because there was always the possibility that the strange encounter and story along the Battery were nothing more than that, a strange but remarkable coincidental encounter and story. The answers, Tony hoped, would be found in Greenville, South Carolina, in the memories of Augusta Camber Thomason, the newest of the old, connected by heritage but disconnected by geography. Tony was cautiously optimistic. If not Augusta, Tony was less hopeful about mining her brother Ben on the return trip north on I-85 to Charlotte, allotting little more than a rest stop on the way back to the airport. For now, though, Tony was following his hunch through the Piedmont, a mixture of rolling hills, giant-peach water towers, automobile manufacturing plants, and lots of signage for a truck stop called Cafe Risque promoting topless talent and a breakfast special. Welcome to the New South.

Driving into downtown Greenville, Tony was awestruck by the streetscape, a tree-lined collection of shops and restaurants that bore a striking resemblance to Charleston, without the age and history but with all the charm and with even more reinvestment. New developments strolled arm in arm with the reinvented while a gently rolling river, little more than a stream, meandered alongside buildings and below picturesque bridges. After checking into The Poinsett, another historic and well-appointed hotel, Tony took in the late afternoon view out his window, thinking to himself that developers in California spent fortunes trying to create this town-center feel with movie set construction and synthetic stucco, but they almost always failed. Then again, as with Charleston, many of the newer Greenville buildings probably pre-date many of the oldest buildings in Los Angeles. Even more, though, there was an order, almost a symmetry to the layout of the small town, and in the distance he could see the Rockwellian steeples and lawns of the oldest churches. Los Angeles seemed to lack both order and religion, Tony thought, but he could honestly say he didn't miss either as he turned to find the digital clock on the bedside table. He was meeting Augusta and Ellis for drinks and dinner at 7:00, but the clock suggested he had sufficient time for a shower and change of clothes before he was back on the street heading north on Main Street, as directed by the concierge, toward Melissa's, one of the trendy bistro-type restaurants that lined Main Street from top to bottom.

As Tony walked in he saw Augusta waving quietly from a table near the back, a semi-circular booth with original oil paintings of lighthouses and other coastal features. As Tony made his way through the small bar and seating area, he noticed ships' wheels and anchors and yachting flags and other nautical fare. As he reached the table, Tony's expression met Augusta's knowing nod.

"Melissa was born and raised on the coast," she told Tony. "But she married a local mortgage banker who refuses to leave Greenville. So she decided to bring the coast to the upstate."

"That explains a lot."

"Wait until you see the menu," she continued. "She has fresh seafood sent up from the coast three days a week. Her father and brothers are big fishermen, so it's really fresh."

"Sounds good to me," Tony replied, sliding into the booth across from Augusta. "How's your mother doing? And how are you doing? Everything returning to normal, as they say?" Tony was intent on holding her gaze to make sure she knew he wasn't simply making polite conversation.

"All good on this end, we think. Can't speak for Margaret, but I think she's moving forward," Augusta replied while holding Tony's gaze. "Life has a nasty habit of injecting itself into a family crisis."

"Yes it does."

193

"Kids still go to school, houses get built, soccer games are played."

"The beat goes on, and the dream never dies," Tony affirmed, "but it's also important to give grief its due."

"I appreciate that, and I think we're doing that. Ellis sends his regrets. Our oldest has a make-up soccer game this evening, and he felt his relevance was greater there than here. I tended to agree."

The waitress arrived and took drink orders and revealed the daily specials of fresh seafood, repeating some of the family connections between the fish and the owner. After they'd explored the options and placed an order for food and beverage, the two skipped the usual pleasantries in favor of getting to the point.

"So where do we stand on the bank stuff?" Augusta started. "You mentioned on the phone that you weren't trying to reconstruct the family meeting, and I appreciate that. I don't know that our schedules would have allowed that in the near term."

"No, that moment is lost, I think. My hope now is to capture some of the time we didn't share, one family member at a time, and look back at where the people and the bank meet."

"Seems sort of general," Augusta said, looking at her watch. "And like I've said, we've never really had anything to do with the bank. I think Ben is likely to say the same thing. So, when you look at it that way, these people, the one sitting here at the table at least, never met the bank." Tick. Tock.

"Well, maybe people meeting bank people might be a more targeted line of inquiry. For example," Tony eased into it, "does the name Wrightman ring a bell?"

Augusta furrowed her eyebrows and looked at Tony. She seemed hesitant and confused.

"Thomas Wrightman?"

"Yes," Tony said enthusiastically. "That's the one."

"Tony, Thomas Wrightman was Old Gus's right hand man for decades, but he retired a while back. How in the world did his name come up?"

"Accountants," Tony lied, making his way through a rationale for asking these questions. "Lots of older entries had his name in the journal notes, and they were trying to understand the role he played. They were trying to rebuild executive compensation numbers to determine expense ratios, I think. Is any of this making sense to you, because it was all Greek to me until somebody explained it."

"It makes sense," Augusta replied, "but I had no idea you were going back that far into the records."

"How far is that far?"

"I think he retired at least ten years ago, but I may wrong about that. I do know it's been a while, and Old Gus never took to his replacement."

"How do you mean?"

"Even as late as last year, right up to his death I guess, Old Gus still seemed bitter about Mr. Wrightman's retirement, like he was going to get lost without him."

"Really."

"That's the way I remember it. But what Old Gus couldn't get his mind around was that most people retire in their 60s, 70s at the latest. Old Gus wanted his hand on the tiller—pun intended," she said gesturing at the nautical decor, "until the very end. And I guess he got his way. He even called Mr. Wrightman before he died. Probably the last call he ever made. Called him from the office the night he died. Never called Margaret or me or Ben, but called an unbelievably loyal employee ten years into retirement who puts on a suit and comes down to the office and finds Old Gus face down on the desk next to a cold cigar and empty brandy glass."

"Why would you describe him as unbelievably loyal?"

"It couldn't have been easy to work for my grandfather for that many years, and that was probably not the first time he'd been called out of retirement.

"Must've been difficult to sustain a family life and that sort of loyalty, wouldn't you think?"

"I don't know. I don't know if he had children. I remember his wife being a very reserved woman, but I really only saw her a couple of times at official functions when I was very young. I wouldn't know her today, that's how long it's been. I haven't even seen him in probably ten years."

"But he was an institution, you might say? Very loyal?"

"If he could have died for my grandfather, I wouldn't have put it past him."

"Why so loyal, do you think? I mean, nothing against your family or your grandfather, but the man you describe, the loyalty you describe, is not common, is it?

"Not anymore, I guess, and I have no idea why. Old Gus was a curmudgeonly man from the longest reaches of my memory. Bitter, unpleasant, and loyal in his own way to the dead men that preceded him. I've never really thought about it before, but maybe Old Gus thought of Mr. Wrightman as the son he never had, since Margaret was never really involved in the business."

"And why was that? Just a cultural taboo to have women involved in daily operations?"

"I guess so. Charleston can be a very small place. But then, I'm the only female headmaster of a large private school in the South Carolina upstate, one out of over 50 in our region. And this is education we're talking about, a field dominated by women but still led by men."

"And you think Mr. Wrightman might have recognized his son-like status through the years?"

"If he did, I can't imagine it being worth the effort."

"Did you ever consider going to work for the bank?"

"Sure, but the invitation was never extended to me. Only Ben."

"Really? I guess cultural taboos cross generations."

"It seems, but remember that the same man was at the helm for both of those generations."

The waitress brought the drinks and appetizers, and Augusta took advantage of the pause to check her cell phone for messages. There were no messages, so apparently Ellis had everything under control. This fact was settling and unsettling at the same time. While Augusta liked to bemoan the male bias of the business world, she also felt pangs of maternal guilt when others were tending to her children. With everything under control, though, Augusta decided to capitalize on Tony's therapeutic responsibility, at least as he suggested during their one failed family session.

"So how long have you been studying family dynamics?" she asked Tony while stirring her drink and eyeing the crab claws on the small plate in front of her.

"Almost ten years, I suppose. I started while I was working on my master's. Read an article that opened my eyes to the dysfunction within my own family and kept going from there. Never expected to be doing this, though. Always saw myself more in your role, the professional academic, the noble educator. Maybe a clinical psychologist or therapist."

"What happened?"

"Phone calls and job offers. You wave enough money in front of a starving grad student and you'll get his attention."

"Do you miss the clinical part? I'm assuming you don't get to do much of that."

"More than I thought I would. The human part of it has always been the most interesting. I enjoy learning about this brave new world of capitalism, and I get to work with nice people like you and your family, but I miss the purely human side of it. Too much of this work is removed from that."

"So what do you think of our little slice of dysfunction?" Augusta asked cutting her eyes toward Tony from the crab claws.

"Dysfunction is the new norm," he replied with a chuckle, "but I am fascinated by the impact of the bank and the Charleston community on your particular brand of dysfunction. I get the feeling that your family has lived in something of a fishbowl for a number of years, generations even."

"Even if that fishbowl is self-induced?"

"We all seem to be our own jailers in some form of fashion, certainly, and Plantation Trust seems to have built fairly substantial walls around your mother. Some your father was never even able to scale, I'm assuming. They must've had an interesting relationship through the years, even before her father died and left the decisions to her."

"That may be stretching it a bit. I don't think he left her with any decisions to make. Just a mandate to sell the bank to Pacific Mergers. Period."

"And how does that mandate make you feel, about your family if not the bank?"

"More numb than anything else. I'm not betraying any confidences when I tell you that I've been trying to figure out a way to keep the bank from being sold. I know that's not what you want to hear, but it is what it is."

"No, please tell me more. Your reasoning is at the heart of what I'm trying to understand, and I've got my therapist hat on now anyway. Let's pretend, if it's possible, that I don't work for Pacific Mergers. Lay it all out there."

"Well," Augusta began guardedly, "we've always been a house divided unto itself, with family distinctions cutting like a razor along bloodlines."

"How do you mean?"

"At official functions, for example, when the time comes for pictures, Margaret has always made a point of separating family from other."

"That seems natural."

"Yeah, but not the way you're thinking. She drew the bloodline in a way that included, initially, only me and Ben. Daddy was excluded somehow as other. And then when I had kids, the same distinction was made with Ellis. And not that he cared. It has become sort of a joke between us, but it was as if he qualified as family only under certain circumstances, like when an architectural or design question came up. Margaret would always ask for a family opinion and go on and on about how great it was to have an architect in the family. Other times he ranked somewhere below sperm donor. But his children were family even when he wasn't. Really strange. Even stranger that I'm telling you about it."

"That does sound peculiar, but pretty tame on the dysfunction scale if that helps."

"It does," she said with a grin. "But that's the way things have been in our house. There was always a distinction between the Cambers and the Middletons, even though Margaret was both. Daddy's job and the church were always separate, as if everybody had a job to do. But for Margaret it always seemed to be limited to that, Daddy's job. We never went to church there, which I always thought was strange. Going to church there, instead of the Camber family church, would've been like banking somewhere other than Plantation Trust, I guess, which we never did. I didn't think much of it until I got old enough to understand it and recognize the politics involved. Mother was absolutely dedicated to the Camber family traditions, including the bank, even though she was never allowed to participate in the business."

The waitress intervened with the dinner entrees and a fresh round of drinks, a break which also afforded Augusta the opportunity to introduce Melissa, the owner and namesake of the establishment, who walked through the restaurant eyeing the slow early evening crowd before stopping at Augusta's table to check on everything. The exchange of pleasantries seemed to lighten the confessional feel of the ongoing conversation, but Tony was eager to get back to the point.

"How did your father deal with the house divided, as you say?" he asked, cutting into his fish taco.

"Built his own wall, I guess. Other than the mission trips, we never had much to do with his work."

"Lots of walls in your family."

"Doesn't that tend to happen over time in families, though?"

"It might, but it doesn't make it very healthy. Has it worked the same way with your family, between you and Ellis?"

"No, not at all, I don't think. Ellis may argue about that, but I don't see it as working the same way. The geography probably works in our favor."

"I'm assuming you've thought about moving closer to the nest."

"Regularly, but usually with the same result. Ellis is not a big fan of the idea."

"Is that because of what's here or what's there?"

"Both. We've made a pretty good life here, his practice, my job, the kids love it here. He says the quality of life doesn't improve with a move. Just the pace and expectations."

"How do you feel about that?"

"I agree in large part, but he doesn't have a fourth generation family business on the block, and Charleston has a way of luring the fruit back to the orchard."

"It is a captivating town. Lots of history. Civil War and all that."

"But we also have walls of our own," Augusta said, the words weighing heavy on her tongue. "Though I also think ours are the normal ones."

"What are the normal ones?"

"Middle age, 15 years of marriage, routine, children, apathy, survival. I think every married couple probably deals with these issues."

"I've never been married, but if it's as tough as the dating process, I haven't got a chance," Tony replied with a grin. "As for the family system or dynamic, these are all issues that affect both the individual and the collective. But in a healthy family, the issues don't typically manifest as debilitating walls."

"I don't think of ours as debilitating."

"The view from the inside can be cloudy. The part that gets really tricky is when families began to cross generations. The kids begin to pay for the sins of the father, and they become conditioned to internalize the wall-building behavior as normal. When it happens, it can take multiple generations for the skeletons to wash out of the system."

"So you're saying I'm just like my mother."

"No," Tony replied quickly. "I'm not saying that at all. I'll leave that for Ellis to decide."

"Thanks."

As he was cutting into his grass-fed Nebraska ribeye and eyeing the huge baked potato and single broccoli spear that framed it, Tony secretly vowed to return to his vegetarian roots when he got back to L.A. The Stockyard, the best steak house in Charlotte as recommended by Ben Middleton, a regular if the staff's familiarity was any indication, had served Tony what appeared to be an entire side of beef. Even the plate seemed larger than life, and the knife he held in his right hand felt more like a saw than flatware. He was thankful that he'd eaten a light lunch earlier that day while driving from Greenville to Charlotte. He had chosen, instead, to take the tour of the BMW plant near Spartanburg, fascinated by the assembly systems as well as the finished product. With his new job, Tony could almost see himself driving a new BMW. Almost. But at this point, he could not see his way to the end of the steak on his plate.

"So, did Gus answer all of your questions?" Ben asked with a grin. "She's more of the family historian than I am."

"She was very helpful," Tony replied, balancing a bite of beef on his fork, "but I appreciate your willingness to talk one more time."

"No worries. Man's got to eat before heading home to watch ESPN highlight reels and Golf Channel clinics."

"Sounds like Twinkle had other plans this evening, with you watching all that sports programming."

"To say the least."

"Well Augusta and I were talking about some of the bank history, as well as some of the family history, trying to understand how decisions were made through the years."

"I'm sure that was a short conversation," he laughed. "Old Gus didn't let too many decisions slide to other folks. He liked to make those himself."

"Yep. Augusta said pretty much the same thing. But there were a few other names that ran through the files."

"Such as?"

"Thomas Wrightman, for one. His name appears in the ledger quite a bit, in the notes section, approving loans or transactions. That name ring a bell?"

"My grandfather's indentured servant?" Ben replied with a chuckle, "sure, the name rings a bell. He did everything but mow the grass for Old Gus."

"What can you tell me about him?"

"More than you'll want to know, I assure you. Why the interest?"

"For no better reason than because his name appears more than others in recent files, and Augusta's description of him as a loyal employee of your grandfather's."

"What else did she tell you?"

"Just that he always seemed very dedicated, and that he was the one who found your grandfather in his office, face down on the desk."

"Well, that last part's kind of tricky, but he was Old Gus's bitch for a lot of years."

"How so?"

"He owned him. I didn't choose the term indentured servant lightly," Ben said, his chuckle masking the growing tension in his demeanor, like a snake had started up his pant leg headed for his shorts.

"What do you mean?"

"Wrightman started out with Old Gus straight out of college and stayed with him cradle to grave. You never knew Old Gus."

"But I've gotten a pretty clear picture of him through this process."

"Sure, and even you'd have to admit that a man would need to really enjoy pain to stick with Old Gus that long."

"What kind of pain are you talking about?"

"The kind of pain that's made even worse because it makes absolutely no sense to the victim, who eventually seems to give up on trying to make sense of it."

"Wow. I'm a licensed psychologist and I think you've just described a malady that I can't classify. There must be something to this. Are you comfortable going into more detail?"

"Like I said, more than you'd ever want to know. But off the record. Any of this comes back up with your boys in California, I'll hang you out to dry."

"Absolutely. Doesn't leave this table. And I wouldn't want you to betray anyone's trust by telling me any of this, so be aware of that as well."

"They're all dead anyway, so no harm, no foul. Except for Wrightman, and he lives in a parallel universe where he's probably still guided by Old Gus's voice."

"So he's still around?"

"In a manner of speaking, but he's crazy."

"But he felt comfortable somewhere along the line to fill you in on the background of all this?"

"Wrightman? Hell no. Walker shared all of this information in one of our father/son bonding efforts. Those sessions were never really successful."

"I picked up on some tension between the two of you."

"Well, you didn't need an advanced degree for that. How that man was my father I'll never know. I seemed to have inherited absolutely nothing from his gene pool, and he always seemed like a stranger, like there was some unnatural distance between us."

"Fathers and sons are like that."

"Well, he was big on these bonding efforts. They seemed mostly artificial, like something my mother was coming up with. She is a master at artificial social arrangements. She arranges people like flowers and then doesn't understand why they seem to wither. But Walker and I were bonding last year at a time when Twinkle and I had hit a rough spot."

"Is that still the case, with you and Twinkle?"

"I'm watching a lot of ESPN and Golf Channel, and you may have noticed that the waitstaff knows me by name."

"I see."

"But when the shit first hit the fan, Walker got wind of it and made his way over here for some pastoral father bonding," Ben said, returning to the past year to draw out the specifics.

"Fidelity is a tough row to hoe for some," Walker said to Ben as they made their way up the cart path along the first fairway. Ben was driving the cart, which afforded him the option of not looking at his father during much of the conversation.

"I'm really not in the mood for a sermon."

"It'd be tough for me to get too high and mighty on that one. Glass house and all."

"What?" Ben said, moving his eyes between his father and the cart path.

"All I'm saying is that marriage is tough enough without that added expectation of monogamy. It can challenge even the most disciplined." Walker moved his eyes across the fairway looking for their drives.

"You saying the Man of God has stretched his legs on roads less travelled?"

"Unlike you, it's not something I'm particularly proud of."

"If you saw the bitch behind the Bible study, I don't think you'd blame me."

"Nobody's blaming you, except maybe Twinkle."

"You think so?" Ben said sarcastically, leaning over his approach shot of some 160 yards to a back left pin. He hit a high draw to the middle of the green and returned to the cart as Walker scuffed a long iron and rolled the ball to the fringe. As Walker sat back in the cart, Ben looked at his father without moving.

"But you've been unfaithful to my mother. A preacher."

"Believe me when I tell you that I'm not the only preacher in that club. I think you hold our profession to a slightly higher standard than you should."

"If only because I've been conditioned to do so," Ben replied, hitting the gas and moving the cart down the path toward the green.

"Maybe so. That's not the stance your grandfather took."

"How did he find out about it?"

"Cause and effect."

"What?"

"Old Gus was the cause, but I'm not sure it achieved the effect he was after." Grabbing their putters out of the bags, the two made their way onto the first green to finish out the hole. As Ben lined up his putt, he wrestled with the ongoing revelation from his father.

"I know he's a strange old hard ass, and I get the feeling that the two of you have never really been the best of friends, but I can't see him throwing his own daughter under the bus like that." He adjusted his feet, eyed the cup and the line, but missed the birdie putt. Walker played for par, lagged the putt up close, and drained for the four. They walked back to the cart, formulating the next stroke of conversation.

"He is a strange old man, and you're right about our relationship. There's always been an edge to it. But the same is true for most of his relationships. Your mother and you kids are the only ones who seem to warrant an unfiltered view. The rest of the world sees life through his lens or not at all."

"Still sounds like a cop-out to me. So you don't get along with your father-in-law. How does that make him the cause of your infidelity?"

"Chess."

"Chess? The board game?"

"Chess. Only Gus doesn't use carved ivory on a checkered board. He prefers humans on the marble floor of his entry hall."

"What the hell are you talking about?" Ben asked as they approached the second tee box.

"Old Gus likes to have small dinner parties followed by a friendly wager over a chess game. The dinner guests and the help put on costumes and set themselves up on the black and white marble tiles of the entry hall. Old Gus faces the opponent from the stair hall that looks over the floor from both directions."

Ben took a couple of practice swings as he listened, all the while shaking his head as if Walker were really reaching. As he stood to line his drive up with the second fairway, he asked some clarifying questions.

"And you've been to some of these dinner parties."

"Only one. You and your sister were very young. You had gone with your mother to New York to shop for school clothes. Your grandfather invited me over for dinner without really filling me in on any of the details. I had assumed it would just be the two of us eating informally in the kitchen." He paused as Ben hit his drive, a slow fade that hugged the left side of the fairway and came to rest in the first cut of rough. Then he hit his own drive, a swooping banana ride that crossed the fairway and threatened the cars on the adjoining road.

"But it wasn't."

"Nope. I got the feeling that the other guests had been through the drill before, some several times. It didn't strike them as odd when, after dinner, Old Gus challenged one of the regulars—Tom Wrightman, you remember him?—to a friendly game. I thought it was pretty interesting at first. I was Old Gus's King, so I didn't move a lot. We got to participate to some extent, which mostly meant shouting directions to the players above or challenges to the other pieces on the board. The game was over pretty quickly. Old Gus is a pretty good chess player, I guess. All the chess pieces were pretty drunk by this point. Everybody was having a great time. When the game was over, the king and queen from Tom's side came over to our side, still in costume, and surrendered. I don't remember my queen or his king, but I remember his queen vividly. It was Tom's daughter, Helen. She walked up to me and kissed me, took my hand, and began leading me off the floor. The other king was leading my queen in the same direction, toward the guest room off the entry hall. The rest of the pieces were cheering and whooping like this was the natural consequence of the win or loss, and I was confused."

When Walker looked up, Ben had stopped the cart at his ball and was looking at him wide-eyed. He got out of the cart and chose a hybrid iron to lift the ball out of the rough and back into the fairway. He addressed the ball and gave a mighty swing. The ball came out of the rough and trickled back into the fairway. Walker climbed back into the cart where Ben's facial expression hadn't changed.

"And you just went along for the ride, so to say?"

"Not exactly. And you have to remember that this was the '60s, the era of free love and key-swapping parties."

"And what?"

"Key-swapping parties. You dropped your car keys in a big bowl on the way into the party and the wives chose keys with their eyes closed on the way out the door at the end. Whoever the keys belonged to got to drive, so to say."

"I hope you're kidding."

"Nope. We never went to those parties, but they were really popular."

"I bet."

"So I get into the room with these three other people, and the other king and queen are quickly going at it, and I look at Helen and tell her plainly that such a course of action is not possible. And she tells me that if we don't go through with it that her father would probably lose his job. She explains that it was an understood part of the game. But I tell her it wasn't understood by me. But she was pretty drunk, and I was pretty drunk by that point, so reason and logic weren't the force they could've been. So I tell her that we could just say we did and nobody would be the wiser. And then she nodded to the large mirror on the wall and said that he would. I thought she had been talking about the reflection of the other king who was by that point thoroughly enjoying the spoils of war. When I told her that the other king would certainly never remember what we did or didn't do, she told me that she wasn't talking about the king. She had been talking about our host, your grandfather, who often retired from the game to a comfortable viewing space in the adjacent room concealed by a two-way mirror."

"You have got to be fucking kidding me," Ben said, still wide-eyed, as he rose from the cart, shaking his head, to select a club for his approach shot to the second green. "And why the hell are you telling me all of this? I think this officially qualifies as too much information."

"Just part of your unique family history, Ben. Might help explain why you strayed."

"I strayed because I'm married to a frigid religious zealot. You suggesting we have common ground?" He punctuates the accusation with a crisp 6-iron that bounces on but over the green. He continues the thought as he makes his way back to the cart. "Or are you suggesting that infidelity is in my genes because you took drunk one night and snagged some free love while the cat and kittens were away."

"I didn't sleep with her. I walked out of the room and out the front door."

"Without claiming your prize? And Tom Wrightman kept his job. So Old Gus was feeling generous that night?"

"Not exactly."

"There's more?"

"Old Gus was feeling Helen that night."

"What?"

"I ran into her several months later in front of the book store on Division Street. We took a short walk from there and she told me about the rest of that night, how Old Gus had availed himself of my absence, how he had told her of his relationship with her mother, Tom's wife. As it turns out, Gus had won her in a chess match a generation before and had maintained the spoils of war for years afterwards, at his leisure and at the expense of her mother's sanity. Upon hearing the news of her daughter's commodification, Mrs. Wrightman had lost her battle with the demons of depression and had hung herself with a genuine silk scarf given to her by your grandfather."

Walker then noticed that Ben had turned the cart around and was heading back to the clubhouse. He looked confused.

"Where are you going?"

"So I told him that I couldn't play golf with him dumping all that shit in my lap," Ben told Tony, returning to his steak and potato, "and that was really the last time we tried to do any bonding."

Tony was almost speechless at the confirmation of the story he'd heard on the porch weeks earlier, but he didn't want to appear too eager to fill in details.

"Have you ever met Helen Wrightman?"

"I never knew Tom Wrightman had any children until Walker told me that story."

"But I'm confused," Tony said. "The way you were telling Walker's story made it sound like he had been unfaithful to your mother, but he never slept with Helen."

"No, but he'd been sleeping with the church secretary for almost seven years when he died."

"Oh."

"I guess I left that little detail out, but I was assuming we were talking about Tom Wrightman and the bank."

"We were. Even within a complicated family, your father was a complex man."

"You don't know the half of it," Ben said with a chuckle. "Since we're talking off the record and you're bound by client confidentiality . . . ."

"Not really on the client confidentiality, but who am I going to tell? And why would they believe me, other than the fact that I couldn't possibly make this stuff up!"

"Well, off the record, the complexity of my father gets deeper and deeper and harder and harder to reconcile with my absolute simplicity. There's just no way I could be his son."

"What could be more complex?"

"It goes back to Tom Wrightman and the night he discovered Old Gus face down at the desk."

"Okay. What about him?"

"Well, first of all, Old Gus never called him that night."

"Okay, but remember that I don't know much about this, only what Augusta shared with me the other night."

"And what Helen Wrightman told you on the porch a couple of weeks ago in Charleston."

Tony froze, unable to decide whether to deny the reference and call his bluff or concede the advantage to Ben and see where the road would take him. He hated to get caught in a lie, much less twice.

"Don't worry," Ben said. "You've betrayed no confidence. And why do you think I would tell you all of that if I didn't think you already knew the answers to the questions you were asking?"

"Now I'm really confused."

"Don't be," Ben said, taking another bite of his steak. "If I'm wired for infidelity, as my father suggested, I also got Old Gus's heightened sense of vigilance."

"I guess so."

"When Twinkle and I hit the rough spot last year, it had been a while since the two of us had made even a little noise, so I had assumed she had taken up with somebody else, and it seemed like a matter of time before she asked for a divorce. So I had hired a firm to keep an eye on her, to collect data that might be useful in a court of law."

"Okay. But why me?"

"For the fun of it, really. Margaret never really told us much about you or your company, and I had these guys on retainer, so I put one of them on you for that afternoon, just for the hell of it. Same reason I had them look into Old Gus's death."

"Didn't the police do that?"

"Sure, but parts of it never made sense to me, especially after Walker told me the bit about Tom Wrightman and I got the initial reports back from the sunglasses that Tom was a nutcase."

"The sunglasses?"

"You know. They always wear sunglasses and talk to their watches. It's not just in the movies."

"Oh."

"So, like I said, I had my own personal investigative unit check it out, and no calls were made that day from Old Gus's office to the Wrightman residence. Not that day, not that week, not that year. And why would Tom simply show up unannounced after all these years just in time to find Old Gus dead at the helm?"

"So you think Tom Wrightman killed him?"

"Thought so initially, but I couldn't make that work."

"But the police report said natural causes, if I remember correctly. There was a copy in my due diligence file."

"Yep. When he discovered the deceased, Tom called Old Gus's personal physician, who was able to pronounce him dead before the ambulance arrived so he could be taken out of the office in a pine box. I'm assuming Helen Wrightman filled you in on that little twist."

"She did."

"So, it seemed likely to me at the time that someone in the Wrightman household knew the place and approximate time of death in advance."

"So you think Helen killed him."

"It made sense at the time."

"But how did she disguise a murder as a death by natural causes?"

"Great question," Ben replied, "and one that I asked as well."

"Why do I feel like I'm reading a Sherlock Holmes novel?"

"You're right. This is probably boring you to death. Let's order dessert."

"No way. You have to tell me how the story ends."

"Very simply, actually. The sunglasses traced the calls to the Wrightman residence that night, and the caller might surprise you. It was Walker."

"Walker?"

"Yep. He called the Wrightman house about an hour before Tom called Gus's physician and Gus was pronounced dead."

"Coincidence?"

"Maybe, but probably not."

"So you think your father might've killed your grandfather."

"Sure, but I'm open to another explanation."

"Obviously the police didn't agree."

"I don't think they ever looked at anything. They arrived to find an old man under lifelong stress face down at his desk with a pen in his hand, his faithful servant at his side, and his personal physician putting a bow on the package. The family never questioned the obvious explanation, and Charleston has plenty of real criminals to fight, so they filled out the paperwork and moved on to the next crime scene."

"So, you've never mentioned this to anybody."

"Nope. Not even to you."

"What about all those people that used to play chess?"

"I have no idea what you're talking about. Want some dessert?"

CHAPTER ELEVEN

The holidays had always been a time of tension and celebration around the Camber household, at least for the last several generations. Margaret could remember the loneliness of her early Christmas celebrations, the stiffness of the staff, the similarity between the Dickens book and the world around her. She had always assumed that to be the norm, so her own holiday preparations had progressed along the same lines after she and Walker had married and moved back to Charleston. She never recognized or understood the distinction of family time like, perhaps, other families did, or didn't, for that matter. There weren't really any other families in the pool, had she any interest in an apples-to-apples comparison. Margaret had no such inclination, anyway, always assuming that hers was the family to which all others would one day and in some way compare themselves. And her intuition had been correct, even if warped by the standards set forth by the Happy Family Commission, if such were ever to exist. Margaret set the standard for what most of polite Charleston society considered requisite holiday decorating and entertaining. Her homes were flawlessly decorated with the charm of her southern roots and the edginess characteristic of much larger markets and the ready availability of labor and creativity. Among the local florists and special events coordinators, Margaret Camber Middleton was the economy, whether the work enveloped one of her residences in seasonal fare or created the idiosyncratic fundraisers of one of the many non-profit boards she had served through the years. Also churned in the wake of her unceasing benevolence were landscapers, tent makers, caterers and waitstaff, security officers and valet parkers, and these vendors were almost guaranteed a short run at unlimited success, at the very least, if their performance met the Camber standard, for there was always a scramble among the guests to surreptitiously secure the names and contact information of the vendors at any of Margaret's functions without, of course, their hostess taking note of their efforts. For a guest to lift what Margaret might've considered but not identified as intellectual property would have precluded him or her from future invitations, and for a vendor to knowingly replicate any feature of a Camber affair for a subsequent client was the kiss of death. The revenue train would stop quietly but abruptly, and the threat was very real. The cross-pollination across the catered affairs of Charleston's polite society was extraordinary, suggesting that 250 people lived in that charming coastal city and they saw each other over and over again, parting only to return to their respective old family homes to count their money and change clothes. Vendor transgressions often required either a change in location or vocation, sometimes both. Likewise, though, Margaret was very generous and loyal to those whom she might have considered but not identified as proprietary providers, those who had gained and maintained access to the Courts of Camber, and she was thankful that she was able to call upon the usual suspects this holiday season to dress the country house in mournful joyousness, having lost her father and husband nine and three months prior, respectively. Nothing over the top, she'd told the decorators, but we do want the grandkids to know that life goes on. She'd told Augusta the same thing, and Augusta had told Ellis, and Ellis had remarked that it seemed an almost unprecedented expression of concern for the children, whose roles in the holiday festivities were usually limited to the bribery and torture related to their smiling assemblage for the annual holiday card photograph.

Augusta had agreed that it seemed noteworthy, evidence almost of a seismic shift in the crust of her mother's emotional geography, and she decided to make an early visit to Charleston, ahead of the usual holiday pilgrimage, leaving Ellis and the children in Greenville after school ended to celebrate the early holiday break parties without her while she excused herself to check on her mother. All seemed happy with that arrangement, even Margaret, who hadn't seen her kids for any extended period of time since Walker's funeral and had done just about all the mourning that she could do or that Charleston could ask of her. And that enthusiasm showed on her face as Margaret opened the front door to welcome Augusta, who was walking up the steps from the front motor court with arms full of luggage and shopping bags.

"Well, Santa Claus has arrived at last!" Margaret said with a grin. "The tree's been looking awfully lonely since Geraldo's men finished setting it up and lighting it last week."

"How is Geraldo?" Augusta asked in return. "Nobody fills a room with flora like Geraldo."

"He's fabulous, just fabulous," Margaret said, crossing her hands over her chest and leaning her head to one side as she said it, imitating Geraldo's actual and body language. "Said so himself."

"Was that before or after you handed him the check?"

"Both, thank you very much. A woman in mourning must make every effort to surround herself with happy faces."

"I see," Augusta said, walking in the front door and dropping her bags in the entry hall, taking in Geraldo's decorating efforts in their presumed entirety for the first time.

"Well?"

"He's outdone himself once again," Augusta said with a wide-eyed sigh and a shrug of the shoulders. "He has a gift."

"I have to agree. Those funny boys have a way with flowers," Margaret said with satisfaction, turning and heading through the entry hall toward the back of the house and the kitchen area. Augusta closed her eyes and shook her head, taking a deep breath to let the statement pass.

"Funny?" she asked, following her mother down the hall. "Is that funny-ha-ha or funny-queer?"

"I think you know what I mean," came the response back over Margaret's shoulder, "and I don't think you should start your visit off with a lecture about political correctness or whatever liberal notion you've got itching the tip of your tongue."

"Well, you have to admit that your chosen expression is a bit ironic in light of our family history."

"Which family history is that, dear?" Margaret had walked through the kitchen and into the den where she was straightening a small stack of magazines on the ottoman in front of a large, plush wingback chair before placing them on the coffee table that separated the chair from an equally large and plush sofa of a floral print. "I've been trying to catch up on the magazines this morning."

"Surely you haven't forgotten the bomb you dropped in the hospital, about Daddy and Uncle Robert? Ringing a bell?"

"Oh, honey, that was college or right after, and it was the '60s. Youthful experimentation," she said, sitting in the blue chair and putting her feet where the magazines had been. "Don't tell me you want to talk about all that again."

"Well, we never really talked about it at all. You just put it out there and expected me to make sense of it." Augusta was still standing, as if her refusal to take a seat on the sofa as expected was just that, taking a stand.

"Oh. That was a tough day for all of us, sweetheart. Your father was talking crazy and it must have gotten the best of me. I didn't mean for it to upset you."

"But it was true? My father was 'funny' when you two met?" She actually used her hands to make the quotation marks in the air, a trait she discouraged in her faculty and students.

"Well, you have certainly arrived loaded for bear this afternoon. Do we really have to talk about this?"

"It's what normal families do, Mother, especially when children are blindsided by details of their parents' lives."

"The Cambers have rarely been accused of being a normal family."

"Well, this is the Middleton family, Mother," Augusta said, taking her seat on the floral print sofa, "and we were making a pretty good run at it until you told me my father was gay!"

"Not when we married and certainly not when you were born."

"So he just flipped the homosexual switch to the off position? That what you're saying?"

"Youthful experimentation. That's what I said. He and Robert had gotten very close as roommates in college—"

"Apparently."

"—and that closeness carried over into the real world for a very short time."

"Until the two of you met?"

"I assume so, yes," Margaret said, becoming visibly uncomfortable as the conversation, one she'd never really had with anyone, progressed. "But your father was always a very physical person."

"You mean physical, like sexual?"

"This is not one of your teacher conferences, Augusta. Must you make this so direct and confrontational?" Margaret raised herself from the seat and walked to the large windows, taking in the view of the pool, the orchard, and the river in the distance.

"I certainly don't mean to be confrontational," Augusta said after a short pause. "I'm just trying to understand what you're saying. Remember, I've never heard any of this before."

"Neither has anyone else, dear. Neither has anyone else. There was never a reason to talk about it. Not sure there is now."

"But by physical you mean sexual."

"Yes, that's what I mean," Margaret responded with a sigh of frustration. "Physical contact was always very important to him."

"But not to you?"

Margaret looked at Augusta from across the room and across the generations with a look of astonishment that she would ask such a question or series of questions.

"Come on, Mother. This is like the Good-Housekeeping conversation we were supposed to have on my wedding day, the whole sex talk leading up to the honeymoon, the expectations and politics of it all."

"I don't remember that conversation."

"That's because we never had it. But we can have it now, understanding that we're adults, married and widowed, but subject to some of the same circumstances."

"Augusta, honey, sometimes you think too much," Margaret said with furrowed brow, returning to her wingback chair.

"Well, you're the one that, in that same conversation, told me that you thought Ellis was 'funny.' Or that certainly the thought should have crossed my mind. So you've been thinking quite a bit yourself lately. And psychologists say that marriages evolve as well as sexual necessity."

"You've been seeing a psychologist?"

"No. It came up at my dinner meeting with Tony last month."

"Tony Gordon? You talked to Tony Gordon about all this?"

"No, not all of this. We just talked about marriages generally. He had asked how you were doing and if I thought you'd be okay with Daddy gone."

"That was very nice of him, but hardly his place to ask. He represents Pacific Mergers, not us." Her expression had become one of grave concern, as if she was circling the wagons with the lions at the gate.

"I didn't give him the combination to the safe or anything. Don't worry. But we talked about how couples often grow differently within a marriage, and sex is one of the most obviously divergent paths. And it sounds like you and Daddy might've experienced that, if his need for physical contact was greater than yours."

"It was. But not at the beginning."

"How's that?"

"Well, in the beginning, when we started dating, I guess you could say," Margaret seemed to confide, her posture changing and demeanor warming, "we were both pretty frisky. We enjoyed our quiet time together."

"And did you know about Uncle Robert?"

"Not at first, no. Well, I had met Robert, yes, but I didn't know about their closeness until Walker and I had moved beyond dating and began spending much more time together. At first Robert seemed hurt and I couldn't make sense of that, being the sheltered Charleston girl that I was."

"How did you figure it out? Did he tell you?"

"Walker did, yes. He told me and I was shocked, absolutely appalled. I explained to him that his relationship with Robert was wrong in the eyes of God."

"And what did he say?"

"I can't remember. Something smooth, I'm sure. Walker was nothing if not a smooth talker. But I took it as a personal challenge to prove to him the error of his ways, the right path, so to say. And that was the first time we slept together."

"Well, it must have worked," Augusta said after an awkward pause. "He stuck with you and we came along."

"It's more complicated than that, but you are correct. And like I said, he was always a very physical person."

"And you weren't as physical?"

"No, not after you kids came along. We jumped through some different hoops through those years, but it all worked out. He and I seemed to part philosophically on those issues, and I tended the nest as they say. You and your brother became my focus. But he found his outlets, I presume, the latest being Darlene, of course.

"The secretary at church?"

"Yep. That's the one."

"Wow. That's really disturbing."

"Well, you started this conversation."

"Did you know all along?"

"I picked up on most of them through the years, but he was discreet for the most part. It reached a point where I adopted a no-news-is-good-news perspective, believing that if I didn't know about it, nobody else did either. We had an unspoken agreement, I suppose. We agreed to disagree. Same bed, different lives."

"Did you still love each other?" Augusta asked hesitantly, not really knowing if she wanted an answer or not.

"I think so. We evolved, like your psychologist said. Our lives remained connected in some ways, disconnected in others."

"Did he ever revisit the 'funny' side of life?"

"Not that I'm aware of. He decided on seminary shortly after we started talking about marriage, and I often think my efforts were stronger than I intended, as if I scared the God into him when most folks were going the other way."

"Why seminary and why preaching?"

"I never really knew. Our only conversations about all of that involved my wanting him to be happy and me to be in Charleston."

"So he had never really mentioned being a preacher until you set your sights on marriage and Charleston?"

"As far as I remember."

"Did you ever talk about him working for Old Gus?"

"Only to rule it out as a possibility. Your grandfather never really took an interest in Walker, and the two would have mixed like oil and water in a work setting, especially one as small and close knit as the bank. There was really only room for one at the top, and you know who that was. And by that point, Mr. Wrightman was in place to catch whatever fell through the cracks, a job that almost drove that man to the looney bin. So, in a way it was a blessing that Walker steered clear of the bank."

"What about you?" Augusta said, standing and moving toward the kitchen. "And can I get you something to drink? I'm dying of thirst."

"There's tea in the fridge. And what about me?"

"Did you ever want to work at the bank, or was that ever an option, when you guys were planning on moving back here?"

"That was never discussed, formally, but I always assumed my father would've mentioned it had it been a real possibility. I really wanted to be a writer, though I didn't do much writing at the time. Just a romantic notion, I suppose. Had I expressed a serious interest in the business, though, it might have been an option. But it would've been a long shot. It wasn't a woman's place to work in management at a bank, much less run one, even if she owned it. It just wasn't done."

"What about now," Augusta asked, returning to the sofa with two glasses of tea.

"Oh, I'm too old to learn new tricks now. And, besides, your grandfather wanted the bank to be sold, you know that. That's why we've been going through all this."

"I know, but what if we could keep the bank in the family, let it remain a defining family asset, as Tony said."

"What else has Tony been telling you? Have they found some issues we need to be aware of?"

"You were there when he said that, three months ago at the Planter's Inn, and I haven't talked to him about any of this."

"Any of what?"

"The idea of keeping the bank in the family."

"Augusta, dear, what are you talking about?"

"I'm talking about stopping the sale of the bank and keeping it in the family," Augusta said, taking a drink from her tea to let the gravity of the simple truth settle in. Her mother looked confused but answered quickly.

"Well, sugar," Margaret said with a consoling if not condescending voice, "we're past that point, I think. The California folks are kicking the tires, as they say, but we have a contract to sell to them, and at a very nice price I might add. Your grandfather made a deal, and I plan to honor it."

"I know all of that."

"Then what are you saying? I'm having a hard time understanding your point."

Augusta had faced this wall a million times in her life, and while the issues had varied, the outcome had been astonishingly consistent, though she had never been able to discern whether her mother's inability to understand her point had been a sincere rhetorical disconnect or simply a way of punctuating an argument Margaret no longer wished to endure. The many frustrating attempts to guide her mother toward the light flashed before her eyes as Augusta tried to reformulate her argument, deciding, in the end, that there had been sufficient revelation for the afternoon.

"I'm saying that it's great to see you and the house looks great and all this talk has made me really hungry. I didn't see the pecan-sugar cookies, so I can only assume you've already made them and put them safely in hiding."

"I have done no such thing," Margaret replied, a relieved smile coming across her face. "I was hoping we might work on those together this afternoon."

Margaret rose excitedly from the chair, patted Augusta on the leg, and almost danced into the kitchen. Augusta, too, was relieved to be free of the afternoon's burden of full disclosure. Her mother's simple and steadfast loyalty to her father was almost comforting in the wake of the new complexities of the Reverend Walker Middleton, but Augusta couldn't help but wonder how she came to be the genetic combination of these people whose early lives were so vastly different than anything she'd ever imagined, and that sense of wonder would soon be rewarded with even more irreconcilable revelations.

"Have you talked to Ben or Twinkle?" Margaret asked, pulling flour and sugar from a cabinet and mixing bowls from drawers.

"I have not. Have you?"

"Not at great length. He never really talks to me when I call, but I get the feeling there might be trouble in Paradise."

"You really think so?" Augusta said, doing a poor job of hiding the facetious tone in her voice.

It was a beautiful day for flying, and Buddy Hill was thrilled to be aloft, climbing through the Lord's blue heavens on his way to Atlanta for his first meeting with the congregation development professionals at the Southern Baptist Association headquarters. It was, for Buddy and the others in the select group of young pastors, an anointing of sorts, a recognition of their commitment and achievement, uncommon this early in their careers. It was time for the home office to reel them in and ensure their paths were straight and narrow, for the future leadership would likely come from their ranks. This was, at least, the consensus among Buddy's peer group, colleagues and pastors from the Charleston area who met on a monthly basis for lunch and mutual support. Buddy was on his way to the top, the big time, the major leagues, a prospect he was excited about. But he was excited about this trip as well, a much-needed break from the everyday, swapping the known and routine for several days of vacation surrounding an afternoon of working and networking with church leaders.

Earlier that beautiful day, a garage door opened in suburban Charlotte and a Volvo wagon emerged with a smiling face behind the wheel and an expensive-looking overnight garment bag hung on the little hook above the rear window. As the wagon made its way along the tree-lined streets, another vehicle, a small pickup truck, entered the light midday, mid-week traffic several cars back, unnoticed by the driver of the Volvo wagon despite her several glances in the rearview mirror to check her hair, make-up, and lipstick. Twinkle Middleton was glowing, she had to admit to herself. She couldn't remember the last time she'd been this happy, this anxious about a trip. The four short hours to Atlanta would fly by, she thought, as she turned the Volvo south on I-85 and set the cruise control at an aggressive 78, even bumping it up to 80 as she felt the cars begin to pass her, not wanting anyone to reach the Galleria Hotel before she did, and feeling certain she could take the risk. She had been so careful with everything else. The hotel had been chosen over the Ritz Carlton in Buckhead, her usual Atlanta home, because she always saw someone she knew at the Ritz, and none of her friends would ever stay at the Galleria, an upscale hotel and convention mall that catered more to the business types and franchise shoppers. Twinkle wasn't even sure she could find it. Ben had offered little resistance to her mid-week shopping trip to Atlanta for, as she described it, last-minute gifts for his family. With her tennis group slowing down for the winter break, Ben had been almost giddy when she declared her intent to leave him alone for a couple of days. Proximity breeds discontent, he'd said under his breath, flipping through the channels looking for the Food Network or ESPN or both, either, anything.

Buddy's plane arrived late, and the Atlanta airport was alive with holiday travelers. Having heard the testimonies of the passengers on his right and left, and having witnessed to them in hushed, reverent tones, Buddy was exhausted but energized as he made his way through the baggage claim carousels and found his luggage and his way to the rental car desk.

As he stood in line waiting for his turn to sign for a tiny Chevy mysteriously classified as mid-sized sedan, Buddy took in the view of the customers around him, dressed mostly in suits and all telling their cell phones that they had arrived and would be on the road soon, asking if the numbers had changed, if the contracts had been signed, if the supplier in Milwaukee could possibly take any longer to ship three simple parts to the warehouse in Orlando. Buddy remembered with fascination his days in the soulless world of commerce, where deals were struck with the devil, and capitalism moved against humanity like a millstone, grinding life to peak efficiency with no accounting for the true cost of goods sold. And he was thankful. Yes, Buddy Hill was thankful that he had been rescued from that world, allowed to walk toward the light, freed from the bonds of the new slavery, a self-imposed attachment to things and stuff for which the pursuit of a buck could never cease. He was not experiencing a feeling of superiority, though, and did not consider his perspective to be condescending as he looked upon his fellow salesmen. He simply felt that he had a better product, one steeped in the economies of the soul and the real investment in the life ever after. And he still felt that he was at the very beginning of a really great learning curve, and yet the more he understood the more mysterious it all became. He had become very fond of that word, mystery, and might've even wondered if religion wasn't, in fact, a commodification of mystery. But Buddy never really drilled that deeply into the business side or the philosophical side of his work, relying instead on the Word of God to reveal all truths and reconcile all mysteries in due time, in His time. Until that time, Buddy thought, the very presence of mystery in our world confirmed the very presence of God. At last, he signed for his Malibu sedan and headed out of the maze that is the Atlanta Airport, turning north toward the Galleria and his rendezvous with another of those great mysteries, Twinkle Middleton.

Traffic moved slowly along the perimeter, or at least it seemed that way to Twinkle Middleton as she examined the broad expanse of concrete from her 12th-floor window, her eyes moving between her watch and the exit ramp that she assumed Buddy would use and should've used by now.

She had already changed clothes twice, first into "something more comfortable" and then back into her traveling outfit, deciding that the new nightie could, in fact, wait until closer to nighttime. She couldn't ignore that she was anxious to see him. Even her breasts ached with excitement as she buttoned and unbuttoned her blouse to determine an appropriate amount of reveal. The irony of her search for propriety escaped her as she, a married woman, continued to stare out of a hotel room window awaiting a widowed preacher who was not her husband. Exasperated by the waiting, Twinkle turned to examine the room as she had assembled it. Candles on the small tables at each side of the king-sized bed, fresh flowers in vases both at the window and on the bathroom counter, a bottle of champagne chilling in the ice bucket on the desk beside the entertainment center, and room service menus placed about to reinforce the idea that they wouldn't be leaving the room that evening. She had even pulled the Gideon's Bible from the drawer of the nightstand, placing it prominently alongside the candle. Twinkle had come to find scripture quite arousing before sex and comforting afterwards, Buddy reading as she ran her fingers through the hair on his chest. She was sure that Buddy would have his own Bible, but sharing a new Bible, a strange Bible, would be in her mind almost like sharing a new position, and she was always open to that. So the Gideons had unknowingly left an appliance or sexual aid in the drawer, though Twinkle would never think of it that way. Instead, she thought the scripture was simply pulling her closer to Buddy, and closer quite frequently. Twinkle thought about the dozens of times that she had been with Buddy, shared his bed, his living room, and even his kitchen counter during one adventurous visit. She felt herself blush as she recounted her sex life from the past several months, a more active life than she'd shared with Ben in several years, and she felt reborn, her very soul filled with new life, as she heard a plastic card key unlocking the door. She turned and greeted Buddy with a hug and an enthusiastic kiss.

"Well, ain't you a sight for sore eyes," he said, holding her at arm's length. All she could do was smile demurely and invite his eyes to take in the full view. "And somebody's been doing some decorating, I see. I like it!"

"I thought you might like some of the comforts of home," she replied, kissing him again, more insistently. "It's been too long."

"Oh, is my little kitty purring?" he asked with a grin. "It's only been a week."

"Nine long days," she said, reaching down to unbuckle his belt, "and I've missed you!"

"I'm beginning to see that. But didn't you want to do some shopping first? Maybe catch a movie?

"Nope," came the reply, as she pulled the belt from his waist and cast it aside. "I think you know what I want to do."

And sure enough he did. And they did. And afterwards he saw the Bible on the nightstand. He looked back at Twinkle and chuckled.

"We did all that in front of God and the Gideons!" he said.

"Yep," Twinkle said, rising and walking comfortably naked to the bathroom as Buddy thumbed through the Bible. He was still turning pages when she returned.

"You lost?" she asked, grabbing the champagne bottle by the neck.

"It's been a while since I roamed with the Gideons."

"Well, you pick the verse while I pour the festive," she replied with a twist of the foil that sealed the cork.

"The festive?"

"I certainly think so," she replied, popping the cork excitedly and pouring into two plastic champagne flutes she'd brought from home. Wedding gifts, if she'd taken the time to think about it, which she hadn't.

"I'm not feeling inspired," he said, closing the Bible and picking up the room service menu as she returned to the bed with the champagne. "But I am getting hungry."

"Oh, Lord," came the reply. "The Reverend Buddy Hill uninspired? What is there to be done?" She straddled his legs and offered him a champagne flute as he looked over the room service menu.

"Not seeing anything on here," he said. "You dead-set on room service?"

"I could be persuaded otherwise. What've you got in mind?"

"Well, there's a spot down the road, if I remember correctly, called something on the river. It's a great little spot, or was years ago. Heather and I went there for her cousin's rehearsal dinner, I think."

While the thought of getting caught put a flutter in Twinkle's heart, she faced an even greater threat in the mention of Buddy's dead wife, a rare occurrence, but one that required a response. The memory of the place on the river, whatever the name, was fresh and dangerous, and Twinkle decided quickly that she and Buddy needed to replace that memory with one of their own. So dinner it was, at that place by the river, and afterwards there was the new nightie, new flutes of champagne, and New Testament readings, all of which accelerated Twinkle's pulse until she fell asleep in the arms of her new lord and savior, whose true gift first manifested itself early the next morning, as the lord himself lay sleeping while Twinkle held the pregnancy test under the dim light of the well-appointed bathroom and watched the blue plus sign emerge in unmistakable clarity.

"Do you have a child I don't know about?" the voice asked after a long pause.

"Say again," Ben said, holding the cell phone tight to one ear and sticking a finger in the other.

"The child, screaming in the background," Augusta repeated, "is there something I should know?"

"Not that I'm aware of," Ben replied, "though the mother is a looker. The kid needs a beating."

"Where are you?"

"At the mall at the peak of the holiday shopping season buying consumer non-durables for my nieces. Where else would Uncle Ben the Hero be on a night like this?"

"Wow. You are my hero," Augusta replied with a chuckle. "Doesn't Twinkle usually handle all of that?"

"She's been busy with other things," he said, leaving it at that. "But I'm walking outside now so I can hear you better. What can I do you for?"

"I was just checking in with you, trying to get a handle on your holiday travel plans. Your mother seems anxious to see you, as always."

"Oh, so she's my mother now?"

"I've been here for almost three days, Hero. The bloom is definitely off the rose."

"I see. Have you stocked the bar?"

"Twice. I'm willing to be an enabler of your probable substance issues if you'll just get in the car and head this way."

"I take issue with very few substances, I'll have you know."

"My point exactly. So when do you think you two will be heading home for the holidays, as the old song goes?"

"Soon enough, I suppose, but the desperation you can't hide in your voice is not becoming for a woman in your leadership position."

"That obvious?"

"When you buy the drunkard brother whiskey for Christmas, you've got a reindeer up your ass about something. You want to pass that thing over the phone or let it squirm around your colon 'til I slide down the chimney later this week?"

"Interesting mixture of holiday images."

"We all have our gifts."

"Yes, and your mother seems to be that reindeer."

"Tis the season. Tell me something I don't know," Ben said, followed by an excited outburst. "Holy shit! You're not going to believe this. The mall Santa just walked past me stoned out of his gourd. Smells like a hash pipe. The elves are having to help him up onto the sleigh. That's the way to approach all of the Hallmark holidays, if you ask me."

"Great," Augusta said with resignation in her voice. "Can we focus on the real issues, please?"

"You have to tell me what the issues are before I can focus on them. That our mother is a lunatic who pushes all your buttons is hardly new business."

"How about the one where your father has been sleeping with his secretary? That news to you?"

"Darlene? That doesn't surprise me, no. She was a real cupcake back in the day."

"My God! Are all men pigs?"

"It's not always the man, my sheltered sister. Women have been known to jump the fence as well."

"Well, how much do you know?" she asked in disbelief.

"About the sex lives of your parents? More than you want to know. More than I want to know, if you really want to know. Know what I mean?"

"Okay. Stop with the knowing. I get the point."

"They're human, Gus. Sometimes they back their cars into trees and sometimes they sleep with their secretaries. Shit happens."

"I hope you can see the abyss of distinction between the tree and the secretary."

"It's all relative, the older we get."

"I don't agree, but I'll move on to the cash in the closet."

"I like the sound of that. Whose cash and which closet?"

"I don't know where the cash came from, but a bunch of it turned up in your father's closet."

"Oh, he sleeps with Darlene and suddenly he's my father. Does that make the cash mine as well? I could use an extra thousand when I go back into that toy store with the stoned Santa!"

"How about eighty-three thousand and change?"

"Holy shit! Are you kidding me?"

"Nope," Augusta replied with growing indignation, sensing the momentum of surprise had shifted in her favor. "Most in hundreds, stuffed in the pockets of all his suits and in his socks."

"Eighty-three thousand. What's up with that?"

"I was hoping you would know. Mom said she found the first clues when she took the burial suit to the funeral home. The technician included almost six thousand in hundreds in a plastic bag with the other personal effects. Said he'd found them in the pockets as he was dressing Walker. When she started cleaning out his closet a couple of weeks ago, she started adding it all up."

"Eighty-three thousand in cash. That's very strange. I'd say it was golf winnings through the years, but he was never really that good a golfer."

"So where did it come from?"

"Maybe he was skimming off the top of the collection plate, squirreling money away for the mission stuff."

"Is that legal, because it doesn't sound right?"

"Church on Sunday is a cash business. Doesn't make it right, but it sure makes it possible"

"What about Uncle Robert? Could he have something to do with it?"

"Sure. So could the Easter Bunny or the stoned Santa who right now appears to be hurling over the side of the sleigh. Oh man, security is trying to pull him out and kids are screaming. Classic. You really should be seeing this."

"The money, Benjamin. Stay with me here."

"I wish I knew how to use the video feature on this damn phone. Prize-winning footage right in front of me."

"Ben!"

"What? What's the difference? You're never going to know for sure. He could've been saving that money in his sock drawer for the last forty years just to spite his father-in-law who happened to be a banker. Or holding a little bit back every month and keeping Uncle Sam out of it."

"Or stealing from the church."

"Or that, sure. Or any of a million other scenarios that we could contrive over the next several years. At the bottom of that balance sheet, though, you're still eighty-three grand in the black, so count your blessings or thank your lucky stars or whatever it is you Episcopalians do in the face of mysterious grace, and move on."

"But what if it's really the church's money?"

"What if it's not?"

"Okay. We'll talk more about this when you get here."

"So you're releasing me to the hurling Santa?"

"Not quite."

"There's more?"

"Maybe, but it's probably nothing."

"What is it?"

"Did you recently interview at another bank in Charleston?"

"Of course not. Why the hell would I do that?"

"I don't know. That's why I'm asking."

"Well, what makes you ask?"

"It's probably nothing, but Daddy had one of your business cards in his wallet."

"And?"

"And on the back he had written B of A, Market Street, 1030A. Is there a Market Street Branch in Charlotte? There is one here. It's the main office of the local bank."

"No. I don't know of a Market Street in Charlotte."

"I didn't either, so I was connecting dots that weren't meant to be connected. I assumed one of the two of you had a 10:30 meeting there, and since it was your card, I just assumed you were involved somehow."

"Nope. Another one of your mysteries."

"Well, I'll hold on to the card and maybe you can figure it out."

"Okay, but it'll cost you about eighty-three thousand dollars."

"Yeah, yeah."

"And change."

"Alright. Go play with the puking Santa."

"Oh he's gone by now. Left a wake of wide-eyed children, though, as he flew out of sight, wishing all a goodnight."

"I bet he did. Poor kids. How do the parents explain all of that?"

"That's the eighty-three thousand dollar question, isn't it? How do parents ever explain the real when it flies in the face of the imagined, smelling of hash and hurling up a food court."

"Okay. Let it go."

"Bounces off me and sticks to you. You're the one that needs to let it go."

"I give up. When do you think you'll be heading this way, Uncle Hero? Or should I check with Twinkle on that?"

"Why don't you check with her and let me know what she says. You can probably reach her on her cell. She's in Atlanta, shopping I think."

"What's she shopping for if she's got you going to the mall?"

"Another really good question. Like to place a value on that one? I know I would."

"No. I'm hanging up now. I'll see you when you get here."

"I'm off to brave the crowds and the puke to get the perfect gifts for your children. No sacrifice is too great, you know!"

"Goodbye, Benjamin."

"Hey, how's the paper coming?" Michael Kelly asked, entering the office and sitting before Tony had even looked up from his computer.

"What paper is that?" Tony replied, giving his boss a confused look and a shrug of the shoulders.

"Oh, come on. You have to be writing all of this down somewhere. That's what you academic types do, isn't it? You write it all down and go to conferences and debate the implications. Solve the world's problems one syndrome at a time while you eye each other's wives at social hour. That sound about right?"

"Sure, but you changed all of that," Tony replied, pushing away from the desk and assuming a more relaxed posture, agreeing to follow Michael on this little exploration. "You boys put me in a suit and gave me an expense account, and now I'm part of the machine."

"But are you happy?"

"More often than not. Why do you ask? Are you happy?"

"Sure, but I'm in the money business. You just play one on TV."

"How do you mean?" Tony asked, locking his fingers together behind his head.

"Simply that. You're like a television anchorman narrating the family story as the deals unfold, looking for that needle in the haystack that might connect the dots in some way that makes sense on a spreadsheet."

"Interesting way to look at it, I guess," Tony offered, "but isn't that what you hired me to do?"

"Precisely, and you have performed the task beyond any expectations that I might've had when we hired you."

"But . . . .?"

"But, we got to let you go anyway."

Tony was unsure how to react. He was stunned, to say the least, but he wasn't sure that Michael Kelly was just yanking his chain. He furrowed his brow and looked at Michael as if he might not have understood what he'd said. Michael's expression, however, didn't even begin to show the necessary transition from grave certainty to gotcha.

"That's the bad news," he continued, "but now we can talk about the good news."

"I'm all ears," Tony said, raising his eyebrows in confused surprise and pulling his hands from behind his head to better support himself in the $1,000 office chair he was just beginning to get used to.

"The good news is that it's got nothing to do with you or your performance."

"Except that it's me losing my job."

"Well, aside from that."

"So what does it have to do with?"

"Statistics, really. I mean, you make a great addition to the team, and you're able to extrapolate the family story in a way, qualitatively, that none of us are really able to appreciate, since we tend to look at all of these deals from a strictly quantitative perspective. But in the end, even in your short tenure here, we've not seen a discernible connection between the story and the spreadsheet."

"Does that surprise you? In our initial conversations you seemed to accept that the approach was experimental."

"Absolutely. I think we both did. And we had, at that time, a generous investor ready to fund the experiment. But his deal's about to close, and we've decided that the results to this point don't really warrant a continuation of the experiment."

"And that's the good news?" Tony asked, beginning to feel the gravity of the situation, having left his tweed jacket with elbow patches for the blue suits of the corporate world only to feel the rug being pulled out from under him. It occurred to him that he hadn't even had the suits dry-cleaned yet.

"No, of course not. That part sucks. Hell, you probably still owe money on the suits. And you're probably sitting there soiling the pants you're wearing right now, with me throwing all this at you out of nowhere."

"It is a bit of a shock."

"No, the good news is that our generous investor is setting you up with an equally generous severance package. How does two-years' salary and benefits sound?"

"Like you've got the math wrong. I've been here less than six months."

"Like I said, generous. But I need you in Charleston for the Plantation Trust closing." Michael began to rise from his chair. "You'll be the face of Pacific Mergers, so make sure you clean those pants before you go."

"This doesn't really make sense. At least not to me."

"That's why you're writing it down. So you can take it to conferences and make sense of it with all the other abstract thinkers and ivory-tower dwellers. And get laid. That'll probably help, too." With that, Michael Kelly gave Tony a consoling wink and walked out of the office, leaving Tony to settle back into his chair and shake his head in wonder.

CHAPTER
TWELVE

It had been that kind of a morning. After a late flight into Atlanta and a brisk jog between concourses, Tony's flight into Charleston the previous night had landed him in the lobby of the Planter's Inn at close to ten o'clock. Even Eueland's ceaseless smile couldn't ease the travel fatigue that led to a restless night's sleep and an early morning fight with the snooze button on the bedside clock. It wasn't until after his shower that Tony realized he'd forgotten to pack his dress shoes. All he could do was shake his head as he stood on the corner waiting for the light to change so he could cross, finally looking down to the bottom of his blue suit pants to find his brown casual travel shoes. It had been that kind of a morning. Under his right foot, a flyer caught his eye, advertising what appeared to be a band party of some sort. Tony moved his foot and bent to pick the flyer up for a closer look. Sponsored by the Charleston Aids Outreach, presumably a local non-profit, a group calling themselves The Chixie Dicks were to be the featured act of what was described as a country/western drag show. Tony was taking in the details as a voice spoke to him over his shoulder.

"Local favorites."

Tony turned to see Ben Middleton standing behind him, hands in pockets, staring at the traffic lights as if willing them to change.

"Hello, Ben," Tony said, still holding the flyer and trying to make sense of it. "So you're familiar with the group?"

"Not intimately, no," Ben replied with a cheeky grin, "but I've seen their show a couple of times. Hell of a show, even if you're not a big country music fan." The light changed and the two started across the street. "They are local favorites, though. Have quite a following."

"Is there a large gay community in and around Charleston?"

"I don't really know," Ben replied. "But these guys have a foot in both worlds."

"How's that?"

"They sing in some of the local church choirs. Paid voices, they call them."

By this point they had reached the other curb and Tony tossed the flyer into the garbage can, still shaking his head in amazement. Ben continued to walk looking straight ahead with purpose, and Tony was content to follow along with someone who presumably knew where he was going. He was still trying to reconcile the flyer choir, though.

"Maybe it's just me, being from California, but isn't there a disconnect between the drag show and the church choir? Does that seem normal to you?"

"You're the shrink, Doc. I really don't know much about normal. But these guys have great voices, and I guess the congregations look the other way about their activities on the other six days of the week."

"But if you watch any of the media outlets, the church is always homophobic."

"And Californians are always flaky liberals. Nice shoes."

Tony chuckled and continued to walk beside Ben as they made their way to the offices of Rosen, Krantz & Gildenstern, Attorneys at Law, specialists in corporate and securities law, and counselors to more than three generations of Cambers. Tony had never actually attended a shareholders meeting and had no expectations. Ben walked as if four generations of family energy were about to be drained from his body. Or maybe he was simply bracing against the cold breeze of Charleston Harbor whipping through the city streets. Or maybe it was just another Tuesday and Ben was walking as rapidly as possible toward Wednesday. They both leaned into the breeze and spoke minimally.

"How's Twinkle?" Tony offered, trying to fill the chilly silence.

"Fine. She's visiting a friend here in town."

"Oh. That's great that she's been able to cultivate some friendships here. She's not from Charleston, is she?"

"Nope. Mississippi."

"Oh. Long way from home. Well, that's great."

Ben wanted to echo the qualification that her new friendship was, in fact, great. Probably greater than Tony could ever have imagined. But something was the better part of valor and, whatever that something was, Ben contented himself with the valorous idea that Twinkle Middleton, like Plantation Trust, would soon be somebody else's problem. They walked the rest of the way in silence.

The offices of Rosen, Krantz & Gildenstern were well-appointed with stuffed leather chairs, hunting art, and shelves of bound volumes. At the center of it all was a large conference room, to which Tony and Ben were quickly ushered after walking in the firm's front door. Neither carried a briefcase or cared to surrender his overcoat. The windowless room was brightly lit and encased in shelved volumes. Seated at one end of the large center table were Margaret, Augusta, and a gray-haired gentleman wearing a bow tie. As Ben led the way to that end of the table, Tony thought it best to hold back and anticipate that Pacific Mergers might occupy a different part of the table. The gray-haired gentleman rose to greet them, Ben first.

"Ben," he said extending his hand and shaking Ben's, "Caleb Rosen. I haven't seen you since you stopped playing football."

"Hello, Mr. Rosen," Ben replied. "What's that no-good son of yours been up to lately? Has he figured out how to catch a forward pass yet?"

"No," Rosen said with a chuckle. "He took up orthopedic surgery. Gave up completely on the NFL. Their loss, if you ask me." With a second chuckle, he moved down the table to greet Tony. "Dr. Gordon, I presume. Caleb Rosen. I'll be your tour guide this morning."

"Nice to meet you," Tony replied with a smile. "I can only assume that you have all the things you need. They didn't send anything with me. I'm more of a spectator than anything else."

"Indeed you are, but we're glad to have you with us. Mr. Kelly and I have gotten to know each other well over the last several months. He was even so bold as to offer Rose Bowl tickets if my beloved Gamecocks ever make it to Pasadena."

"His money's safe," Ben replied while making his way around the table to sit beside his mother.

"Probably so," Rosen replied over his shoulder to Ben and then looking back at Tony. "We have all the things we need, yes. But if you have any questions, please feel free. And have a seat anywhere you like."

"Thank you," he said, making his way around the opposite side of the table as Ben and leaving a chair between his and Augusta's. He exchanged greetings with Augusta and Margaret as he sat down, remembering to ask Augusta about Ellis and the kids.

"Well," Rosen said in an official tone to the small group, "I guess we can get started. As with most family businesses, I suppose, Plantation Trust is closely held, and all but five percent of the outstanding stock is held directly or in trust by those seated here at the table. The majority of the rest of the shares are held by current or former members of the Board of Directors, and I hold signed proxies for each of those, voting unanimously in favor of the sale." Here he paused and looked at Margaret. "Augustus was nothing if not thorough." There was a knock at the door and all heads turned as it opened.

"Mr. Rosen," a secretary said, "the Wrightmans are here."

All eyes widened and turned toward Rosen, except Margaret. Her expression never changed. Rosen stood to greet the Wrightmans, Tom and Helen, father and daughter, and Tony rose as they selected chairs close to his. If they recognized him, Tony thought, they gave no signs of such.

"I was just explaining that all shares had been accounted for," Rosen told the Wrightmans, "including yours, Tom, and that proxies all voted in favor of the sale. Have you changed your mind and wish to vote your shares differently?"

"Not at this point, no," Thomas Wrightman said quietly. They took their seats and folded their hands neatly in their laps. "Am I correct in assuming, though, that there will be a time for comments at some point in this process?"

"Well," Rosen said, looking at everyone else and sweeping back to the Wrightmans, "this is an informal gathering, Tom. With a very formal purpose, of course, but I think comments would be welcome at any time you, as a shareholder, would like to make them."

"Thank you. I'll wait, for now." Helen Wrightman still showed no interest in the proceedings at all, except that she appeared to be calmly on the verge of tears.

"Very well, then," Rosen said, returning to the group and shifting gears to a more formal demeanor, a skill that must be taught in law school, the capacity to differentiate between the people and the purpose, the addition of pomp to the right circumstance. "Margaret, as Chairman of the Board and majority shareholder, you have before you an offer to purchase Plantation Trust. You also hold the proxy shares of all other members of the board in addition to your personal shares and those you hold in trust for your grandchildren."

Margaret straightened her already perfect posture and nodded in bright-eyed assent. Unsure of whether she was supposed to say anything or not, she continued to look to Rosen for a cue, though he had returned his gaze to the papers on the table in front of him.

"Augusta and Ben, you hold significant minority positions outright and in trust. Tom, you hold the remaining shares in a trust for which Helen is the sole beneficiary. As of today, that is a complete accounting for all outstanding shares of Plantation Trust. Does anyone here know of any shareholders of record not mentioned in that accounting?"

All present looked at Rosen without looking left or right or giving any indication that other shareholders existed to their knowledge, assuring themselves that such questions were a formality intended to cover the transaction agents—the lawyers—as they stepped through the process.

"Seeing none," Rosen continued, "we can move forward to the voting process. Have all shareholders been made aware of the details of the pending transaction? Are there any questions? Does anyone need additional information?"

Again, no response from anyone in the group.

"If there are no questions, it is my assumption that all shares have been voted and counted, in favor of the sale. If there are no objections," Rosen asked, scanning the table for objections as he produced a small stack of papers and slid them across the table to Margaret, "I'll ask Margaret to review and sign the transfer agreement on behalf of the board and the shareholders."

"Is this the same document?" Margaret asked as she picked up the pen that had weighed heavily on the table in front of her.

"Yes. This is the same document you and I reviewed earlier. And the same document reviewed with Michael Kelly yesterday afternoon," he said with a quick look to Tony. "No changes."

As he was completing the last statement and Margaret was signing the form in the spots marked by yellow flags, there was another knock at the door as Rosen's secretary quietly opened the door and gave him the secret signal that a situation needed his attention.

"I'll just be a moment," he said to the table in general, and then to Tom, "and then we'll open the meeting for comments, if you like." He followed the secretary out the door.

"Well, Tom," Margaret said, finishing the paperwork and sliding the signed copies back across the table to where Rosen had been sitting, "we certainly do appreciate the loyalty you've shown to our family through the years. My father was a big fan of yours from the very beginning."

"Your father was a good man," Tom Wrightman said without looking up from the spot on the table that had held his gaze since sitting at the table.

"That was Michael Kelly," Rosen said, walking back into the room, "calling from the West Coast to check on the progress and glad to hear that the transfer was complete." He resumed his seat and collected the papers, checking to make sure they were signed in all the right places. "Margaret," he continued, "I think Augustus will rest easier knowing that this has been settled. Augusta and Ben, it seems life has taken you in different directions, and this potentially resolves a lot of questions that naturally arise as family businesses grow across generations." His efforts to fill in the patriarchal gap were quickly interrupted by Margaret.

"It's what Daddy wanted," she said. "We'll be just fine."

"Indeed, that seems likely," Rosen shifted gears with a sincere grin, "given the substantial cash settlement that will be wired to the accounts you specified. And does anyone have any questions about the wire transfers or funds disbursement process?"

Nobody had any questions, and Margaret began gathering her things, her anxiousness a product not so much of seller's remorse as the simple need to move on. Sensing the emerging urgency, Caleb Rosen moved smoothly but quickly to retain control of the meeting.

"Tom, if you had comments, now would probably be the right time."

As Tom Wrightman straightened in his chair and began positioning himself to offer some comments, the conflict that had defined his life and his relationship with the Camber Family seemed to rest heavily on his furrowed brow, lifting only as he exhaled deeply and prepared to uncork the bottle of vintage emotions. He raised his eyebrows, took a deep breath, and opened his mouth to speak and, at that very moment, a knock at the door bid him pause and reconsider. Frustrated by the continued interruptions by his secretary, Rosen flashed a look of apology toward Tom Wrightman.

"Come in, Cynthia," Rosen called to the closed door, but when the door opened it wasn't Cynthia's hand on the knob. It was, instead, the hand of an older gentleman who seemed ill-placed in the blue suit that followed the hand into the room.

"I'm afraid I wouldn't make a very good Cynthia," the voice said as the blue suit and full head of gray hair came into view.

"Uncle Robert!" Augusta said, pushing the chair back as the first to recognize the visitor and making her way around the table to offer a hug. "What in the world are you doing here?"

"Had some business to take care of, Princess," he replied as they exchanged a hug. His use of her childhood pet name only added to the asymmetry of his presence in this meeting, and even Charleston for that matter, since he had never visited them before. As they parted, Ben was there to replace Augusta with the offer of a handshake and quick hug, and confusion seemed to settle like an early morning low country fog across the room. Margaret kept her seat but offered an appropriate if questionably sincere greeting.

"Welcome to Charleston, Robert," she said, "but I'm not sure this is a good time." Sensing the tension, Caleb Rosen again worked to regain control of the meeting, looking past the intruder through the conference room door as if willing his secretary Cynthia to explain the interruption.

"May I help you with something outside, Mr.—?" Rosen said, extending his arm back toward the door through which Robert had just arrived.

"Tinsley. Robert Tinsley."

"Yes, well Mr. Tinsley, we're concluding a meeting and need just a few minutes to wrap this up."

"Oh, I'm sorry," Robert replied. "Michael assured me that the deed was done and champagne would be flowing."

"Michael. Kelly?"

"One and the same, Consiglieri. One and the same. Said he had just spoken to you not five minutes ago."

All eyes at the table sought out all other eyes at the table in an effort to make sense of the situation. Tom Wrightman, who had maintained a ready position, the comments resting steadily on the tip of his tongue, eased back in his seat almost out of fear. His experience in conference rooms had been limited mostly to meetings run by Augustus Camber, and any deviations from the carefully planned agenda were resolved quickly, the intruders dispatched summarily. This stranger seemed to have a recently established connection to the firm that just bought the bank, and he also seemed to be related to the Middleton family, even though Tom Wrightman had never heard of him. He cast a sideways glance down the table to Margaret whose look of confusion made the circumstances all the more interesting to him.

"Of Pacific Mergers?" Augusta asked. "That Michael Kelly? How do you know him, Uncle Robert?" Her eyes moved back and forth between Robert Tinsley and Tony Gordon. Robert made the connection.

"Business associates," he replied to Augusta before turning to Tony. "And you must be the good Doctor Tony Gordon."

"Yes I am," Tony said in surprise. "But have we met?"

"Not before now, but I've been a fan of yours for several years. Or of your work, I should say."

"Well, thanks. Have you studied family systems theory?"

"Not until I encountered your article on business succession and leadership in Forbes a couple of years ago. Insightful to say the least."

"So how do you know Michael Kelly?" Tony asked the question that everyone seemed to need an answer to, "because he didn't mention anything about your joining us for the meeting."

"I hired him to purchase a business for me."

"Really?" Augusta asked, excited that he might actually have legitimate business interests.

"Really," he replied with a shrug of the shoulders and a slight raise of the eyebrows revealing a sideways glance at Margaret. "Why should that be so surprising?"

"What business did you buy?" Ben asked, genuinely curious.

"This one," Robert responded without the slightest change in tone or demeanor, though punctuating the statement by taking a seat at the table.

"What?" Margaret asked excitedly from the other end of the table. "What did you just say?"

"I said I just bought this business," he replied calmly, anticipating but enjoying the turmoil he was plowing.

"I don't understand," Margaret said, moving her eyes between Caleb Rosen and Tony Gordon as if both were traitorous leeches feeding off of her family name. And the fog of confusion crept in from the walls as Augusta and Ben stepped back from where Robert had taken a seat, as if the news had been delivered with a physical blow. They turned to look at Tony.

"Is that true?" Augusta asked Tony.

The fog began to settle around Tony, creeping around the room to envelope the focal person as the strange tableau played out. Tony was still glowing from the praise of his work and, quite frankly, had no idea who Robert Tinsley was or why it should make a difference that he had purchased the bank. He was keenly aware, though, that the family was unhappy, and he was not interested in being made into a scapegoat because Michael Kelly had not been as forthcoming as he could have been.

"I'm not privy to any information about partnership structures on the buy side of the deal," Tony said. "I was never made aware of any of that."

"There are no partners," Robert said calmly.

The gravity of all of this, at least for those who knew the connections and history, was astounding. For Tony and Tom and Helen, the revelations grew more and more fascinating. For Caleb Rosen, whose temples burned from the laser stare of Margaret Camber Middleton, confusion was never a good thing, especially if confusion had you against a wall.

"Caleb," Margaret asked calmly, too calmly, "is this true? Have we just sold my family's bank to this man?" When Caleb didn't answer immediately, still trying to formulate a reasonable response in his own mind, Robert offered his own clarity so, if for no other reason, that it might spare the innocent any collateral damage.

"Actually, no. You just sold your family's bank to Pacific Mergers, just as the all the paperwork indicated."

"Now I'm really confused."

"Don't be. Pacific Mergers, in a separate agreement, assigned sole ownership of Plantation Trust to JRT Ventures, Inc."

"John Robert Tinsley," Margaret recalled quietly.

"One and the same. So you didn't sell the bank to me as much as I bought it from you."

"So all of this is true? You really did all of this?"

"All of this is true," he replied calmly, "and I did all of this."

There was a pause as the fog of confusion was displaced by the pall of certainty, as the compounding revelations began to sink in and Margaret could only shake her head, caught between her inability to completely understand what had happened and a feeling of powerlessness to change the outcome. She could only shake her head and stare at the stack of papers where the ink had only just dried. Surely her father would never have let such a thing happen, and she began formulating an apology to him in her mind. When she got to the part about why it happened, though, she got no traction.

"Why?" she asked Robert. "Why would you do this?"

"Simple, really," Robert replied, "and you of all people should understand. It's been a family business, and I wanted to keep it that way."

"But you're not family, Robert."

"Maybe not," he replied with a shrug, "but Augusta is, for both of us."

"Leave them out of this, Robert. This is between you and me."

"Not anymore, Margaret. That was then. This is now. And this is one situation that is no longer in your control."

"Okay," Augusta said, "this is getting even more confusing by the minute. Does somebody want to fill us all in here," she continued, gesturing to the entire table, including Tom and Helen Wrightman, whose deep sense of anxiety, so palpable when they had arrived, seemed lifted as they sat wide-eyed in witness to the strange confrontation. A Camber at a disadvantage? The tectonic plates beneath Charleston Harbor seemed to be shifting.

"Again, very simple explanation," Robert said calmly to Augusta. "I bought the bank and I want you to run it." He didn't say any more and everyone at the table looked at him like he had three heads. Before Augusta had a chance to respond, Margaret voiced her opposition.

"Robert, you're being foolish. Not that it's any of my business, since you seem to own the bank at this point, but Augusta's a teacher, an educator."

"Headmaster, Mother," Augusta clarified. "I've managed every aspect of our school for almost ten years, and I know my way around a balance sheet."

"I know, honey. I know. And I'm sure you do. But your brother is a banker and a businessman. Your grandfather always had hopes that he would, you know, one day . . . ."

"Margaret," Robert interrupted, "I think you're right. This is none of your business. And if I didn't think Augusta could handle it, I wouldn't ask it of her. Besides, Walker used to marvel at her business sense, for years and years, struggling to understand why Old Gus never recognized the possibilities, always trying to force the square peg through the round hole." And while he said all of this very calmly, the saying of it cast a paralysis over all in the room except for himself and Ben, the latter chuckling to himself and breaking the tension.

"I'm glad you can find humor in all of this," Margaret said sternly to Ben. "Your family name bought into drug money and all you can do is laugh." Ben kept a smile on his face as if her comments didn't really register.

"That's been a long time ago," Robert said to Margaret, "and while that was an unfortunately profitable place to start, the real money's been made in real estate and, ironically, banking."

"Still drug money no matter how you look at it."

"Well maybe you're right again," he said with a knowing grin, "but before you make me out to be the only turd in the punch bowl, maybe we need to revisit the origins of Plantation Trust, because if I'm not mistaken, the Camber seed money for this little bank of yours came through the slave trade, right around the corner from where this building stands. Humans bought and sold on the open market, with the Camber Brothers building a fortune one trade at a time."

Margaret was visibly shaken by this reminder. She was aware that the family lore had included slaves, but no Charleston family of any depth could hide from that. If the Cambers had been involved extensively in the slave market, though, her father had never really talked about it. Regardless, she felt the need to defend her family honor.

"The early Cambers were cotton merchants."

"I'm sure they were," Robert replied calmly. "There was a lot of that going around. But you'll have to remember that I've had the time and reason to dig into all of this."

"Well," she said with a huff, "you may have done the digging, but I'm not going to sit here while you throw all the dirt back in my family's face. This meeting is over." And with that, Margaret Camber parted ways with Plantation Trust. After the dust had settled from her hasty departure, the quiet hum of the halogen sconces was replaced by Ben's voice.

"This is really starting to make sense to me now," he said, nodding his head in the affirmative.

"That's great, Ben," Robert replied, pointing toward the Wrightmans, "but who are these people?"

"These are the Wrightmans," Caleb Rosen replied, returning to the room after escorting Margaret as far as the front door. "Tom and daughter Helen. They are, or were, stockholders in Plantation Trust, and Tom was about to offer some comments when you arrived." Then, gesturing in Tom's direction he asked, "Tom, did you want to offer those comments at this time?" Caleb Rosen realized that, much to his dismay, he had lost control of the meeting.

"No sir," Tom replied with a shake of his head, rising from his chair and assisting Helen in the same. "I think enough's been said in this room to last a lifetime. Mine, at least. You sir," he said to Robert, "I'm afraid I never caught your name either, but you put on a hell of a show. Caleb," he turned to face Rosen and walked toward the door, "will you see if that wire transfer has been made before we leave? This man's got me holding on tightly to my wallet, like there are more surprises yet to come."

"Sure thing, Tom. We can check it on the way out." And then to the remaining few, "I guess this meeting is officially adjourned, but use the room as long as you like. Sounds like you may have some details to sort through."

And then there were three. Plus Tony.

"So," Robert said to Ben, "tell us what you've learned thus far, since all of this is really making sense to you now. And then," he turned toward Augusta, "we'll talk about our little family business."

"That's good," Augusta replied with a stifled chuckle, realizing that she was the only person still standing now, having stood with her mother but suppressing the urge to leave with her. "Because all of this seems to have come out of nowhere."

"Hardly," Robert said, "let me assure you."

"I would have to agree with that," Ben intervened.

"You knew about this?" Augusta said with a glare before taking a seat next to Ben.

"No," Ben replied quickly, "but a lot of other stuff is crystallizing, even for a square-peg idiot banker like me who's not round-hole management material."

"I never said—" Robert interjected.

"I know. I know. I'm just yanking your chain."

"You have the ability," Robert assured. "Always have. But aptitude is a fickle mistress, and now you have the means without the expectations. You can find your niche without having to drown your soul in sour-mash whiskey."

"You're starting to sound like my old man."

"Well, funny you should mention that."

"Hold on. Let me tell you what I've made sense of so far," Ben said, pushing back on the table with both hands as if trying to stop either time or the flow of conversation, or both. "The part I could never get my head around until today was why the feds were still mining that same old vein and trying to drag Walker into all of that."

"Are you talking about the time they questioned you over coffee?" Augusta asked.

"Yeah, that and a couple of other times as well, but I think they were using the DEA files to dredge up an old pipeline for the IRS."

"And why would they do that?" Robert asked with a knowing smile.

"Because you've been moving money back into this country for years."

"Many years. And some of it never left."

"But has that been legal?" Augusta asked. "We've always assumed you had been expelled from the country."

"Only by your mother, I'm afraid."

"What?" Augusta replied with a jerk of the chin and darting eyes beneath a furrowed brow. "What's that supposed to mean?"

"Part of a deal we struck a long time ago," Robert replied with a long sigh.

"Wait for it," Ben replied quickly. "The IRS was trying to freeze your assets, but they couldn't nail you to any crosses, so they went after Walker hoping the church would force him to come clean. But he pulled the plug instead and told them nothing. That sound about right so far?"

"Well,—"

"Come clean about what?" Augusta asked.

"Being an early mule," Ben said, keeping his eyes on Robert, waiting for a sign that he was right or wrong as he was piecing it together, "before the term even meant anything."

"What are you talking about?"

"That's where all the cash came from," he replied as if she would recall immediately what he was talking about, though she obviously didn't. He had to remind her. "The cash in Walker's suit pockets? Ring a bell?"

"Yes," Augusta said with frustration, "but?"

"Walker was a cash mule. Like a drug mule or a jewel mule, except he carried or received cash here in the states and distributed it, I'm assuming," he continued to look to Robert for clues, "through random accounts in small amounts that could then be manipulated across larger balances over time, leaving a forensic accountant to beat his head against a wall tracing it. That sound about right?"

"Interesting so far," Robert said smugly.

"And the cash in the closet," he turned back to his sister, "was either awaiting distribution or meant to be Walker's fee or cut. But," he said turning back to Robert, "there's no way he could have laundered enough over time to put this amount together, to pull this off. I'm not bragging, but this is adult money in this transaction, and eighty grand in a suit pocket ain't a drop in the bucket. So you've got me there."

"So," Augusta filled in, "you're saying that our father, the preacher and missionary, laundered drug money so that his college roommate could buy the bank that has been in his wife's family for generations. Is that what you're saying?" She was almost apoplectic. Ben didn't respond immediately, as if the retelling of his story wasn't as plausible as he'd imagined.

"Not exactly," Robert said finally.

"And now you want me to run that bank?"

"Well, yes," he agreed, "that part is correct."

"And the rest? Is Ben right about the rest?"

"Not so much. Especially the part about the drug money. And, for the record, your father would often carry cash back from mission trips, but always amounts within the legal limit of ten thousand dollars. And the money wasn't distributed among accounts. It was his to spend on the two of you. Because the Camber dollar was ever-present, and because the church dollar was what it was, Walker allowed me to subsidize his parent cash."

"With drug money," Augusta said, adopting her mother's facial expression from moments before.

"Again, not exactly. Yes, in the early years, and it was the sixties, and I was an early pilgrim in the South American land of promise, and while I would have potentially enjoyed the fame and fortune of drug-lording, my involvement in that trade was recreational at best. But I had friends and colleagues, much better suited to the edge, who sought my advice on financial issues and taxation, and I offered it freely to all in the beginning, establishing a sort of financial services practice that evolved into banking and real estate and so on and so on, and here we sit."

There was a pause, a palpable silence, while Augusta and Ben both worked to assimilate these latest revelations. Each was forming his or her own questions, but both seemed to struggle with reconciling the Uncle Robert of yesterday and the Robert Tinsley of today. The hum of the halogen sconces again emerged through the silence until Ben shook his head and ventured a question.

"Banking. Really?"

"Not as exotic as drug-lording, I'll admit, but you have to remember, if you ever knew, that I was an accountant when your father and I lived together. I'm assuming you know by now that we lived together in New York, before he met Margaret."

"That we know," Augusta confirmed.

"But the accounting is new information," Ben added.

"Well," Robert concluded, "there it is."

"But what about those goons who worked with me in college, when I was part of the network, or so I thought? Didn't they work for you?"

"Friends of friends, not traceable to me in any way, much to the DEA's displeasure, I assure you."

"And Jimmy Taylor, the bartender I sort of grew up with. Was he recreational as well?"

"Oh, yes. Young James. He mentioned having seen you recently. A lovely boy, but he was no Walker. None of them were, or could've been. And he had a substance problem."

"An ironic line for you to draw, don't you think?" Augusta asked.

"Perhaps."

"Or maybe not," she continued, "since this whole drug-lord story seems to have been an elaborate fiction. But I don't understand why you would keep it up, perpetuate the myth for all those years."

"Who says I have?" Robert asked calmly.

"But that's been the story forever," she continued, "even when we went down for all of those mission trips. That's really when it started, when we got to know you. It was always understood that we shouldn't ask too many questions about you or your work. At some point the drug-lord label just sort of stuck. And then there was all of that with the prodigal son over there," she concluded, pointing at Ben.

"Just a boy rebelling against a father," he said, "who also happened to be a preacher. Walker expected it, knew all about it, and even asked me to get involved to keep an eye on him. Through the goons, as you called them."

"No shit," Ben said. "Guess that explains why we never talked about any of that at the time."

"I think he figured it would just make it worse, though he was no child psychologist."

At that point all three seemed to remember that Tony Gordon was still sitting solo at the other end of the table, and all three looked in his direction, making him almost self-conscious about being a silent party to the conversation. He sat calmly, close to the door end of the room beneath a bust of Joshua F. Krantz, who along with Ignatius Rosen, Caleb's great-grandfather, had apparently founded the Charleston firm shortly after the War of Northern Aggression. At least that's what Tony had learned from reading the history of the firm the week before on their website. From the look of the bust, Krantz was also a lover of cigars. But as all eight eyes met over the long conference table, Tony raised his brows as if to ask if he was supposed to be hearing all that he was hearing.

"You getting all this down, Dr. Gordon?" Robert asked with a smile.

"I'm sorry," Tony replied sheepishly. "I should have excused myself with the others." And he rose to leave.

"Nonsense," Robert said. "You're still on my payroll for a couple of years, and we're just getting to the good stuff. Keep your seat." So Tony sat back down.

"There's more?" Augusta asked in disbelief.

"Small details to sweep up," Robert replied, turning back to face Ben. "But Ben seems to have those figured out, don't you Ben?"

Ben sat back in his leather conference room chair, hands in his lap, staring at the hunting print on the opposite wall from him, a resting spot for his eyes between Robert and Augusta. It was obvious that he was trying to work through something.

"I have that part, yes, but I'm still trying to figure out why on the drug-lord thing," Ben said, punctuating the thought with a strong glance at Robert, whose expression didn't change and gave no clues. "I mean the who is obvious."

"Margaret," Augusta said as if pronouncing a foregone conclusion.

"And maybe the whys are connected to the whos, because the whos seem to have been."

"This is starting to sound like a Dr. Seuss book," Robert interjected, "but I think I know where you're going. Why don't you take us there?"

"Please," Augusta pleaded, shifting in her seat. "I'm lost in all of this."

"But you remember earlier," Ben said, "when Robert told Margaret he was keeping the business in the family?"

"Yes. That's why he wanted me to run it."

"Yes and no," Ben said without taking his eyes off of Robert, "or not exactly." He reached into the vest pocket of his suit jacket and pulled out a small stack of folded papers and slid them over to Augusta. "There's more to it than that."

Augusta unfolded the papers and began making sense of them as Ben and Robert read each other's eyes. She turned page after page and finally looked up at Ben for an answer.

"Where did you get these? And how long have you had them?"

"Safe deposit box 1030A at the B of A Market Street Office," he said calmly, still holding Robert's gaze.

"The mysterious business card," Augusta confirmed with a nod.

"Opened the box this morning on the way here. Didn't seem to mean much until the new owner of the bank showed up."

Augusta shifted her eyes to look at Robert who slowly returned the favor.

"Is it true?" was all she could ask.

"Yep," Robert answered quietly but without hesitation.

"So you are the biological father of Margaret Camber's children?"

"If you mean the two of you, yes. I can't account for any others."

The last part didn't really draw a laugh or reduce the tension as he thought it might. He had played this scenario out a number of times in his head, but a smooth option for discussing it never really emerged. The tension remained, like an extra presence in the room, an observer like Tony but with years of family history to embolden it. Ben sat quietly to allow Augusta some time, since he'd had the benefit of the walk from the bank to the meeting to shake his head in wonder. The hum of the halogen sconces provided the harmony line to the family melody now playing, each monotonous and offering both unlimited and nonexistent points of access. Where does one begin recasting that many years of family in this new light?

"So Daddy was sterile?" Augusta finally asked. "Or is it impotent?"

"Walker was not impotent, I can assure you," Robert replied. "But he was sterile. The result of a genetic condition passed through from his mother's family, if I remember correctly."

"And you were a donor?" Augusta asked, referring back to the small stack of papers to reconsider the details listed under a letterhead from a lab in New York City.

"Yes."

"So I guess," Augusta said looking back at Robert, "since the rest is fairly self-explanatory, the only question I have is why we're only finding out about this now. I mean, not that it makes any difference."

"That, as I mentioned before, was part of the deal that was struck many years ago between your mother and Walker and me."

"The same deal that forced you out of the country?"

"One and the same, yes."

Augusta put both of her elbows on the table and held her cheeks in her hands. The morning's deluge of information was taking its toll on her. Ben sat quietly trying to piece the scraps together. His emotional connection to the family wasn't as pronounced as his sister's, so he could objectify the players and interactions more readily. To him it was more like trying to solve a puzzle or a riddle. It appeared that Augusta might harbor some more significant questions.

"But why?" she asked finally. "I mean, I know I've asked that a lot this morning, but a forced exile on the biological father of your children seems a bit extreme. And if she felt that way about it, why would she allow us to go on those mission trips? Why allow us to know you at all? That would've been easier than perpetuating this whole drug-lord story, wouldn't it?"

"While I hate to repeat myself as well, and especially in this case, it really is quite simple, in your mother's convoluted sort of way. Old Gus's last will and testament required an heir, as did his father's and his father's and so on. If at any point along the way the last standing Camber at the helm failed to produce a clear line of succession, the Company Charter required that the bank be sold to the highest bidder."

"That's ludicrous," Augusta said. "Plus, we are Margaret's children. She gave birth to us. Old Gus was in the waiting room for all we know. That doesn't even make sense."

"Well, the need for and insistence on a clear line of succession didn't start with the Cambers, and it's not all that uncommon in family businesses. Is that right, Dr. Gordon?"

"Not uncommon, no. The standard for biological birth parents, though, drills down into the case histories deeper than I'd considered before. And the markets and banking regulations have evolved to the point that family businesses aren't as idiosyncratic as they once were."

"But remember," Robert added, "that Plantation Trust started essentially during Reconstruction, and the fear of hostile takeover by lawless carpetbaggers was very real."

"And what does all that have to do with your exile?" Augusta asked.

"Margaret was afraid that her father wouldn't honor children conceived outside of the normal definitions of marriage, whatever those are, and in the end her fears were realized. But to protect her interests and yours, she agreed to the artificial insemination if and only if I disappeared."

"So she did it for the money?" Ben broke his silence.

"Not exactly," Robert said.

"There's a lot about this that's not exact," Augusta said.

"Your mother has always been a mystery, at least to me, but I don't think she's ever been motivated by the money, if only because she never really understood much about it. She has always been fiercely loyal to the men around her, though, and I think she felt a responsibility to produce an heir so that the great line wouldn't end with her father, so he wouldn't have to pull the trigger and put the bullet in the head of the family legacy. They were always very close because of her mother's death at a such a young age."

"If she felt that strong a loyalty to her father, why didn't she divorce Walker and marry someone who could provide an heir?" Ben asked, without losing the ironic connection to his own marital woes.

"Loyalty to your father, mostly, but also to her father, since divorce had always been derided by the Cambers as a sign of weakness. They were more of the 'get married and make it work' stock, apparently. And she also felt like she had won a hard-fought moral victory in Walker, pointing him down the straight and narrow, as it were, though apparently that didn't work out very well for her either."

"You know about all of that?" Augusta asked.

"I lived with Walker, remember? When he left me for Margaret?"

"Damn, this is a strange conversation," Ben quietly offered.

"But I think it's going well," Robert added. "Would you agree Dr. Gordon?"

"With both of you, I think." Tony was taking it all in.

"So why did she let us, including Walker, go on those mission trips?" Augusta asked, wrapping up the last of her questions.

"That was my stipulation, that somewhere along the line I be granted some interaction, and the mission trips were a great vehicle for that."

"So that wasn't Walker's Christian spirit and enthusiasm at work?"

"I wouldn't think so. Walker was an atheist."

"Shit," Augusta said, dropping her head from her hands to her crossed arms on the table top. And then her muffled voice rose from the pile, "Tell me you're kidding."

"No," Robert said quietly. "Now would not be the right time to start kidding."

"But you just said Margaret got the moral victory when she married Walker and he changed his ways and became a preacher," Ben argued, not ready although more than willing to accept this latest development.

"That was her moral victory. The events themselves were unrelated."

"How's that?" Ben replied. "They get married, he becomes a preacher, end of story. You saying the whole preacher thing was a sham, too?"

"Aren't they all?" Robert asked calmly.

"No," came the muffled voice from the pile of arms. "Some of us still believe in Santa Claus and prefer it that way."

"Be that as it may," Robert continued, "Walker's decision to become a Baptist preacher had more to do with your grandfather than with your mother."

"Really," Ben said, and Augusta raised her head to listen.

"Yep. When they decided to get married, Margaret had made it clear that she wanted to return to Charleston to live and raise a family. So when the time came for Walker to ask Old Gus for his only daughter's hand, Old Gus made it very clear that, while his daughter might have fallen for his bullshit, Plantation Trust would never put him on the payroll, being a nameless hippy from the Baptist hinterlands of South Georgia. He was never good enough for Margaret Camber in the eyes of her father, so Walker figured the best way to get back at him was to become what Old Gus seemed to despise the most, a Baptist. A real fire and brimstone Baptist. Well, maybe not real."

"So that was a fiction as well?" Augusta asked, thinking to herself that her entire childhood was unfolding to be a facade. "Because he really seemed to get into the spirit, if you know what I mean. It moved him, and he seemed to move others."

"That's the most interesting part," Robert agreed. "He got really good at it. So good, in fact, that he painted himself into a corner. But it also served to keep his life very separate from the Cambers. Each could compartmentalize the other, and he almost lived in a different Charleston."

"She had children," Augusta said, "and a clear line of succession for Old Gus, but you said her fears were realized, that her father didn't recognize us as successors? Something like that, a little while back. What did you mean?"

"Exactly that. Did you ever wonder why the relationship, after you two reached a certain age, seemed to be one-dimensional, like Margaret was working it but Old Gus wasn't buying it?"

"Sure," Ben responded, "but he was always a strange bird, and he was old when we came along, and I always assumed he was just always working, you know, married to the bank."

"That may be the case, but there was a tipping point for Walker, sometime when you guys were kids. He never talked much about it, but he had some sort of run in with Old Gus, at one of his dinner parties when Margaret wasn't with him. Some kind of fucked-up chess game, he told me. They exchanged words and Walker let go of Margaret's secret, threw it in his face like he was casting down a gauntlet. In the end, you kids took the hit for it, not him. I don't think he ever forgave himself for that. That's why he was so willing to help with this little project."

"Wait," Augusta stopped him. "Are you saying he knew you were trying to buy the bank?"

Robert smiled softly and chuckled just a bit. "Know about it? Princess, it was his idea. Once he realized you two were damaged goods in the old man's eyes, and that it was his fault more or less, the nameless hippy from South Georgia set about to shift that man's paradigm. And here we sit. Just a damn shame he didn't live to see it. This is his moral victory."

Augusta had reached critical mass at the conference table and excused herself to step outside to get some air. She had planned to take a quick stroll around the block to stretch her legs and clear her head before returning to talk through bank details with Robert over lunch at a sandwich shop close by. As she hit the steps and sidewalk below and felt the cold, wet air, she began to feel like a crane would be required to lift the morning's news from her shoulders.

"Augusta, isn't it?" A voice was calling her from outside of her peripheral vision. She turned back toward the steps to find Helen Wrightman waiting just beside the building.

"Yes," she said, "and you're Helen, right?"

"That's right."

"Yes, well I'm sorry for all the confusion this morning. The day started out to be so simple, despite the conclusion of four generations of ownership. I guess it didn't work out that way. And I'm sorry your father didn't get to say his piece. He is an establishment unto himself, as my grandfather used to say."

Helen nodded in affirmation, and the two women endured an awkward pause, both nodding and acknowledging the other like a watered-down Korean introduction, rubbing their hands together against the chill. Finally Augusta broke the sequence.

"Well, I've got to stretch my legs and get some air."

"Do you mind if I walk with you?"

"No, not at all," Augusta replied, hesitating before continuing. "Have you been waiting out here to talk to me?" She began to wonder if the morning would ever end.

"Yes," Helen replied without apology. "I took Daddy home after the meeting."

"He seemed really eager to be heard right up until the end, when the two of you left."

"Yes," came the matter-of-fact reply. "I think the confusion finally got the better of him."

They pause to cross the street. Helen reached to push the traffic control button to change the signal as Augusta looked her over, as if her agenda were hanging unnoticed like a price tag on a new suit. There was no tag to be found though, and Augusta shifted her tired, anxious gaze to the traffic signals and waited for Helen to carry the conversation, hoping she would do so quickly. Helen, however, remained silent, and Augusta restarted the conversation, hoping to move it along.

"It did get confusing this morning. I'm still trying to make sense of it."

"I think Daddy went the other way," she replied, her voice beginning to carry an edge. "Gave up trying, resigned himself to loyal silence."

"You feel differently, I suppose?"

"Yes."

"Well, if you don't mind me asking," Augusta said, her voice taking on an edge of its own, "what is it that you feel he should've unloaded? I mean, it's been that kind of morning. What the hell."

They both look up in time to see the signal change, and they join the several other pedestrians making their way across the street to greener pastures and better sandwich shops on the other side. As they reached the other sidewalk and turned right to follow the lunch crowd, Helen began the unloading process.

"It's about your grandfather," she said, "about the night he died. My father thought you and your brother should know the details, though by the end of the meeting he'd decided otherwise."

"Okay. So you're here to clear the air on that one. I understand completely," Augusta said, seeing an opening to offer Helen the catharsis she seemed to need, and trying desperately to resolve her issues and continue the walk as originally intended, solo. "From what I remember, Old Gus called Tom from his office that night, but by the time Tom arrived, Old Gus was dead in his leather chair. Is there more?"

"Only that your father killed him," Helen replied shortly, sensing Augusta's desire to politely but flippantly cast her to the curb, continuing to walk in percussive punctuation of the next in a series of morning revelations. Augusta stopped behind her and watched her from under a heavily furrowed brow, shaking her head once again in disbelief.

"What the hell are you talking about?" she said, calling Helen back to relevance and proximity.

"What part of the statement was unclear to you?"

"The whole thing. Are you kidding me? Even by this morning's standard, the idea that my father would kill anyone is ludicrous. And this was Tom's big secret? Really? I think the two of you should get some help." As she starts walking again, leaving Helen to follow with her eyes, Augusta seemed to have reached a boiling point, shaking her head and shrugging her shoulders almost violently before stopping, standing straight, and returning to Helen.

"Was your father laying under that damn park bench when he told you this story? Has he slipped into another world and wants to create conspiracy theories to ruin us all?"

"I was there," Helen replied calmly without acknowledging the slight.

"Where? You were where exactly?" Augusta's voice was rising in intensity but not volume, tempered by her awareness of others on the sidewalk, and her use of her hands to punctuate questions was becoming more pronounced.

"Old Gus's office. The night he died."

"Why is that?" Augusta asserted, still hesitant to allow that the story had merit.

"Because your father called me and asked that Daddy and I get to Old Gus's office quickly. So we did. And when we got there, we found Old Gus slumped over his desk and Walker sitting across from him drinking a scotch and staring calmly at the portrait of Margaret that was hung over the credenza."

"And when did the assumption of murder come into play?"

"We never assumed that. We assumed, as did the police, that Old Gus had simply worn out, died in the office as predicted."

"What changed your mind?" Augusta asked, still incredulous.

"Walker cleared it up immediately when we got there. He said calmly that Old Gus had taken the game too far."

"Game? What game?" Augusta threw her hands up at the seemingly endless series of riddles.

"The chess game."

Augusta's face showed her immediate surprise, as her posture straightened and she moved her glance between Helen's face and the storefronts across the street, finally locking eyes sideways with Helen.

"What would you know about all of that?"

"I know that we were both losing queens to the same winning king, though many years apart."

"But how did you know that?" Augusta asked, holding Helen's gaze and still hoping to find the flaw in her claims.

"I didn't. Walker told us that night."

"What exactly did he tell you?"

"He said it was one thing to drag a disgruntled son-in-law through that social gauntlet, but to test his own granddaughter's loyalty by placing her on the chess floor was unthinkable."

Augusta looked away as the air of contention seemed to leave her body, resigned to the idea that Helen knew what she was talking about. As she turned to face the shop windows immediately behind her, she saw the two of them reflected in the glass and moved up the sidewalk toward the dull brick face of the adjacent streetscape. Clear of her reflection, she faced Helen again, eyes wide with pain.

"But, that means . . . ."

"Yes," Helen concluded with an edgy finality that seemed at once vengeful and cathartic, "that means that your father had the courage to do what mine did not, to kill the man whose warped sense of loyalty included rape and incest. The same man whose emotional bondage drove my mother to an early grave was ushered into judgment by a weak-hearted man of God. The irony would be breathtaking if it weren't all so desperately human."

And just as suddenly as their walk had begun, Helen turned and made her way back to her father's house, her own issues to resolve, her father's life of loyal inaction to reconcile. Augusta, for the first time since checking on the kids that morning, pulled out her cell phone to call Ellis. The bank news needed immediate delivery. She was beginning to realize, though, that maybe some of her family history, the ugly bulk of which she'd compartmentalized and contained, needed some long-overdue air as well. But as Ellis answered the call, Augusta could only slide down the dull brick storefront wall to a seated pile on the sidewalk and cry.

The view from the porch was extraordinary, though Ben hadn't paused in years to consider it. The houses of the neighborhood along the bay were spaced so that even those removed from the waterfront had a view of the marshes and the rivers and the ocean beyond. As a kid he'd never really given a shit about pretty views. He was always in a hurry or in a mood when going in or out of the front door of his parents' townhouse. The furniture on the porch was probably the same as it had always been. He wouldn't know. The chairs and tables of some kind of wicker. He never sat in the chairs as a kid, and he wasn't sitting in them now. Instead, he was sitting on the top step, his feet a couple of steps down, arms across thighs, and hands joined together around a Coke can. It was mid-afternoon, several hours removed from a hellish morning meeting that dredged up more family history than Ben considered possible, and the cocktail hour was upon him. He rolled the can between his hands, his wedding band adding a percussive beat with each pass. Percussive. If anything, his life lacked a beat.

He looked to his right where the driveway passed beside the house and met a patio and small garage to the rear. Close to the porch, Ben's small BMW coupe sat with a light dusting of winter leaves and straw. He hadn't really driven anywhere since arriving two days before, and the previous night's rain had taken its toll. Behind his, though, was Twinkle's Volvo wagon, clean as a whistle despite sitting under the same trees as the BMW. The fresh look might've been attributable to Twinkle's compassion and concern for Ben and his family, and her offer to join him in Charleston, at the townhouse, following the family meeting. And that would make perfect sense, except Twinkle had arrived in Charleston ahead of the previous night's storm, arriving early because of the storm, a change in plans revealed to one more person than Twinkle had anticipated.

Ben looked back toward the water, across the street and through the houses, rolling the can between his hands and thinking about what his niche might be, as a late-model Buick sedan pulled slowly to the curb in front of the house, leading with a license plate boldly proclaiming CLERGY in the shape of a fish bolted to the front bumper. Ben watched as Twinkle emerged awkwardly from the passenger seat and looked up at the porch to make eye contact. He withdrew his eyes to the can as she opened the rear door to retrieve her Vera Bradley overnight bag from the back seat. She opened the small iron gate where the city sidewalk met the herringbone brick pattern of the walk to the porch, and the Buick eased away from the curb and headed toward Church Street and the Central Business District. Twinkle carried her bag up the walk and up the steps. The click of her heels on the brick and the tinny thump of his ring on the can formed a slow drumbeat that seemed very loud in the absence of street traffic or songbirds. It was the closest they had come to making music together in quite a while, but their eyes never met. When she reached the top of the steps, she set the bag down and took a seat next to him on the top step.

"How did my car get here?" she asked, more out of curiosity than surprise, enjoying the same view that Ben seemed to be enjoying.

"I had it towed early this morning," he replied without passion and without shifting his focus from the marshes in the distance between the houses. He had stopped rolling the can between his hands and took a drink, a pause for refreshment, as the ads used to say.

"You want something to go with that?" Twinkle asked.

"I'm okay for now," he replied with a nod and a closer examination of the ingredients. "Thinking high-fructose corn syrup may be the new drug of choice for a while."

"I tried to call, but something's wrong with my phone."

"Nothing wrong with the phone. I terminated the service."

"You've had a busy morning."

"Sold a bank, too. Been one of those days, I guess. Hoping to cure cancer before dark."

They let the humor settle in, both realizing that the marriage had been over for a while, if it had ever started. Anything worth fighting over had long since passed, and even Twinkle had to agree, at least to herself, that the car and the phone had been clever punctuation marks to her own games. And the fact that he'd pursued his own strategy without confrontation suggested to her that he shared her interest in an amicable conclusion to their story. As they both stared ahead toward the marshes, the Buick sedan passed slowly in front of the house from the right to the left. Twinkle closed her eyes and shook her head. Both smiled.

"You obviously told him about my history of violence."

"He's just concerned. For both of us."

"Oh," Ben said with a chuckle. "Well, I think we'll be okay, though I appreciate his pastoral concern for me as the cuckolded husband."

"That's not what I meant," she said quietly. "I meant both of us." Her emphasis included a small gesture toward her belly as she turned to face Ben with the beginning of a tear in each eye."

"Oh," he replied, shifting his focus between Twinkle's eyes and lap. "Well, there it is. Seems like you've been busy as well. I guess congratulations are in order." The awkwardness became difficult to sustain and, as usual, Ben defaulted to humor. "Well, I think you should know that, based on my family history, that child may not be mine." They both chuckled and turned back to face the marshes. The view seemed to ease the conversation.

"Do you love him?"

"Since the first moment I met him," she replied with a demure smile seasoned by the reality of a failed marriage already under her belt. "He's a good man."

Ben let slide the opportunity to fish for a compliment, trusting his confidence that he, too, was a good man. Just not the right man. No need to squeeze self-esteem from your estranged wife, especially when she's high on prenatal hormones and carrying another man's child. Zero-sum game, at best.

"So what happens next?" he asked calmly, running the can through his hands again. "I'm assuming you've talked through all of this with him."

"I have," Twinkle replied, excited but hesitant. "He wants to get married and build a strong Christian family."

"I guess family can be a good thing," he replied, considering the generous evidence to the contrary that he'd waded through earlier in the day. "If you're into that sort of thing. If that's your niche."

"I'm into that," she repeated the obvious, "but you know that better than anybody by now. I think it's what defines us in God's eyes. That was what attracted me to you in the first place. A big, happy family with strong Christian values and a history of doing good things for the community. I want the same for my own kids, my own family."

"Be careful what you wish for," Ben said with a laugh and a wry smile, replaying the last several months and especially the last several hours, "because you just might get it."

They sat quietly enjoying the view, discussing the details of domestic mergers and acquisitions. The Buick drove past again slowly. And somewhere in Charleston, Plantation Trust, a fourth-generation family business, was reborn. Maybe Twinkle was right. It's all about family.